About the Author

When Laurie is not running after her two young children, her husband, or just plain running, she loves nothing more than disappearing into the fictional world of her characters, preferably with a large coffee and a slab of chocolate cake to hand.

Laurie lives in the heart of the Dedham Vales on the Suffolk/Essex border, and when she in the thick of a character crisis she can often be seen walking around the village chatting (and occasionally laughing) away to herself.

Dedication

I would like to dedicate this book to everyone who has supported me. You know who you are.

Laurie Ellingham

THE RELUCTANT CELEBRITY

AUSTIN MACAULEY
PUBLISHERS LTD.

A CIP catalogue record for this title is available from the British Library.

ISBN 978 1 78455 449 1

www.austinmacauley.com

First Published (2015)
Austin Macauley Publishers Ltd.
25 Canada Square
Canary Wharf
London
E14 5LQ

Printed and bound in Great Britain

Acknowledgments

A special mention must go to the Machines because you girls are awesome, and to my mum and her many hats – grandmother, proofreader, general voice of reason, to name but a few.

One

THE DAILY
FRIDAY, FEBRUARY 14TH
THE MOST ROMANTIC GUY IN BRITAIN

Britain's top hunk, Guy Rawson, has swapped the catwalk for the recording studio to pursue his "one true love."

In an exclusive interview with The Daily's celebrity reporter, Sara-Marie Frances, Guy, 27, said: "I've really enjoyed modelling, it has got me where I am today, but my passion has always been for music. It's something I have to do now."

The model who shot to fame five years ago as the face of *GiGi* Sportswear, and has since dominated the catwalk with his famous moody pose, was nothing but smiles as he explained: "The last six months have been the best. I've spent every day in the studio writing and recording. I really hope the public love my album as much as I do."

But when the topic moved to romance, the star was quick to dismiss rumours of a relationship with a well-known blonde Hollywood starlet, and instead intimately revealed that he was still hopelessly in love with his first girlfriend, Juliet. "I didn't realise it at the time, but every song I've written has been for her. Juliet is the most fantastic person I've ever met. I still love her."

Speaking about his debut single 'Regret' he revealed: "It's how I feel every day when I think about her. I was young and stupid. She was my first love and has been my only love."

With other songs on the album including 'Who is your Romeo now?' and 'A goodbye Fool' it looks like Guy will need his very own cupid this Valentine's Day.

'Regret', officially released on Monday, has already climbed to number 10 in the charts through radio play alone, and is tipped to go straight to the top spot in Sunday's chart show. The album, also titled 'Regret', is released later this month.

Good luck Guy, *The Daily* will be first in line for the album.

Above: Gorgeous Guy and his sexy ex, Juliet, then 20

Saturday 15th February, 6.45pm

'Oh no. No no no no no,' Jules shrieked as she stepped into the darkness of her new house, instantly covering her chocolate brown Uggs in a thick layer of dust.

Clumps of what looked like plaster covered every available inch of her living room. The bare lightbulb from the hallway was more than enough to illuminate the gaping hole into the bedroom above.

'This can't be happening,' Jules cried out again as she struggled to comprehend the mess in front of her.

'Hello? Did someone just say something?' A woman's voice called out from somewhere above her.

'Yes, hello,' Jules called back, swallowing hard in a futile attempt to push back the lump of panic which had ballooned in her throat. 'I'm the new owner.'

'Hang on lovey; be with you in a tick. DAN, JASON, GET DOWN HERE WILL YOU, SHE'S ARRIVED AND BE CAREFUL WHERE YOU'RE STEPPING THIS TIME!' A shower of dirt streamed from the ceiling as what sounded like elephants stomped above her.

'Oh thank goodness! I thought I was hearing voices again.'

Jules spun around to find a small forty-something woman in white overalls hopping through the debris towards her. Two tall and lanky teenage boys trailed behind her.

'But here you are,' the woman smiled, reaching Jules and instantly enveloping her in a tight hug.

'Voices?' Jules asked, releasing herself from the embrace.

'It's the—' one of the boys began before the woman cut him off.

'Never mind about that Daniel, can't you see this lady has had enough of a shock without you adding to it?'

'Sorry mum,' he mumbled.

'Um, would someone mind telling me what exactly is going on here?' Jules asked, waving her hands across the wreckage.

'Gosh, where are my manners, eh? I'm Terri and these are my boys, Daniel and Jason. We're Cottinghale's one and only builders and decorators.'

'I'm Jules Stewart.'

'How pretty. Short for Juliet is it, lovey?'

'No, it's just Jules.'

'Well, we were expecting you yesterday, Jules. That's what Dennis told us, but he often gets in a muddle about his days.'

'Dennis the estate agent?' Jules asked, thinking back to the boy barely out of school who had stammered his way through the house viewing last month.

'That's right, lovey. He's my nephew. A sweet boy, but as thick as two short planks, wouldn't you say?'

'I ... I'm still not sure what has happened?' Jules asked again, hoping Terri wouldn't press her for an answer about her nephew and the level of his intellect.

'No, of course you're not. The thing is...' Terri paused, casting a stony stare back towards Daniel and Jason, still lingering in the door way. 'These two ... God, there isn't even a word for them. You raise them up as best as you can. I'm a single mum, you see. Their dad ran off with bloody Dawn from the Post Office, leaving me with two boisterous toddlers eating me out of house and home.

'You do what you think is best, help them with their homework, teach them a trade, that kind of thing, all the while assuming they are developing a sense of right and wrong. You see a light at the end of the tunnel, they show some basic human skills, and then like bloody criminals, they sneak in here for a look about and-'

'Alright mum,' Daniel cut in. 'We get it. We know we were wrong and we really are sorry, but how were we supposed to know the whole ceiling would come down? We barely even stepped into the bedroom and it just went.'

The look Terri gave her son reminded Jules of the look her own mother used when she battled shoppers for the best bargains in the January sales.

'The important thing,' she said, turning back to Jules, 'is that we will fix it. I've taken a look and from what I can see it's just one or two lathes that need replacing, the rest are fine. We'll have this mess cleared away and a new ceiling back up in no time. I've already put a call in to my brother, Tom, he does plastering you see. Anyway, he'll pop in as soon as we're fixed up. Give us a week and it will be like it never happened.'

'Right,' Jules nodded at Terri in a way that she hoped masked the feeling of helplessness threatening to overwhelm her. What were lathes? And what kind of hell had she just walked into? Jules attempted a calming breath, filling her mouth with the millions upon millions of dirt particles floating in the air.

'For free, of course, and we'll pay for your stay at Mrs Beckwith's whilst we clear out this dust. Lord knows you can't stay here.'

'I'm sorry, who is Mrs Beckwith?' Jules choked. It felt as if she had tuned into a soap opera halfway through and couldn't quite figure out what was going on.

'You'll love her. She runs a bed and breakfast down the road. She's as sweet as apple crumble. I phoned earlier so she's expecting you.'

'I can't believe this,' Jules mumbled almost to herself as she cast another look around the room. To say her first project as a solo property developer wasn't off to the best of starts was an understatement of drastic proportions.

'I'm truly sorry,' Terri said, taking Jules's hand. 'Very, very sorry.'

'It's not your fault. Well actually it is, but it's okay. I just ... I just feel a bit out of my depth,' she admitted as the painful lump expanded back into her throat.

'Come on lovey, let's get you outside. Staying in this room too long is no good for the lungs. It will all look better in the daylight tomorrow,' Terri soothed, pulling Jules gently towards the front door.

'What are all these papers doing here?' Jules asked, noticing for the first time the knee-high stacks of newspapers piled neatly against the wall, leading all the way from the front door to the kitchen.

'Oh don't worry about those. Stan at the shop can explain,' Terri answered quickly, 'We'll clear them out with the rest of this mess just as soon as the skip arrives.'

'But I didn't order any papers. There must be hundreds of them.' Jules felt the first throb of a headache wind its way behind her eyes.

'From what I gather the previous ... err ... owner paid for a lifetime's delivery in her will and, well, Stan didn't want to go against her wishes.'

'But that's ridiculous,' she exclaimed, picking up the newspaper nearest to her, 'This one has yesterday's date on it. Why on earth would anyone keep delivering ...' Jules broke off as a gut punch of recognition ricocheted through her, sucking the breath out of her lungs.

She staggered back, pulling away from Terri's hold, her mind failing to make sense of what her eyes were showing her. The girl in the photograph on the front page was sickeningly familiar. The bleached blonde pixie cut, the pink highlights and the clashing red platforms. It was nothing like how Jules looked now with her long brown hair, always tied back, and her understated wardrobe, but that wide smile grinning back at her – Jules knew it instantly, even after all this time.

'Are you alright, lovey?' Terri asked, cutting into Jules's racing mind. 'You look like you've seen a ghost.'

'I ... I ...' Jules stammered, her voice barely a whisper. 'I'm fine. I just thought I saw something, it's nothing,' she replied, noting the looks of concern crossing between the boys and their mother. Had they seen the photograph too? Did they know it was her? Jules wondered with escalating horror, stuffing the newspaper deep into the pocket of her olive green Parker.

'Right everyone, outside before we all breathe in any more of this dust,' Terri commanded, moving her arms to shoo her boys and Jules outside. 'Once you've had a hot bath and are tucked up with a cup of tea at Mrs Beckwith's none of this will seem so bad.'

Jules noddedas she allowed herself to be ushered into the clear crisp February evening. Five years of being in control of her own life and just like that, he could swoop in and destroy it all again.

As Terri's headlights disappeared from view, Jules fought the urge to pull out the newspaper from her pocket. The full moon, which had illuminated her driveway a short time earlier, had since been swallowed by endless cloud, leaving her in complete darkness. For the first time since her arrival in Cottinghale, Jules stared out at her surroundings, which at that moment looked like a wall of inky black closing in from every direction.

Jules stumbled one foot in front of the other towards Mrs Beckwith's guesthouse, filled with a sudden longing for the familiar orange streetlights that had blanketed Reading, and which she had, until that very moment, loathed. The silence she had longed for in the city now seemed eerie.

What she wouldn't give for the incessant hum of a motorway to comfort her – anything, in fact, that would make her feel more like the confident, independent woman she was, instead of a character from the opening scenes of a teen horror film; the one that always got killed. As if answering her wish, a bright security light jumped on, lighting her way to a blue front door.

Before Jules could knock, an elderly woman in a floral housecoat and fraying thick cardigan opened the door, peering at Jules through one-inch thick glasses.

'Mrs Beckwith? I'm Jules Stewart. I believe Terri has booked me a room.'

'Of course. Welcome, welcome, please come in. How nice to meet a new resident in our little hamlet. I can't tell you how excited we all are to have you here.'

Jules opened her mouth to correct the elderly lady. She had no plans to remain in Cottinghale long enough to be considered a resident, but as she stepped into the hallway the words disappeared.

In the instant the front door closed behind her, Jules felt the tiny hairs on the back of her neck prick up, as if a million pairs of eyes had set their gaze on her. Yet, other than the frail body of Mrs Beckwith, they seemed to be alone. That was until she saw them, lining the shelf above the radiator, and every other available surface in Mrs Beckwith's house. Tiny brass animals of every kind imaginable – owls, tigers, mice, monkeys – their beady black eyes staring out at her.

'This is the living room,' the old lady explained as she led Jules into a room at the front of the house straight out of the 1950s.

Four high-backed maroon chairs with white lacy doilies on the arms and headrests consumed the room, all pointing at an old television with wood-panelled sides that looked as if it had been there for more years than Jules had been alive.

'I've got my own annex off from the kitchen so you're welcome to spend as much time in here as you like. I'm afraid you're the only guest at the moment so you might find it a bit quiet, but once you've got to know everyone you'll feel right at home.'

'Great, thank you,' Jules mumbled, her gaze falling to a tall sideboard opposite the doorway. On the top, above a stack of decrepit-looking board games and a shelf of nameless red books, sat a row of multi-coloured bottles which seemed to beckon Jules like a hot bath on a cold night.

'Help yourself,' Mrs Beckwith nodded, following Jules's gaze. 'From what Terri told me, you'll need a drink,' she added with a chuckle.

'Thanks,' Jules replied with a weak smile.

Mrs Beckwith shuffled on to a room towards the back of the house, bumping into a side table as she moved and scattering the ornamental animals resting on it. Lucky they were brass and not porcelain, Jules thought, wondering if Mrs Beckwith's glasses needed to be a few inches thicker.

'And here's the dining room,' she began, leading Jules into an equally dated room with a long, dark wood table, complete with a lace tablecloth.

'I do breakfast anytime you like, from toast to the full works. I can also do evening meals. Just let me know each morning if you'll be wanting something,' the old lady explained, knocking into a chair and letting out a loud trumpet fart. 'Oops, do excuse me, my dear. It's this high-fibre diet those pesky doctors have got me on," Mrs Beckwith chuckled.

Jules stifled a smirk. 'That's very kind of you Mrs Beckwith. Err, shall we say coffee and toast at eight tomorrow and go from there?'

'That's fine, dear.'

It took another ten minutes before Mrs Beckwith showed Jules to her room. The old lady talked as slowly as she moved, bumping into several more tables before she made it to the narrow staircase. Each knock unleashed more noises from the landlady and more detail than Jules cared to know about high-fibre diets.

'I've got three rooms I hire out, all the same apart from the colours. I've put you in the yellow room; it's the nicer one.' The old lady smiled at Jules, showing off a row of gleaming white dentures.

As Jules stepped through the open doorway she fought the urge to laugh at the room before her. Compared to the rest of the house it was almost completely bare. A single bed rested against the only radiator, just below a single-paned window looking out into the darkness. A mustard yellow bed cover and matching curtains provided the only colour to the room.

Apart from the bed, a thin wardrobe and a chest of drawers were the only other pieces of furniture in the room; both tucked against the wall opposite a beautiful mahogany fireplace, which looked like it belonged in a national heritage home rather than Mrs Beckwith's strange guesthouse.

'Nice and spacious,' the old lady said from the doorway, as if the room needed the extra description. 'A little plain I know, but you wouldn't believe the amount of trouble I've had with hikers stealing my precious animals. In the end I had to move them all downstairs. Never trust a hiker, that's my motto.'

Jules nodded, unable to think of an appropriate response.

Mrs Beckwith continued regardless. 'The bathroom is just at the end of the hallway. As I said, you've got it all to yourself so feel free to leave any toiletries in there. And on that note, I will leave you to it. Just knock on the kitchen door if you need anything. Sleep well, dear.'

'Thank you Mrs Beckwith,' she replied, lifting her hand in a small wave as she closed the heavy wooden door.

It could be worse, Jules told herself, dropping onto the lumpy bed and shrugging off her jacket; but as her hands felt for the newspaper still hiding in her pocket, she struggled to see how.

Two

The fifth long and sickly swig of bright green out-of-date crème de menthe caused two thin trickles of liquid to fall from the tiny china mug and down the sides of Jules's mouth. The alcohol finally defrosted the ice blocks of her feet from beneath the bed spread.

Did out-of-date crème de menthe increase the alcohol content or reduce it? Jules wondered. At least the arctic temperatures outside the bedroom kept the disgusting drink too cold for her taste buds to protest. It was alcohol after all – alcohol she so desperately needed. Jules let her eyelids close for a moment as she felt her thoughts drift to the hidden crevices of her mind.

'How could he do this to me?' Jules whispered to the empty room, the hit of alcohol finally allowing her to unleash the thoughts that had been bubbling under the surface of her consciousness since she'd seen the newspaper that now lay across her lap. It should have been another layer of warmth, but each time her eyes scanned the wretched article it chilled her to the bone.

It was dated yesterday, Valentine's Day. Her picture had been plastered across the front page of a trashy tabloid for twenty-four hours and no one had contacted her. How could that be? But even as Jules asked the question, she knew the answer.

Each new project meant, among other things, a new location and a mobile upgrade. She had replaced the number this time too, not bothering to tell anyone but her parents of the change, and they were two people as unlikely to read the tabloids as she was to keep in touch with old friends. Her eyes flicked back to the headline.

'Bastard.' The involuntary sound startled her as it slipped out from somewhere inside. A sense of *déjà vu* spread through her. She had been here before: a newspaper open in front of her, Guy's face staring back. But this time it was her grinning face next to his. The photograph, like a hundred others that had been taken throughout the years of their relationship, showed her and Guy arm in arm on a night out, grinning at the camera without a care in the world. Had she really ever been that happy? she wondered suddenly, staring at the young girl with the smile so wide it seemed to stretch across the entire length of her face.

Five years without a single word and then this, Jules thought, cutting off the memories from invading her mind. She had vanquished Guy from her head a long time ago and had no plans to let him back in now. Why, after all this time, would he be trying to drag her back into his life? It was the most impersonal form of communication, yet the worst possible intrusion.

It had to be a publicity stunt, she realised. Nevertheless, it was another slap in the face to the truth of how wrong she'd been about him (and herself, for that matter).

With each sweet sip of the green alcohol, Jules melted closer to numbness. She forgot if it was anger or hurt that she was supposed to feel at Guy's pathetic attempt to boost his career and stomp over her private life in the process. Then, without warning, the *déjà vu* probed again at the doors of her mind: the flash of another cold bedroom, another lifetime, and the other newspaper spread in front of her; the familiar feeling of alcohol coursing through her, the haze luring her into a dark nothingness.

A bitter taste of bile rose to the back of Jules's throat as she recalled the empty bottle of vodka and the crippling sadness that had hounded her. Just the thought of that time in her life was enough to start the hammering in her chest. How close had she been? Always the same question, never the same answer. But she was a different person now, her own person, she reminded herself, pushing the cup out of reach on the bedside table. She shuffled further under the covers as she pushed the images and the questions back to their hiding place, until her mind stopped churning and sleep took her away.

The constant early morning drizzle soothed Jules's hot face as she pounded her legs harder into the hillside. Her limbs seemed to move on mechanical autopilot as she fought for one cold breath after another. The wispy shrubs of winter scratched against the bottom of her calves in the space where her leggings stopped and the cold started. Woodland stretched before her, the leaves from summer still spread across the floor, crunching like orange and brown cornflakes beneath her feet.

Jules liked running. She liked the power it gave her and the way it kept her body lean, but most of all she liked the healing force of running, the way it never failed to clear the remnants of a bad day.

With each mile of ground she covered, Jules began to feel herself again. In fact, as she threaded her way up the valley, she felt almost normal. The betrayal of Guy's lies meant nothing. One newspaper, one headline, one very old and unrecognisable photograph, it would all be forgotten. She had been the victim of a cruel publicity stunt and a slow news day. Nothing more.

Jules felt as if she could run forever with her head down against the cutting February wind, her mind pushing away the anger and hurt of Guy's betrayal, and the fear and frustration she felt towards the mess of her new house. But as her feet fell upon the flat grassy hilltop, Jules stopped. A sudden break in the clouds unleashed a weak beam of sunshine, causing a momentary brush of light to touch her face.

As she turned slowly on her heels, her eyes absorbed the view. Tangled branches sprouted out from the woodland covering the slopes before her. Beyond the hills, scattered beams of light dropped from the thick cloud like spotlights on the dark and empty farmland. The sweet smell of fresh morning dew filled Jules's senses. It felt like a different world compared to the bleak cement of the bedsit in Nottingham, the flat in Slough, and the townhouse in Reading. Their images deteriorated into one grey block in Jules's mind compared to the landscape before her.

Not for the first time, Jules wondered how she'd come to own a property in such an unusual place as Cottinghale. There had been none of her normal meetings with the property management companies she'd worked for; no renovation cost calculations or profit analysis completed; and none of the methodical planning she'd applied to her life and her work over the past five years.

Within a matter of hours from setting eyes on the detached stone house at the top of the hamlet, Jules had found herself making an offer and beginning the extraction of her small life in Reading. She still recalled the lure from that first showing. The late autumn sunshine had shone through every window, illuminating high ceilings and huge rooms.

She had felt a pull towards it, as if something in the house had called to her that day. It needed so much more than a new coat of paint and a laminate floor: it needed her love, something she felt unqualified to give to anyone or anything.

Whatever it was that had made her ignore the moulding wallpaper, the fraying carpets, the desperate creaks of the stairs under her feet, she had responded to it. It seemed she had finally found the solitude she'd been craving for so long.

As her breath slowed, Jules felt the first tingle of cool air penetrate through the thin layer of sweat cloaking her skin. Time to head back, she decided, lifting her shoulders in a shrug as if apologising to the beauty that lay before her – except that, in the few short moments Jules had been standing on the hilltop, each pathway leading back into the wood looked exactly the same. She had no idea which twisting path led back to Cottinghale, Jules realised on the verge of panic. She had been so lost in her thoughts that she hadn't bothered to keep track of her route and now she really was lost.

It was early on a Sunday morning in the middle of nowhere. She could keep running for miles in the wrong direction and find nothing but pneumonia and exhaustion.

Then, out of nowhere, a rustle sounded from the undergrowth directly in front of her. Shit! Do they have wolves in the English countryside? No, of course not, she silently answered her own fear, but what about the panther sightings she'd heard about a few months ago? Had that been near here? Where was here?

Just as Jules prepared herself for a diving sprint to the cover of the woodland behind her, the creature revealed itself. Galloping out from its hiding place, a brown and white springer spaniel, not much older than a puppy, bounded full pelt towards her with his bright pink tongue flapping in the air at the same rate as his giant floppy ears. Hardly the vicious creature she had feared, Jules realised with relief.

'Hello there,' she cooed as the dog sniffed her outstretched hands. His stubby white tail wagged so hard that the whole back half of his body wiggled from side to side. Jules ran her hands over the dog's hot, damp back as she crouched down to his level, leaving her hands covered in white and brown hairs.

'I hope you've come to show me the way home.'

At the sound of her voice, the dog wriggled with even more fury as he shoved his cold nose towards her; the force causing Jules to topple back onto the damp grass as he flapped his hot wet tongue across her face. A sudden smell of rotting fish overtook the fresh morning dew.

'Yes, yes, I've said hello,' she grinned, pushing the dog back so she could sit up.

'I hope that's how you greet everyone up here,' a man's voice said from behind her as a pair of green wellingtons stepped into view beside her.

'Oh, sorry, I was saying hello and your dog pushed me over,' she replied, her eyes widening at the sight of the rugged, immensely tall blond towering over her.

'I can see that,' he replied with a broad smile, brushing a tassel of windswept hair away from his face. 'Now, Maximus,' he said, turning his attention to the dog, 'how many times do I have to tell you, it's customary to take a girl on a date before you slobber on her.'

The unfamiliar sound of a laugh escaped from inside Jules as the dog barked his response. Taking advantage of the dog's wavering attention, Jules scrambled to her feet, pretending not to notice the outstretched hand of the man offering to help her up from the cold ground.

'Well you've already met Maximus, Max for short, and I'm Rich, and guessing by the look of you, you're lost.'

'Jules,' she replied, wiping Max's saliva from her face and looking up towards the dog owner. Even standing, Jules couldn't help but feel taken aback by his height. She barely reached his chest and she was hardly short herself at five foot ten inches.

'And I'm not lost; I was just taking a breather,' she replied, the lie falling from her lips before she had a chance to consider why.

'Really?' Rich raised his eyebrows.

'Yes,' she said, a little more hotly than she intended.

'Well, I'll let you get on with your run then.' Rich took a step back allowing Jules to choose her direction, his gaze on her face unfaltering.

But she couldn't leave; she still had no idea which way led back to Cottinghale. Damn, why hadn't she just admitted that she was lost?

'Everything alright?' he asked.

'Yes thanks, I'm just deciding which route to take back,' she lied again.

'And where is back?'

'Cottinghale.'

Before Rich could reply, Max let out a loud piecing bark.

'It looks like we're heading back together then if you don't mind? Max wants his breakfast.'

'Sure,' she replied, feeling a mixture of relief and embarrassment.

'It's beautiful, isn't it,' Rich said, looking out across the valley, but making no move to begin the journey home. 'Be careful round here though, the ruins of the Cottinghale estate are dotted all over the place; it's easy to lose your footing, especially after all the rain we've had this year.'

'Right,' she replied, brushing aside his warning without a second thought. Her independence always seemed to bring out the protective side in some men, as if they couldn't quite believe she was happy on her own.

'Seriously. This whole area used to have stables and other out houses all over it. A fire destroyed the lot back in the eighteen hundreds but Lord Cottinghale had a love of cellars apparently and a lot of the land you now see is covering up some pretty dangerous holes. We normally have to rescue the odd hiker in the summer.'

'How did it all burn down if the estate was so spread out?' Jules asked, uncertain whether to believe him.'

'Lord Cottinghale burnt it all down himself. He was a terrible gambler and lost everything he owned in one poker game, if you believe the local gossip that is. Apparently he couldn't bear for anyone else to have his home so he set fire to it before taking his own life.'

'That's terrible.'

'Thankfully he didn't get round to the servant quarters further down the valley, otherwise Cottinghale as we know it wouldn't exist. Those old servant houses are now the main high street of the Hamlet of Cottinghale. If you can call one farm shop and one pub a high street.'

Another bark from Max mirrored Jules own impatience to get back. She could feel her fingers turning numb from the cold.

'Shall we go then?' she asked.

'Lead the way.' Rich waved his hand in the direction of the woods, the edges of his mouth twitched with a smile.

'Sorry?'

An unfamiliar sensation wound its way into Jules's stomach. The mischievous twinkle in his smiling blue eyes combined with his broad physique unsettled her.

'I thought you were deciding the route back? Me and Max don't mind, do we Max?'

The dog barked his agreement.

With no other options available to her, Jules stepped in the direction of Max; hoping the dog would lead the way for her.

'Um—'

'Something wrong?' Jules asked, frowning at the amused expression on Rich's face.

'Nothing. I'm just surprised you want to go this way,' he said, falling in step next to her. 'Don't mind getting your feet wet crossing the river, I guess.'

'No, I was just—'

'About to admit that you are actually lost and ask the friendly dog walker for assistance,' he cut in.

'Fine. I'm lost, but in my defence I only moved here yesterday.'

Rich's deep laugh reverberated in her ears.

'Now that wasn't so hard, was it?' he said, shrugging off his waist-length black coat to reveal a fraying grey jumper, complete with what looked to Jules to be a Bolognese sauce stain spread down the front.

'Here, take this.'

'Thanks, but I'm fine.'

As if she hadn't spoken, Rich placed the coat over her shoulders.

'Take it, if for no other reason it saves me having to carry you home when you collapse from hypothermia, which by the look of your blue lips is any moment now,' he explained, eyeing her lips and creating another wave of unsettlement to dance inside her.

'Thank you,' she muttered, feeling as small as a doll as she slipped her arms into the enormous sleeves, still warm from Rich's body.

'Good, now come on then, Max, this way.' Rich clapped his hands at the dog, striding towards the same path Jules had chosen moments earlier.

'Hey, what about the river?' she quizzed, half running to keep pace with his long strides.

'Oh, there's no river. I just wanted you to admit you were lost.'

'Well, thanks again then.'

'You're welcome.'

'I was being sarcastic.'

'Really? I didn't notice. Us local folk don't know much about sarcasm,' he replied, the amusement never leaving his voice.

They walked in silence for a moment, following a zigzag path down through the woodland. Max galloped around them, dividing his attention between the delights of the undergrowth and the ear scratches from his new friend.

'So how is Mrs Beckwith treating you?'

'What?'

'Mrs Beckwith, the landlady of the B&B.'

'Yes, I know who she is, but how did you know I'm staying there?'

'Ever lived in a small place like Cottinghale before, Jules?' Rich asked.

'No, but—'

'Didn't think so. Let me tell you exactly what it took me a month to realise. Everyone knows everything.'

'Really?' she replied in a mocking tone.

Rich grinned at her. 'Your name is Jules Stewart, you've just bought the old Mayor House, and you're staying at Mrs Beckwith's because the house isn't safe. Oh, and apparently you don't like being called Juliet. Did I miss anything out?'

'Or "lovey",' she replied, hiding her discomfort at how much he seemed to know about her. 'I don't like being called "lovey" either.'

'What about darling?'

'Nope.'

'Peach?'

'Definitely not.' The unfamiliar sensation of a smile began to form on her lips.

In what felt like no time at all, Jules found herself standing outside the blue front door of Mrs Beckwith's guesthouse.

'Here we are then,' Rich said.

'Well, thanks for... err... keeping me company on the way home.'

'You mean thanks for saving you from hypothermia and certain death?'

'I wouldn't go that far, but thanks,' she smiled.

'You're welcome, Jules.'

Seconds past between them as Rich's smiling eyes never left hers. He stepped towards her. 'Any chance I could have my coat back then?'

'Of course. Sorry.' Jules felt her cheeks colour as she shrugged the cosy layer from her body and handed it back to Rich. A shiver travelled across her skin at the chilly void it left behind.

'Say goodbye, Max,' Rich said.

'Goodbye Max,' she responded without thinking.

'I was talking to him,' Rich corrected with another amused grin, nodding his head towards Max's panting body.

'Right, bye then.' Jules turned towards the guesthouse to hide her flaming cheeks.

As she stepped into the quiet house, Jules caught sight of her appearance in the brass hallway mirror and gasped in horror. Max had left more than just mud and drool on her already red face. She had what appeared to be clumps of dried green snot on either cheek. With that and the frizzy damp hair and yesterday's smudged mascara, she looked like she'd been dragged through a hedge backwards and sneezed on by Shrek. What must Rich have thought? Jules cringed.

Shaking her head at her own pathetic reflection, Jules forced thoughts of the tall blond stranger from her mind. The only thing she wanted to concentrate on was a hot shower and the hole in her ceiling, she reminded herself.

Three

THE DAILY
MONDAY, FEBRUARY 17TH
WHEREFORE ART THOU JULIET?

We at *The Daily* are not ones to stand in the way of star-crossed lovers and judging by the overwhelming response from our readers after model turned singer Guy Rawson exclusively revealed that he was still deeply "in love" with his ex, Juliet Stewart, neither is Britain.

So with the UK still firmly in the grip of winter blues, we hope to bring some early sunshine and help true love along the way with our brand spanking new campaign, Wherefore Art Thou Juliet?

Come on folks, we need your help to reunite Britain's hunkiest man and his beautiful muse, Juliet, the girl responsible for his chart topping single 'Regret', which hit number one in Sunday's chart show.

If you have a story to share about our love struck pair then contact Sara-Marie Francis on 0800 559 119, sara-marie@thedaily.co.uk NOW!

And just in case you need another reason to get involved, here's what Paul Atkins, a close friend of the pair during their days at Loughborough University, said: "Guy and Juliet were so much fun. The three of us were always out on the town having a laugh. They really were the perfect couple, always together and the happiest people I knew … it's tragic, we all thought they'd be together forever.'

Left: The couple in happier times just months before they split.

Guy threw his body onto the giant leather sofa, feeling at ease among the mess of brightly coloured toys littering his sister's North London terrace house.

'Nuncle Gy,' a tiny voice shrieked from the doorway.

The sight of his nephew sent a wave of love spiralling though him for the blond bundle tottering towards him. 'Sam the man. Come give me a hug.'

'Gy, nucle Gay.'

Sam stretched his stubby arms above his head as he reached the sofa, letting out a squeal of delight as Guy lifted him high in the air before resting him with care on the edge of his knees.

'Un-cle G-u-y,' he prompted, sounding out the letters of his name.

'Nuncle Gay,' Sam yelled, ignoring his uncle's pronunciation lesson as Debbie shuffled her round pregnant belly into the room, balancing two steaming mugs, a bottle of Sam's milk and a plate of chocolate Hobnobs in her hands.

'Sammy,' Debbie laughed, side stepping a yellow duck waddling its way musically across the living room.

'I bet you taught him to say that,' Guy accused his older sister with a grin as he set Sam's wriggling body to the floor.

'Guy, he's 18 months old, he is getting everyone's names wrong, yours just happens to be funny,' Debbie teased, ignoring Guy's frown.

'Yeah right.' Guy took the hot coffee cup from his sister. 'Ever heard of this great new invention called a tray?' he joked.

'Ever heard of washing? You smell as bad as Sam's nappies,' she retorted with a grin.

Guy looked down at yesterday's Levi's and dirty black t-shirt. Debbie was right, he did smell. Why hadn't he stopped to grab a shower and some fresh clothes after the early call from his publicist?

His local Primrose Hill newsagent had hardly been in danger of selling out of the damn thing. His 'daddy's trust fund' neighbours as likely to leave the house before 8am as they were to shop anywhere off Knightsbridge.

'Sorry Sis,' he replied with a shrug.

'Oh, Guy, I have to tell you something,' Debbie began, waving the plastic milk bottle towards Sam.

'Ta,' she said, as he gripped the container with both hands and plodded towards the television at the end of the room. 'The other day it was so funny, we were watching TV with Carl's parents and that clothes advert you're still in came on. I didn't realise how much Sam could pick up, but he started jumping up and down shouting "gay gay gay," honestly I thought I was going to wet myself. Although I feel like that most days,' she smiled resting one hand on her bump as she dropped to the other end of the sofa.

'Now,' she began, between mouthfuls of Hobnob, 'What brings you here so early? Sam's not even had his nap yet.'

'Nap? It's barely nine.'

'You try getting up at five every morning and see how you feel by this time. Now don't avoid my questions, I'm your big sister and I can tell when something's wrong.'

Guy sighed and unravelled the newspaper from its previously twisted position in his fist.

'It's this.'

Despite the creases, Guy watched his sister's eyes fall straight to the double E cups of the red head sprawled across the page.

'Oh dear,' she said, after swallowing the remainder of the Hobnob.

'Bloody hell! Not that, this, this is what I'm talking about.' Guy jabbed his finger at the story on the opposite page to the half-naked girl, causing a dark splash of coffee to burn through his jeans.

'Guy,' Debbie hissed, nodding her head in the direction of Sam, his gaze unfaltering from the television screen and the episode of Peppa Pig he was watching with trance-like interest.

'Shhi … Sorry, I always forget,' he whispered, rubbing his hand across the scalding damp patch on his thigh.

Guy watched his sister scan the article between loud slurps of a red coloured tea. She had the same high cheekbones and dark eyes, but the features which had earned him a small fortune in modelling contracts were, drawn and weary on his older sister. Until the same crooked smile lit up her face, that was.

'Why are you smiling?' Guy asked, failing to see even the slightest amount of humour in the story, which had jolted him from his sleep like a cattle prod to the head.

'Because this is typical you, totally overreacting. You are such a drama queen.'

'How?' he cried out. 'How am I overreacting?' Guy took a breath. Ever since he could talk, Debbie had been able to make his voice rise to the pitch of a 12-year old choirboy. 'I don't even know anyone called Paul, or where the hell they got this photo from,' Guy added, staring at the picture of him and Juliet lounging in the sun during their final summer together. It seemed a million years ago now.

Guy tried unsuccessfully to push away the memories poking at the edge of his mind.

'What's the big deal, it says here you got to number one, and congratulations by the way,' Debbie touched his arm, 'but other than that, it's not even about you.'

'That's the point, Debs. It's about Juliet.'

'Well, have you phoned her to see if she's okay?'

'Come off it. We haven't spoken in five years and I'm just supposed to pick up the phone and dial a random number on the off chance it's hers? I have no idea how to contact her. I wouldn't know where to begin anyway. I still can't believe what an idiot I was for telling that journalist about her in the first place. Does off the record not count for anything?'

'Exactly my point.'

Guy let his head fall against the soft cushioning of the headrest and closed his eyes. 'I'm sorry, what is your point?' he mumbled, not liking the direction the conversation seemed to be taking.

'For goodness sake, there have been hundreds of stories printed about you, most of which have been total rubbish, and you've always shrugged them off or had a good laugh about it. Why are you letting this one get to you? Surely the extra publicity is helping to sell your music?'

'You sound like Sonja. She acted like it was a lottery win when the first story came out. "You can't buy publicity like this",' he added, replacing his faded South Yorkshire tones with the mimicked squeak of his high-strung publicist.

'So you expect me to believe that you just happen to reveal some juicy details about a relationship which you never talk about to anyone let alone to a complete stranger just as your new career is taking off? A bit of a coincidence, don't you think?'

'What? How can you even suggest …' Guy let out a deep sigh, rubbing his hand against the sandpaper of his day old dark stubble. It tickled against the coarse edges of his fingertips, dry and rough from so many hours spent plucking the strings of his guitar.

He tried again to explain. 'Look, it was an accident, okay? We were in my flat, just me and the journalist. The interview was over. We were sifting through photos of my old playing days and one of Juliet cropped up. I should have just said she was an old friend, but something about seeing her face again, it sparked something in my stupid head and I just started blabbing. She stole the picture too. I mean, how rude is that?'

Debbie paused for a moment, sniffing the air. 'If you'll excuse me, there is now a worse smell in the room than you.' She pushed herself to her feet, resting a hand against the small of her back and letting out an exhausted sigh.

'Come on Sammy, let's get that nappy changed and have a little nap, and then mummy will take you to see the ducks.'

'Duck,' Sam repeated, allowing Debbie to guide his tired legs towards the door.

'Oh right, so he can say duck perfectly but he can't say Guy,' he mumbled, unable to conceal a smile at Sam's quacking noises.

At the door, Debbie turned back to the sofa. 'Just one other thing – if this wasn't just a stunt, then did you mean what you said?'

'I … err …' Guy spluttered, their eyes locking as Debbie's eyebrows shot to the middle of her forehead.

'I'll let you think about that one, shall I?' she cut in, leaving Guy alone with her question still ringing in his ears.

Did he mean it?

The emotions had felt real enough when he'd spoken about them to that bloody journalist. But every time he tried to conjure the same feelings it left his stomach in knots; hardly the most concrete declaration of love, he conceded, running his hand over the short spikes of his dark brown hair.

Whatever his feelings, he knew they had started long before the interview. Ever since the modelling contracts had began to leave him feeling hollow and pathetic. Ever since he'd dusted off his old guitar and started strumming his fingers against the strings for the first time in years.

Something in him had changed. The same something that had finally driven him to walk away from modelling and start singing again. It had unlocked him. As if he had been in a long coma, only to wake up and find the world had turned upside down. He hadn't recognised the pampered reflection staring back at him from the mirror.

But even after the unexpected success of his first single and the feeling that he had finally began living his dream, a part of him still felt missing.

A number one single – he should be jumping from the walls, but instead he felt unfazed, numb even.

Whatever Juliet had to do with his feelings, he didn't know, but day after day he couldn't stop the memories and the feelings from creeping back.

Guy swallowed hard. Unleashing his emotions into the lyrics of his songs detached them somehow. Admitting them in the bright morning light left nothing to hide behind.

'Right,' Debbie said, dragging Guy's thoughts back into the room. 'I have exactly sixty minutes before Sam's batteries recharge to max. Have you got an answer?' Her movements were similar to the waddling yellow duck as she dropped back to the sofa, lifting her feet onto the glass coffee table.

Guy turned his head towards her, noticing again the dark circles under her eyes and the grey sheen covering her usually rosy cheeks. 'Hey.' He reached out for her hand feeling suddenly protective. 'Are you okay, Sis?'

She met his gaze with a weak smile. 'You're avoiding my question.'

'No, I'm serious, are you okay? Do you want me to take Sam out today, give you a chance to have a break?'

'Thanks but I'm fine, honestly. It's just the usual pregnancy tiredness, and chasing after a toddler all day and most of the night. But Carl has been running around after me like a guide dog for the blind so I can't complain. Ask me again next week and I'll take you up on your offer.'

'Any time. I mean it.'

Guy continued to stare with a growing concern at his sister. At four years older, she had always looked out for him. Guy had been too young to remember when their parents had died in a car accident, but Debbie hadn't. Putting her grief aside, she had looked after him, reading to him late at night when he couldn't sleep and staying with him whenever he had nightmares.

They'd been lucky. Their aunt and uncle had given them a happy childhood in Doncaster, but Debbie had never stopped mothering him. Now the years of worry were written across her face.

When she'd met Carl three years earlier at a conference, Guy had been a little sceptical about their relationship. Carl was a nice guy; the reliable type, but hardly the most exciting man in the world. It had taken Guy a while to understand that Debbie liked that about Carl: the stability and the unquestionable love that they had for each other.

'Earth to Guy?' Debbie grinned, waving a hand in front of Guy's eyes.

'Sorry Debs, I was miles away.'

'You don't exactly look like the picture of health either, you know.'

Guy looked down at his creased t-shirt again. 'I know. Last night was my first gig since my single came out. I never realised how tiring it would be.'

'So that's why you smell like a brewery rat, is it? How did it go? Oh and we heard your interview on the radio, very cool. And don't let me forget to get a few autographs from you; they are like currency at playgroups. I've had more offers of play dates than I know what to do with.'

'Yeah, sure. It went pretty well. A great crowd for a Sunday night in Angel and they seemed to like me.'

'Great, now back to Juliet,' Debbie began with a wicked smile. 'You can't tell me you don't know how you feel?'

'Err … I … look, that's not the point.' Guy shifted position, unable to get comfortable under Debbie's stare. 'The point is that Juliet, wherever she is, is probably scared out of her wits right now. Wouldn't you be if some tabloid had started a campaign about you?'

'Rubbish,' Debbie said with a light laugh.

'What?'

'I may not have known Juliet as well as you did, but on the times we met, I don't remember her being the weakling you seem to think she is. Her only problem back then was the way she let you walk all over her, but you sorted that one out, didn't you?'

'That's not true.' Guy stood up, moving across to the large bay window at the end of the room.

'Right.'

'It's not.' He turned towards his sister, surprised at the anger in her voice.

'I spoke to her, you know, after you broke up,' she said before he could carry on.

Something in Guy's stomach lurched. 'Really? Why?'

'Because I wanted to tell her I was sorry that it hadn't worked out.' Debbie rested her hands across her bump. 'She told me what happened.'

'You never said.'

'Nor did you.'

Guy turned back to the window and took a long breath, the silence hanging between them. Why did he suddenly feel more tired than he could ever remember feeling?

'Look, Guy, my hormones are everywhere at the moment, I'm seven months pregnant for goodness sake,' Debbie paused, her voice softening. 'I've never commented on how you live your life and we are all so proud of your success.'

'But,' Guy added, his voice barely audible as he stared out onto the empty street.

'But when are you going to grow up? You're my little brother and I love you, but ever since we were kids you've always thought normal life didn't apply to you. And in some ways you were right, you are an amazingly talented singer.'

'Debbie,' he cut in, 'just say what you want to say.'

'Fine. You're selfish.'

Guy felt the slap of her words. He had heard the same from a few women over the years, but he'd always thought they hadn't understood him. Hearing it from his sister cut deep.

'Sorry, Guy, that came out wrong. What I mean is that you are an amazing brother and a great uncle to Sam, but with everything else you seem to have this one-track mind. I never asked you what happened between you and Juliet when you turned up on my doorstep and slept on the sofa-bed for months. I knew you'd tell me if you wanted to.

'But whatever happened, it changed you. You threw yourself into becoming a success, even though it was obvious you hated modelling, and you didn't stop for breath until a few months ago. And now you're doing the same thing all over again with your music. Except this time, it's something you love. So why are you trying to drag Juliet back into it?'

'I'm not, like I told you it was an accident, I had no intention of getting her involved in my life like this,' he said again, suddenly wishing he hadn't left the comfort of his huge studio flat at all that morning.

Having a sister that lived only ten minutes down the road in Finchley had its good points, but none of them sprung to mind at that moment.

'But you have, so what are you going to do about it?'

'I'm not sure there's much I can do, I have no control over what the papers print,' Guy sighed. He knew he sounded lame.

'There you go again, turning your back on anything that doesn't fall into your lap. You've been so lucky with the modelling and now you are finally doing what you love, and you're great at it, how many people can say that?' She paused for a moment. 'If I thought you were happy I wouldn't be saying this, but I don't think you are.' Debbie stopped, her words hanging in the air between them.

'Right,' he nodded, negotiating his way over the toys back to the sofa.

Kneeling beside his sister, he pecked her on the cheek. 'I'm off then.'

'Wait. I've said too much haven't I? Don't go, come and feed the ducks with me and Sam, I promise not to say any more.'

'No Debbie, you're right, you're always right,' he said, stretching his athletic body back to standing. 'I'm going to do something.'

'Hang on, Guy, don't rush into anything. Let's talk about this. What are you going to do?' his sister asked, her voice taking on a desperate tone.

'I have no idea. Do what I should have done years ago – find Juliet,' he replied, already striding out of the room. 'Love you Sis. Give Sam a kiss from me; see you next week for babysitting duties.'

'Guy wait, don't slam the …'

The loud bang of the front door drowned out the remainder of Debbie's plea.

Two hours later, a freshly shaven and considerably cleaner Guy jumped into his black Jaguar XF and set off.

Four

Loughborough University, Freshers' week, eight years earlier.

The sudden halt of Guy's body almost threw him off balance as his tattered trainers scraped along the floor of the empty corridor. For a split second he had no idea what had pulled him from his trance-like walk. And then the scent caught him again.

The smell like the Woolworth's pick and mix counter – sugar and sweet and just out of reach. He made a mental note to add the line to one of his new songs, instantly forgetting the tune he'd been humming.

He took a long breath in, filling his senses; his feet already moving towards the source as if his body had become disconnected from his mind. Finally, Guy lifted his gaze from their usual view of the concrete floor, finding instead a girl with the biggest green eyes he had ever seen.

Guy found himself unable to take another breath as he took in the bright blonde hair, cut short and messy, and a black loose knit jumper showing the lace of a bra and the milky colour of her skin.

He wanted to touch that skin.

As if hearing his thoughts, the girl flicked her eyes towards his, her pupils wide and clear like a wild animal startled by the headlights from a passing car.

'Hey,' Guy said, fighting the urge to grin like the village idiot.

'Hey.'

'You look lost.'

'I am,' she said, with a smile that hit him like a wave of warm sunshine washing over him.

'Need a hand?'

'I don't know. Can you tell me where lecture room four is? I've been walking around this building for the past twenty minutes. I've found one, two, three and five, but four seems to have been pulled into a parallel universe or something. All these corridors look exactly the same and I'm going to be so late,' she finished, throwing a hand in desperation along the mottled blue walls.

'Ah yes, the mysterious lecture room four, I had a class in there yesterday.'

'Great,' she replied, the relief visible across her face.

Fuck, she was amazing, Guy thought, as the green oceans of her eyes drew him closer. His mouth stretched into a lopsided smile that he was powerless to stop.

'Can you tell me where it is then?'

'Yeah sorry, it's this way, I'll walk with you,' he replied, his cheeks reddening. Pull yourself together, man, before she thinks you're a total moron.

'Thanks.' She smiled, falling into step beside him.

'So you're a musician?'

'Yeah, how did you…?'

She nodded her head towards the long black bag on his back. What a moron, of course he had his guitar with him. The weight on his back so familiar it was like a second skin.

He took a deep breath and tried to slow down his racing heartbeat, pounding like a bass drum in his ears.

'What's the lecture?' he asked, changing the subject before he could embarrass himself any further.

'You wouldn't believe me if I told you.'

'Oh come on, how weird can it be?'

'The history of fashion buttons.'

'Seriously? You're right, that is pretty unbelievable.'

'I know, it sounds ridiculous, but in the past fifty years buttons have lost a lot of their functionality and are being used more and more as part of a design rather than a fastening device.'

'Yeah I get it,' Guy nodded, as if her explanation made total sense. 'Like the chocolate kind.'

To Guy's amazement, the girl threw her head back and laughed, the sound as enchanting as it was surprising.

'I'll have to remember that for my essay,' she grinned, turning her face to meet his. 'What about you? I'm going to guess you study something to do with music.'

'Business studies,' he replied with the nonchalant shrug he gave when mentioning anything in his life which stole him away from his dream. 'It's just a backup plan, if my singing doesn't take off.'

'Oh, I'm sure it will. Hey, lecture room four, thanks.' She grinned at him for a moment longer before darting into the theatre.

And just like that, she was gone. Before he'd even had a chance to ask her name, let alone when he could see her again.

The realisation caused an emptiness to spread through him.

He looked first towards the door, swinging closed before him, and then down at the empty folder in his hands, waiting to be filled with his own lecture notes.

What if he never saw her again?

It took a moment for his eyes to adjust as he darted into the dark lecture theatre. Directly in front of him, down a steep row of steps, stood the lecturer, clicking through a slide show of cushions, all with various types of buttons.

Twenty or so students had spread themselves around the hall, all of them staring intently at the projector and scribbling notes. None of them was her.

Damn. What now? Stop the lecture? Sit and wait? What exactly was his plan here?

Suddenly, he felt a tug on his arm pulling him into the back row. In the dull glow of the projector light, Guy could just make out the deep wells of her eyes and the bright white of her huge smile.

Before he could even whisper a second 'hello' or try and explain why he'd followed her into a lecture about buttons, her lips touched his. Her tongue teasing open his mouth and causing an explosion of excitement and desire to run through him like an electrical current.

His whole body sprung to life as he began to kiss back.

Reaching out a shaking hand, he brushed his fingers against her cheek.

He had never felt so alive, Guy realised, knowing how crazy his thoughts sounded.

And then, just as suddenly as it had started, she pulled away.

'Sorry,' she whispered. 'I ... I've never done anything like that before, you must think I'm nuts.'

Guy had no idea how to respond, or even if he was capable of speech. Instead, he leant forward and kissed her again.

It took one week. One week of non-stop talking, of opening up their lives for one another. One week of laughing and touching; of falling into bed together as if it was the most natural thing in the world. One week before Guy could no longer remember what his life had been like before Juliet.

He'd never bothered with girlfriends before. They'd always seemed too much work and a distraction from his music.

Juliet was different. She slotted into his life and his thoughts without pushing anything out. The passion she'd unleashed inside him drove him harder to write the best song, to play the best gig.

A dream that had always seemed so far away now felt almost in reach.

Five

Jules manoeuvred her car into her driveway and killed the engine. Instead of opening the door and climbing out, she sat in perfect silence and stared up at her house.

Her house. Her dream.

If she stayed in her car and simply stared at the grey stone walls bathed in the morning light then the mess that lay beyond the front door didn't seem so bad. She didn't need to think about the hole in the ceiling, the mould in the walls, the aubergine bathroom suite, or the dank kitchen, which lacked even the basic kitchen necessities like a fridge and an oven.

She didn't have to wonder what kind of garden was buried underneath the wall of brambles and weeds, or how quickly her bank balance would run down to zero, and beyond, trying making her dream a reality. She could sit in her car on her wide sweeping driveway and just stare at her dream in solitude.

The feeling of peace did not last long. Her eyes soon strayed to Terri's old red van, parked next to the yellow skip that had appeared in her driveway on Sunday morning, and the debris that now filled it after she'd spent two days working alongside Terri, Dan and Jason to rip out what was left of her ceiling, and clear the piles of rubble from her living room floor.

A few minutes later Jules fastened the top button on her navy work overalls, opened her car door and slid out, scrunching her eyes shut for a moment as her muscles cried out in protest. The combination of hard running, hard labour and a hard mattress had taken its toll on her body.

'Morning guys. I've got biscuits. Who wants a cuppa?' she called as she stepped through the open doorway, almost tripping over Dan and Jason as they stood whispering at the bottom of the stairs.

It was the first time she'd seen them do anything other than work in two days.

'Everything okay? Where's Terri?' she asked.

'Err ...' Dan began. 'Mum's in the kitchen. Someone is here to see you.'

'Great, is it your uncle? When did he say he could start the plastering? I can't wait to have my own space again,' she said, stepping down the hallway without waiting for a response.

'Hello,' she said, stepping into the kitchen, smiling at Terri before moving her gaze to the man leaning on her kitchen counter.

Her stomach lurched as a force of emotions hit her. 'Guy,' she gasped.

'Juliet.'

For the smallest of moments everything fell away as the noise of the sea roared between her ears. For that one single second, before her mind could catch up, it felt to Jules as if someone had turned on the lights when she hadn't even realised it was dark.

And then reality hit her. 'What are you doing here?' she asked.

'I came to make sure you were okay.'

'But ...' Jules thought for a moment.

Guy had changed. The slim body she remembered was gone. Now a muscular physique filled out a jet black t-shirt and tight faded jeans. The tangled unkempt hair was also gone, but the dark pools of his eyes remained the same. They still possessed the ability to scorch into her, filling her with uncertainty.

'How did you find me?' What a ridiculous question to ask, she realised too late, as if they'd been playing a very long game of hide and seek, and she'd finally been discovered.

'I drove to Bath yesterday. Your parents gave me this address. They haven't changed a bit,' he answered, a smile touching his face.

Typical of her parents, Jules thought. They wouldn't think twice about helping Guy. Even after everything that had happened, they still seemed to idealise him.

'Go back to why you are here … you've come to check if I'm alright, why wouldn't I be?' The anger from so many years of hating was suddenly clear.

'Well, with the newspaper …' Guy trailed off.

'Yes, I've seen that, thanks very much,' she replied, her tone dripping with spite.

'Juliet, I …'

'Stop calling me that. It's Jules now.'

The space behind her eyes began to hammer in pace with her heartbeat. Why was he here? Now, after all this time?

'But you always hated Jules,' Guy replied, his gaze moving around the kitchen as if searching for someone to step in and help him.

Jules had not noticed Terri inch silently out of the room. No doubt listening from the hallway at her conversation with the famous celebrity, she thought with a flush of embarrassment.

'Guy,' she began, focusing her gaze on a point just behind the man standing in front of her. She couldn't trust herself to look into his eyes any longer. 'I really don't understand what you are doing here. You don't know me anymore. Whatever publicity stunt you're pulling, just leave me out of it.'

'Wait, Juliet, I mean Jules. It wasn't a stunt, I thought I was speaking off the record the first time and then the ridiculous article yesterday, I had nothing to do with it, you have to know that?'

'No. There was only one story, not two…' Her voice trailed off as Guy's words sunk in.

There was another article she had not seen, how could that happen again?

'I thought you'd seen it. That's why I'm here.'

'Whatever. Look it doesn't matter now, it's done. As you can see, I'm fine. So you can go back to wherever it is you came from. Okay?'

'Juli… Jules, it's not done, it's not finished. The paper has started a campaign. They are gathering information about us, and they won't stop until they know everything.'

He pulled a scrap of newspaper from his back pocket.

'About me, you mean. They already know everything about you.'

Panic began to trickle through her as she snatched the outstretched paper and scanned the article. It didn't make sense. She was a nobody. Why would anybody want to read about her life?

'Look, I understand that you're angry and I wanted to say that I'm sorry,' Guy said.

Hot red spots spread across her cheeks.

'Sorry?' Jules looked up, scrunching the paper into a tight ball in her fist. 'You think saying sorry for everything you've done is going to help now? It's too late, Guy, years too late.'

They both fell silent for a moment, before Guy spoke. 'I meant…'

Jules cut him off. 'Oh, you meant you're sorry about the newspaper, didn't you?'

A strained laugh escaped from her throat as she realised her mistake. 'And I am not angry,' she hissed.

'Juliet please, I am trying to help you. Just listen for a minute,' he pleaded, taking a step back and breaking the bubbling tension that seemed to be circling around them like a tornado.

'I don't have to…' she stopped mid-sentence as his eyes found hers, sending another wave of indecision through her. 'Fine,' she sighed. 'Say what you've got to say.'

'They are asking people to send in stories of us, of you,' he corrected as she narrowed her eyes. 'Like I said, they are going to dig around in the past until they have published every story they can find or the public get bored, which believe me, can take a while.'

'But I'm not famous.'

'To them you are. But look,' he said, pulling a pink card from the back pocket of his jeans. 'If you give this journalist a call and agree to go on the record with a few quotes on the condition that they stop the campaign, then there's a good chance we can end this.'

'We can end this?' Hot rage coursed through her. 'You started this. You. I was here, minding my own business, getting on with my life and YOU dragged me into this. And now I'm supposed to give an interview? And what am I supposed to say exactly? Or have you got that written down too?'

Jules took a step forward, the grip on the biscuit packet in her hand tightening. 'Oh hello, is this *The Daily*?' she mocked. 'I just wanted to phone and say thank you for publishing all this crap about me, I've always wanted to be famous and now I am. Oh, and please buy Guy's music because it's great.'

In the silence that followed, Jules could hear only her own heavy breathing and the fierce thundering of her heart.

'You need to do this Jules, otherwise they'll keep printing stuff; some of it will be lies but some of it won't, you can't tell me you want that?'

'Don't tell me what I need, Guy, and don't tell me what I want.'

'Please, Juliet; I am trying to help you. I know things didn't end well between us.'

Another strained laugh escaped Jules's throat.

He ignored it and continued, 'But you have to believe me, I know what I'm talking about. Please, just phone them. For your sake, not mine,' he said, holding out the card for Jules to take.

'Fine,' she snapped, snatching the card from Guy's hand, unable to avoid her fingers touching his. Her senses absorbed the familiar rough tips, causing a wave of nostalgia to throb through her.

She took an uneven step back.

'Was there anything else, then?' she asked after a long pause.

'I wanted to tell you …' Guy paused. 'I wanted to ask if you've listened to my album?'

'God, you haven't changed a bit. NO, I haven't listened to your album, and I don't plan to either, so sod off will you,' she yelled, surprised at the venom in her own voice.

His eyes continued to bore into hers.

'Okay,' he replied, pulling out a slip of paper from his jacket and sliding it onto the counter. 'Here's my number if you need me.'

'I won't ever need you.'

With her words hanging in the air, Guy stepped past her, striding quickly towards the door and out of her life for the second time.

She tasted the blood before she felt the pain, her teeth piercing into her tongue as she fought the urge to cry out after him.

Seeing him again had brought back more than just old memories. When his eyes met hers, the old weakness returned too. She couldn't let that happen. Not again.

Out of nowhere a large cracking sound filled the air, followed by a thunderous crash as the pane of glass in the kitchen window shattered to the floor, covering Jules's work boots in glass.

'What the…' Terri exclaimed as she rushed back into the room. 'Are you okay?'

'The window broke,' Jules mumbled, nodding towards the shattered glass. It must have been all the banging we've been doing in the living room. Something else to add to the "to-do" list, I guess,' she said with a weak smile.

Terri glanced at her two sons, something exchanging between them.

'What, what is it?' she quizzed, her eyes darting between them.

'Nothing. Nothing at all. Are you sure you're okay, lovey? You're not hurt, are you?' Terri answered, wrapping an arm around Jules's shoulders.

'No, I'm fine,' she replied, as a red heat crept along her cheeks. 'I'm sorry you had to hear all that.'

'Don't be ridiculous, lovey.' Terri smiled, steering Jules away from the broken glass and into the hallway. 'I've seen my share of lovers' quarrels in my time, I can tell you, and that was nothing.'

'Guy and I are not lovers,' she corrected. 'Nothing could be further from the truth.'

'Well, whatever it was, the important thing is that you are okay. Now how's about letting us take you to the pub for a drink after work today? I dare say you'll be needing it, and meeting a few more locals will make you feel right at home. Rich does a great curry on a Tuesday.'

'Rich?'

'The landlord, lovey, but don't you worry, you'll meet everyone soon enough.'

Six

Squeezed between Terri and her boys in the front of Terri's van, Jules felt the words of protest form in her mouth as they trundled, without stopping, past Mrs Beckwith's guesthouse.

She had tried three times throughout the day to postpone her drink with Terri, Dan and Jason, but each excuse she'd given had been overruled by Terri.

Seeing Guy again had drained her confidence. She'd replayed their conversation over and over in her head, scraping away the wallpaper in her hall with such fury she'd damaged the plaster underneath more than once.

At five o'clock, she'd changed her overalls for the spare jeans, jumper and pumps she always kept in her car for the times she needed to go out straight from working on a property and didn't want to wear her overalls. She may not feel like socialising, but for once she didn't feel like being alone either.

Alone gave her mind a chance to wander. Alone meant thinking about Guy and the emotions he'd unleashed inside her.

'Here we are then lovey,' Terri grinned, cutting into Jules's thoughts. 'We'll have a drink in you in no time.'

Jules nodded as she slipped her body from the van, pushing thoughts of Guy back to the deepest depths of her mind as she breathed in the sweet smell of burning embers drifting from the chimney of The Nag. Sitting in a cosy pub with a large glass of wine suddenly seemed a lot easier than spending another evening shivering in the tiny single bed at the guesthouse.

Ducking her head, Jules stepped through the low doorway, finding the inside even more welcoming. A large brick fireplace dominated the interior, complete with a roaring fire which cast a dancing orange blaze onto the cream walls and dark beams.

As if completing the picture, Max lay with his body stretched out as close to the fire's heath as he could get. His ears twitched as they closed the latch on the heavy pub door, but he made no other signs of giving up his space by the heat.

Dark wood tables and matching chairs had been dotted throughout the pub without any apparent pattern to their positioning, but it was clear from the scattering of people that the main activity focused around the long bar, which covered the entire width of the back wall.

Standing behind the bar was Rich, in a chequered red shirt that stretched tight across his large frame. He slung a bar towel over one broad shoulder as he laughed with two men sat to one side.

His height, which had seemed large against the elements the first time Jules had seen him, now appeared giant next to the old pub's beams, which hung low from the ceiling and almost touched the waves of his blonde hair.

'Rich, my favourite landlord,' Terri called as they weaved their way through the tables. 'Get this lovely girl one of your cocktails – she needs it.'

'No,' Jules protested as her eyes met his. 'Um, I mean a glass of wine would be fine, thanks.'

'Nonsense,' Terri replied, 'All new residents must try a cocktail. You'll thank me for it. And three ales for me and the boys, of course.'

Rich turned his body towards Jules as if waiting for further protest; instead she lifted her shoulders into a shrug. 'I've learnt not to argue with Terri,' she explained.

'A cocktail it is then,' Rich nodded, reaching for a glass. 'It's nice to see you again, Jules.'

She smiled and tried to ignore the feeling of unsettlement which danced in her stomach whenever he looked at her.

'How is it going up at the house?' he asked.

'Fine thanks.'

She knew she should say more. She wanted to elaborate; to share Rich's easy smile and laugh along with Terri's good humoured conversation, but the words wouldn't come out. Guy's reappearance had left her feeling raw and vulnerable.

'Poor Jules,' Terri began, hopping onto an empty bar stool and taking a long sip of the pint Rich placed in front of her. 'She had a terrible run in today with—'

'The kitchen window,' Jules cut in quickly. 'The glass shattered.'

She stepped forward and slipped her body onto the stool next to Terri's at the end of the bar.

'Well that, but it was your ex—'

'Yes,' Jules interrupted for a second time as she caught Terri's eye, 'and the ceiling as well. Things haven't been going my way.' She shook her head, hoping Terri would understand her silent plea. The thought of talking about Guy right now left her wanting to cry.

To her relief, Terri scrunched her face into a slow wink and brushed her fingers across her mouth as if closing a zip.

'Here you go,' Rich said, placing a tall tulip glass complete with a bright green umbrella in front of Jules. 'Although I feel it's only fair to warn you that this is my most lethal cocktail. Grown men have been stripped to blubbering idiots after drinking this.'

She looked at the glass in front of her. It looked innocent enough. It looked just like orange juice.

As she picked up the glass Jules felt every set of eyes in the place on her. Rich leant on the bar across from her, the smile never leaving his face. Terri, Dan and Jason, held their glasses up towards her, and the handful of men at the other end of the bar had stopped their conversation to watch.

How bad could it be? she wondered, putting the glass to her lips and taking a small sip. It tasted just like orange juice too, with a slight tangy fizz she couldn't put her finger on. It didn't even taste alcoholic. Obviously, Cottinghale's idea of lethal was a lot tamer than she was used to, she decided, brushing Rich's warning aside.

'Very nice, thanks.'

It took Jules another two gulps of cocktail before she felt the relaxing hit of whatever alcohol lay hidden beneath the zesty tang. The feeling caused a trickle of peace to worm through the mess of thoughts in her head.

Before long, Jules found herself leaning against the wall, allowing the gentle hum of conversation to reverberate through her. As far as she could tell, the main theme of conversation centred on the weather: what the continued cold spell was doing to the fields, what the next week would bring, and what it might mean for the spring ahead.

Everyone seemed to have an opinion to share. She would need to start paying attention to the local weather reports if she was going to spend more time in The Nag, something Jules suddenly liked the idea of.

As more people entered the bar they greeted Jules as if she was a long lost relative. Rich, never far from her side, introduced the array of locals, their names vanishing from her memory within seconds.

'Another one?' Rich asked after returning from a trip to the kitchen.

Jules dropped her gaze to her glass preparing to shake her head, but to her surprise it was empty.

'Thanks.' She felt a warm glow course through her, and before she could do anything to stop it, a loud hiccup escaped her mouth.

Jules darted her eye towards Terri, still lost in conversation about the weather, and Rich, who had turned his back to the bar as he fixed her drink. Nobody had heard her embarrassing outburst.

'Err, Rich?'

'Yep,' he answered, keeping his back to Jules as he prepared her drink.

'What exactly is in your concoction?'

He spun around with a grin. 'My cocktail you mean. I'd tell you but then I'd have to kill you.'

She felt a smile cross her face as she swallowed down another hiccup.

'Terri, Dan, Jason,' Jules nodded to their glasses, 'another one?'

'We won't say no, will we boys?'

'Nope,' they chorused.

Jules reached into her jacket pocket for her purse. She felt the scrap of paper brush against her fingers, but the cocktail had clouded her mind and for the briefest of moments she forgot the danger lurking at her touch as she pulled out her purse.

It was too late. Before she could do anything to stop it, the balled up piece of newspaper fluttered to the floor, the movement destroying her warm glow with a sobering jolt.

'Did you drop this, lovey?' Terri asked, unravelling the newspaper article Guy had shown her that morning.

'It's nothing,' she spluttered.

'Holy Moly, is that you?'

'Unfortunately yes,' she mumbled, dropping her face into her hands.

'You look... so—'

'I know, my fashion sense was a little questionable,' Jules replied with a weak laugh, hoping in vain that an attempt at humour would distract Terri from going further.

'No, I mean yes, but it's your face, you look so... so... oh, I can't explain it.'

'This is very cool,' Dan chipped in from over Terri's shoulder.

Jules shrugged, hiding her discomfort in a long sip of the fresh cocktail Rich had placed in front of her.

Rich leant over the pumps, his blue eyes moving first over the photograph and then back at Jules. 'You do look different.'

'Yeah well, it was a long time ago,' she replied, a lot louder than she'd intended, avoiding his gaze.

A voice inside her shouted at her to leave. To run back to the bed and breakfast and hide away. But she couldn't leave. Her aching legs felt like jelly.

'This is unbelievable,' Terri laughed, reading the article and turning her attention back to Jules. 'I mean, it's really unbelievable. I... I just can't believe it. How exciting.'

'Exciting?' Jules responded in disbelief.

'Well yes, I mean, Guy Rawson, he's really famous.'

'So? He's also a total bastard, launching this... this ridiculous thing.'

'Oh, I see.' Terri paused for a minute, looking back at the article. 'But it says here he loves you.'

'The only thing Guy loves is himself,' she replied, wishing her voice would stop echoing around the pub.

'You know,' Rich began, sliding the scrap of newspaper back to Jules, 'If you hate it so much I'm pretty sure you could get an injunction or something and stop them printing anything else.'

'No,' Jules replied, shaking her head. 'Anything I do will be playing straight into his hands.'

She took another gulp from her glass. The sticky taste of the orange was beginning to churn in her empty stomach.

'Let's forget it, okay? It's nothing really.' Her eyes darted between Rich, Terri, Dan and Jason. From the expressions on their faces it seemed the only person convinced by her comment was her. 'Seriously guys, no one is going to remember this story tomorrow. It's over.'

'Sure,' Rich nodded.

'Oh, of course lovey,' Terri chirped.

'Thanks. Now, Terri,' she began in a final bid to change the subject. 'You haven't told me how you got into the building trade?'

'Well, that would be all down to my ex-husband you see. He was the builder really, not me. But like I said he ran off with Dawn from the post office, leaving me with a business in debt and two boys barely out of nappies. So when someone called in search of a decorator, I thought why not, I can do that.

'I put myself through a few trade courses and haven't said no to a job yet. Of course, if my boys—'

Jules let Terri's voice wash over her as she slipped the scrap of newspaper back into her pocket and finished off the contents of her glass.

'You okay?' Rich whispered as he leant towards her. His body was so close she found herself breathing in the scent of his aftershave.

She nodded, unable to disguise another hiccup from escaping.

'I'll get you some water.'

Leaning her head back against the wall, Jules took a long intake of air, feeling the dizzying effect of the alcohol she'd consumed. It felt good. Her thoughts merged into a single blur. She didn't care about Guy. She didn't care about *The Daily*. All she cared about was maintaining this feeling for a little while longer.

'And a glass of dry white please,' she called out to Rich.

Maybe all she needed was a distraction, she thought. Something that would keep Guy out of her thoughts, something fun. Jules let her gaze follow Rich's body as he moved easily around the bar, biting back another hiccup as he stepped back towards her.

Seven

Who, who knows you baby?
  Who, who sees you baby?

How long had he been sitting there, watching the people and their cars go by? The scorching tea he'd purchased now sat tepid and untouched in its wallowing cardboard cup.

The sticky icing of the untouched Danish Swirl had begun to congeal. Guy had a hunch that stale food and dishwater tea were compulsory components of all roadside services.

Expectation, a dangerous connotation

He reached into the grey Armani jacket Giorgio had given him on the shoot in Japan less than a year ago, a night he'd prefer to forget. His fingers fumbled for the tattered notebook and pencil, as he hurried to scribble down the lyrics before they evaporated from his consciousness.

What the hell had he been doing for the past couple of days? Guy wondered. What had possessed him to drive across the country and track down someone he hadn't seen or spoken to for five years?

He heard Debbie's voice in his head: 'You're selfish.'

But look what happened the minute he did something selfless, he argued back to himself. Juliet hadn't even been grateful for his advice, let alone pleased to see him. He could hardly be blamed for the paper's decision to make a story out of one offhand comment.

An image of Debbie shaking her head floated before him. The scraping lead of his blunt pencil blotted her out.

What, what happened to the girl?
  What, what happened to you baby?

For a single second she had looked happy. For a single second the same girl who had loved him with every bit of her heart and told him so every day had stood before him. The same girl he'd promised never to leave, and the one he'd been thinking about every day since.

More than just thinking about, a voice echoed from somewhere deep inside his mind. In that first moment the time between them had disappeared. The feelings he'd shared with the journalist had reared out of nowhere, crashing in his head like two brass symbols.

Then the moment had vanished and reality had hit him. The pixie blonde with a smile that reached to the edges of her face, and the craziest clothes he'd ever seen, had changed. That first split second had been a terrible trick of the mind, disappearing at the same rate as his resolve.

After that first second had past Guy had looked at the woman in front of him. Her slim frame hidden behind dark overalls; her long brown hair tied back. Even the set of her face seemed different somehow.

If it hadn't been for the startling green of the doe-eyed stare he remembered so well, he might have believed that an imposter had taken over her body.

The Juliet he had known would never have laughed at him with a sound so hollow it chilled him to the bone.

She had changed almost beyond recognition, but why?

The question surprised him. He had a feeling he knew the answer, but before he allowed his thoughts to travel further towards it; the pencil in his hand began moving again.

Where, where did you go?

Where, where are you now?

If I could win back the years, I would stop the tears

'Years too late.' She had thrown the words at him like a dagger.

Guy felt a stab of guilt twist in his gut. He had made so many mistakes. Had he really thought seeing her again could undo anything? Juliet had moved on, she couldn't have made that clearer to him. She had done more than just put the past behind her; she had buried it twelve feet under. So why did he feel so hell bent on digging it up again?

It's not like he didn't have his own life to lead. A successful life at that. His first single at number one; an album ready to be released; a sell-out UK tour lined up for the summer; not to mention a string of endorsement offers from people who finally wanted more than just his face on a magazine cover.

As if in agreement, his mobile vibrated from the passenger seat next to him. The name of his publicist flashed up at him.

'Hey Sonja.'

'Guy, where have you been?' Sonja's shrill voice jumped from the phone.

He moved his hand, widening the gap between his ear and his mobile.

'I've been looking for you for ages.'

'Really? Why?' he asked.

'I'm outside your flat ringing the doorbell.' As if to prove it, Guy heard the familiar buzzer of his North London flat. 'We scheduled a meeting last week, remember?'

'Shit, sorry Sonja I totally forgot. I had some personal stuff to sort out. I'll be back in an hour. Can you hang on?'

'Personal stuff? Guy, are you keeping something from me?' she quizzed in a soft purr.

'Nothing for you to worry about,' Guy replied, cursing himself for saying too much.

Sonja had the uncanny knack of dragging every last piece of information out about someone and finding a way to twist it into sales figures. An amazing talent, but not one he needed at that particular moment in time.

'I won't be long,' he added. 'There's a good pub on the corner called The Engine. Get a drink and I'll join you soon.'

'I hope you're not trying to sweet talk me into dinner, Guy,' she said, her tone conveying the opposite of her words.

'Dinner?' Guy's stomach growled its agreement. Had he mentioned dinner?

'I have a surprise for you,' she continued, ignoring him. 'We can discuss it tonight, but let me just whisper the words *Radio One's Live Lounge* to you.'

'Really? They want me? That's amazing.'

'Better get here soon, Guy, before I give the slot to one of my other clients. One who doesn't forget our meetings.'

'I'm on my way.'

Guy's hand reached for the ignition as he threw his mobile onto the passenger seat.

Live Lounge would be a great set. A real sign he'd broken away from modelling and been accepted into the music industry, and he had Sonja to thank for it. She might be a bit of a ball ache at times, but she'd earned her salary three times over, and did it without breaking a nail on her perfectly manicured hands.

It was a shame she wasn't his type because he was sure she had a thing for him. He could tell by the way she looked at him. It reminded him of a tiger getting ready to pounce. A beautiful redheaded tiger, but a predator none the less.

Maybe she could be his type? he wondered to himself as he accelerated out of the motorway services. He needed to get Juliet out of his head, he decided. And how better than with a good-looking woman?

The memory of Japan flashed in front of his eyes; a warning from his unconscious, Guy thought. The elfin blonde model with pale skin so soft it had filled him with instant desire. And yet something had gone very wrong. He could still hear her callous laugh, just like Juliet's had been earlier, or Jules, he corrected himself.

It was time to stop looking back. Forget Juliet once and for all, like she'd forgotten him. Forget the model in Japan. One time, that's all it had been, he reminded himself, moving the Jaguar into the outside lane as he sped home.

Time to get back in the game, Guy told himself, pushing aside the memory of Juliet's emerald eyes glistening with anger and the feelings it had stirred in him.

Eight

Something was definitely wrong. The thought nagged at Jules like a persistent alarm clock determined to get her out of bed, but in her pre-waking minutes she had no intention of moving from under the weight of the warm duvet, or lifting her head from the squishy cloud-like pillow.

She must be dreaming. At some point soon the alarm on her mobile would start to beep and she would find herself back in the shivering cold of the guesthouse, with the carpet as prickly as pine needles beneath her feet, and a shower so hot it left her skin raw.

If only the thought would stop poking, trying to wake her from the comfort of her dream.

With her eyes still shut, Jules wriggled her foot out of the bed, waiting for the icy air to hit like a shot of caffeine. Nothing happened. Maybe Mrs Beckwith had cranked the heat up for once, she wondered as she drifted back to sleep. Then someone moved next to her and all notions of sleep disappeared.

Jules's body tensed. In an instant she realised four things: she was in someone else's bed; that someone lay asleep next to her; she had a throbbing headache, and a mouth that tasted like sour feet.

The person next to her let out a deep sigh, causing a thick stench of manure and raw meat to fill her nose. If she ever had the misfortune to discover a decomposing body, she had a feeling it would smell a lot like the breath of the person next to her.

The person moved again, nudging something wet and warm against the back of her neck.

She had been kidnapped, she realised, as fear gripped her. Drugged and kidnapped. It was the only explanation. And now the kidnapper with the dead body breath and the lovely warm bed had decided to subject her to some kind of unspeakable torture.

'No,' Jules cried out as something sloppy flapped into her ear.

Opening her eyes, she shifted position to face her attacker, preparing to fight.

'Max,' she sighed, her body relaxing at the sight of the dog lying on top of the duvet next to her.

Shrugging her arms free of the cover, she spread her fingers through Max's smooth fur.

'Morning,' a voice called from the doorway.

Jules's eyes darted to bedroom door as horror filled her again. 'Oh.'

She had not been kidnapped. She had not discovered a dead body. But she had slept in someone else's bed, and that someone stood in the doorway with two steaming mugs and an amused smile. Shit, Jules cursed herself.

'I made you a cup of tea,' Rich said as he crossed the room; stepping over what looked like her clothes, spread across the pale laminate floor.

In a flash, Jules moved under the covers, relieved to feel the fabric of her underwear still intact.

'Don't worry, I stopped you before you stripped totally naked,' he said, reading her wide eyes and open mouth.

'What?' Red heat crept across her face.

Feeling suddenly exposed, she pulled the duvet up to her chin, struggling to pull a whining Max with her as she shuffled to a sitting position.

'Here you go.' Rich handed her a hot mug.

'Thanks.'

'How you feeling?' Rich asked as he moved back to the door, leaning his tall body against the frame.

Like she'd had a fight with a very angry bear swinging a baseball bat and lost, she thought.

'Not bad,' she lied, running her tongue across the ridge of her mouth. The taste had the fur of a bear's arse feel to it.

'Remember much from last night?' He took a long sip from his mug, keeping the blue of his eyes on her.

'Most of it, I think.'

Jules willed her mind to uncover the memories of the last twenty-four hours. She remembered finding Guy in her house. She remembered, with a wave of anger, the second newspaper story; and she remembered sitting in Terri's van. She had a hazy image of entering the pub and drinking several of Rich's cocktails, but nothing more.

'Dancing on the bar?'

'WHAT?' she cried out, the decibels of her own screech sending another wave of throbbing pain through her head. 'I did not do that.'

'Okay, okay, I was joking.' Rich held up his mug-free hand. 'You didn't dance on the bar.'

'Good.'

'Just on the floor,' he added, his face stretching into the same grin she remembered from their first meeting. 'I'll be in the kitchen whenever you're ready, there's no rush,' he continued before Jules could question his comment.

'Rich wait,' she called after him, trying to ignore another wave of nausea flooding her system.

'Yeah.' He turned to face her.

'Seriously, what happened last night? Between us, I mean.' Another rush of heat crossed her cheeks.

He paused for a minute, a light smile touching his face. 'Nothing, Jules. You were upset about the stories in the paper. Terri asked me to make you one of my specials. Two shots of Gordon's, ginger ale and orange juice. Well, they are pretty lethal and—'

'And that's when you thought you'd invite me back here and take advantage?'

The second she saw Rich's expression change she knew she'd made a mistake. The amusement fell from his face.

'No, actually. Funnily enough, paralytic women are not my type,' he shot back. 'You had a few too many, and if you must know, I didn't invite you anywhere, you invited yourself. You practically begged me to sleep with you. I stayed in the spare room, okay? Come on Max, it's time for your breakfast.'

He strode away, followed by an obedient Max.

Had she really thrown herself at him? Jules wondered as vague memories of the previous night filtered back. She remembered taking off her jumper and the heat of Rich's body as she'd leant towards him, but what had she said?

To Jules's horror, she recalled the answer to her question: 'I really fancy you.' The memory caused a shudder to take hold of her body. It was all her. She had been the one to instigate whatever had led to her being half-naked in Rich's bed. What an idiot.

This was all Guy's fault, Jules fumed. If he hadn't turned up yesterday, she wouldn't have felt the need to drink herself stupid, have a total personality malfunction, and woken up in Rich's bed. She had just managed to ruin any chance of getting to know Rich properly, if that was something she even wanted, she wondered.

A few minutes later, moving very slowly, Jules rescued her jeans and jumper from the bedroom floor. Her jacket, shoes and socks appeared to have been flung off at a different point during her mortifying drunkenness, along with her hair band. The waves of her long hair fell over her shoulders, messy and out of control, just like her life, she thought.

Jules closed her eyes as she padded with bare feet into a bright yellow hallway, each step sending another throb of pain into her brain.

Suddenly the bold colours she'd chosen for her new house seemed like a bad idea.

Rich's flat above the pub had the same stripped beams and high ceilings as the pub below. He had kept the old features, but clashed them with modern touches. She had a feeling the bright colours would have made her head pound even without the hangover.

Another agonising rush of nausea hit her as she entered the green and chrome kitchen.

'Hi,' she said in a low voice.

Rich kept his back to her, making no sign that he'd heard her meek greeting.

Jules took a breath. 'Rich, I'm sorry. I know you were just looking out for me...' she trailed off, waiting for him to respond in some way.

'It's fine.' He turned towards her. 'Grab a stool; I'll put some toast on. Orange juice?'

Jules's stomach gave an agonising churn. How many cocktails had she had last night?

'Err, no thanks, but I'd murder for some pain killers if you've got any please?'

A smile touched his lips. 'Last cupboard by the sink, help yourself.'

'Thanks, and I am sorry about what I said. I'm seriously embarrassed, it's not like me to be so...' Jules searched for the correct word – drunk, pathetic, needy – 'Forward.'

'That's not what you said last night.'

'What?' Jules exclaimed, before she saw the creases of Rich's smiling eyes. 'Oh ha ha, very funny.'

Rich's light teasing continued as they shared toast and coffee. In that moment, and even through the haze of her hangover, Jules felt something pass between them. She just had no idea what it was, and more importantly, what she wanted to do about it.

'Right. Well I'd better take Max out in a minute. Do you want to come? The fresh air might do you good.'

'Thanks, but I'd better get up to the house and see what's going on with the ceiling and getting some new glass for the window in the kitchen.'

'So last night didn't put you off then?'

'What about last night?'0

'What they said about your house?' he prompted.

Jules pushed her mind back through the bottomless pit of broken memories last night had created. It was blank, totally blank.

'Oh yes, that,' Jules chose her words carefully, she couldn't let Rich see she'd forgotten everything. 'No, not at all.'

Rich raised his eyebrows.

'I'd better head off now too. I guess I should check the papers on my way,' she added, the thought of another story filling her with dread. Surely no one would bother telling the paper about her, it's not like she had any enemies.

'Yeah, of course.' Rich opened his mouth to say more, but closed it again.

'Does everyone know?' she asked.

'About you staying here?'

'About the stories in the paper. Why, did I throw myself at you downstairs too?' She didn't think last night could have been any worse, but she had been wrong.

'Well they definitely know about the newspaper. You had a pretty good rant about it. A violation of human rights, I think you said.'

Jules slumped her head into her hands, for once grateful for the loose waves of her hair covering her flaming cheeks. Of all the places to share something so personal about her life, why did she have to choose a tiny community she had to live in for the next few months? Please let that be the last of the stories, Jules begged to no one in particular.

'And as for us, well it's a small place. It only takes one person to see you leaving here for people to start talking. If they haven't already. But don't worry, it really is harmless. Everyone is really nice; they take an interest in each other, that's all.

'It takes a while to settle into a small community,' Rich continued, 'as I'm sure you'll find out for yourself in a few years.' He paused for a moment as he took a gulp of orange juice. Perhaps waiting for her to correct him.

She knew now was the time to tell him that she had no plans to be in Cottinghale for more than a few months, let alone years, but for some reason she couldn't bring herself to do it. The house was her dream, but she knew she wouldn't stay. She liked to keep moving.

'You make it sound like you're not a local. How long have you lived here?' she asked, dragging her sore head back from the table.

'I moved out from London about five years ago now, I wanted a change of scenery.'

'A change of scenery? This is more like changing planets. Did you have a bar in London too?'

'I was a chef actually. Had a crazy notion that this place would make a great country gastro pub.'

'Wouldn't it?'

'I'm sure it would if there were enough people interested. But not many people pass through here. After a while you kind of like it that way.' Rich ran his hand through the tassels of his hair. Despite being indoors, it still had the same windswept look from the first time they'd met. 'I do a Sunday lunch once a month and specials on bonfire night, that kind of thing.'

Before he could continue a loud bark pierced the air, sending a new wave of pain ricocheting around Jules's head.

'Okay mate, we haven't forgotten about you.' Rich stood. 'You good to go?' he asked.

'Yeah sure, but I can't find my jacket or shoes,' she answered with a shake of her head, deciding not to add the missing socks into the conversation.

'Try the stairs,' he laughed.

'Really?'

'Hey, it was your seduction routine not mine.'

'Oh no. I am so sorry.'

'Don't worry about it,' he said, collecting a blue lead from the back of the kitchen door, which caused a fit of excitement to attack Max as he danced around them.

'I'm always looking for someone to try new recipes out on if you...' The rest of his words disappeared behind Max's excited barking as Rich led him down the stairs.

'Sure, sounds good.' she replied, following behind.

She didn't need to hear the rest of Rich's sentence to know that he'd invited her for dinner. After the way she'd behaved, she would be glad to show him that she wasn't a deranged alcoholic.

'Great. Saturday night okay for you? Stan helps out behind the bar at the weekends so I get a chance to take a break.'

'This Saturday?' Jules stuttered, suddenly feeling claustrophobic on the narrow staircase as she forced her feet into her cold pumps, and choosing to ignore the still missing socks.

A meal with Rich at some point in the future sounded good, but now, with her life already such a mess, it didn't feel right.

'Yeah, why not?' Rich called out, unleashing a rush of cold air as he opened door at the bottom of the staircase.

'Um... okay,' Jules replied, her head too sore to think of an excuse.

It wasn't a date anyway, she reasoned. Not after her drunken antics last night. Rich was probably just trying to make her feel welcome, she decided, unable to decide if it was disappointment or relief that her assurances stirred.

An easterly wind fell from the bleak grey clouds and forced its way down the wiry branches of the bare woodland. As its icy touch hit the scattered stone houses of Cottinghale it split, howling into the soot-filled chimneys and lashing through the twisting lanes of the hamlet.

It smacked Jules like a cold hand striking her cheek as she stepped from the back door of the pub. For a moment, her eyes saw nothing but brown. The thick streams of her hair relished the freedom from an elastic bobble as the wind whipped it across her face.

By the time her hands had swept it aside and she'd regained her sight, Rich and Max had disappeared along a footpath to the east and out into the open farmland.

She stared after them for a moment, but the fierce wind caught hold of her again, its wispy talons pushing their way through to her bare skin. Suddenly the idea of Mrs Beckwith's scalding shower didn't sound so bad, especially for her sockless feet, which had already started to feel numb.

Jules stepped as fast as the thumping in her head would allow up the deserted street in the direction of Mrs Beckwith's guesthouse and the Cottinghale farm shop.

It was the first time she'd seen the hamlet surrounded by looming storm clouds above the tall grey homes and manicured shrubs that followed the curve of the lane perfectly.

The dark skies suited Cottinghale, as if the little place suddenly had secrets and mystery beyond the quaint stone walls.

In between the houses to her left, she could see an almost black skyline lying low and heavy above deserted fields, still in the midst of their winter's rest.

To her right, as she struggled to keep her watery eyes open against the harsh wind, she could see that the rain had already fallen in the distance. Past the gloom of the woodland and up over the valley, she could just make out a hint of brightness.

She just hoped her own problems would disappear at the same rate as the dark clouds moving above her.

Guy had to be wrong. He had to be lying to her about more stories, she decided. If he wanted her to give an interview, then it had to be helping his career in some way. Once upon a time she would have done anything to help Guy, but those days were long gone. She had no intention of helping him now.

Jules felt a pang as she recalled their argument.

Seeing him again had done something to her. She didn't feel herself around him. He had achieved what they'd always dreamt about, but now the reality of him back in her life filled her with an indistinguishable mesh of emotions. The very thought of him made her want to crawl into bed and hide forever.

Jules gulped in the smell of fresh raindrops about to tip from the sky above, and pushed thoughts of Guy aside.

Everything would be fine. She had weathered a tiny storm of mortifying embarrassment from the newspaper, Guy, and her own foolish behaviour, but it would be sunshine from now on, she told herself.

He wouldn't be back. Her bitter comments had seen to that, she thought with an unexpected burst of sadness. Before she could dwell on the feelings, Jules summoned the image of her face on the front page of a tabloid. The sadness disappeared as quickly as it had arrived, replaced by the familiar comfort of a slow burning anger.

Just then, the rattle of an engine brought Jules out of her thoughts.

A muck covered Land Rover, that looked like it might once have been black, roared up the lane and stopped when it past her. Jules heard the gears crunch with a sense of growing dread as the vehicle sped backwards.

A blonde woman, only a little older than Jules, leant across to the passenger side and pumped the handle of the car window. 'Jules, lovey, how are you?'

Jules did not know how to respond. Ever since she'd felt Max's breath on the back of her neck that morning, nothing seemed to be making sense.

The woman had the craziest hair she'd ever seen. Giant blonde frizzy corkscrew curls sprung out in every direction, as if the woman had a stream of electricity running through her.

'Sally Pegg,' the woman added, reading the confusion on Jules's face. 'Bill's wife. We've got the farm up the hill. We met last night, although I'm not surprised if you don't remember. I've had the pleasure of Rich's lethal cocktails on more than one occasion.'

Jules nodded and smiled. 'Hi.'

She wished the haze of her hangover would clear and her memory return. The tight grip she kept on her life seemed to be loosening by the minute.

'Look, I can't stop,' Sally continued. 'One of the cows is as constipated as a cement block. Just wanted to remind you about the invite to Sunday lunch soon, okay? The kids are dying to meet Cottinghale's very own celebrity,' she said without taking a breath. 'And I need to hear all about THE Guy Rawson, what a hunk.' Sally grinned.

'Great,' Jules answered through gritted teeth, keeping her mouth in a smile as tiredness overwhelmed her.

It was one thing for *The Daily* to force a ridiculous celebrity status on her, digging up her past and stomping over her present, but if she had to deal with the same from the residents then her stay in Cottinghale would be nothing like the tranquil seclusion she'd envisaged several months ago.

Why did she have to get drunk and open her mouth in the first place? Jules berated herself.

This was all Guy's fault.

'Brill.' Sally crunched the old 4x4 into first gear. 'Oh, by the way,' she shouted back to Jules as she began to pull away. 'We checked the paper and you're off the hook today.'

'What?' Jules asked, more to herself than to Sally, who had already sped up the lane before Jules had chance to process her last sentence.

Nine

THE DAILY
WEDNESDAY, FEBRUARY 18TH

GUY HIT SMASHES RECORDS

Guy Rawson's debut single has become the most downloaded song of the year, just two days after its release. His smash hit 'Regret' jumped to number one on Sunday from radio play alone and looks to stay there for some time based on sales figures released today.

Since turning his back on modelling, the 27-year old has established himself as a successful solo artist. Within a matter of months, the London born singer has swapped his super-groomed catwalk style for what editor of our style magazine, *Lips*, Tracey White has termed 'The retro stubble look'.

But far from lower his status as Britain's top hunk, White has tipped Guy to be voted Hottie of the year in next month's poll. "Not only is Guy more visible to the public now, but his music really hits a chord with women."

Nominated for best newcomer at next month's Lotus Awards, Rawson looks set to take the music biz and women everywhere by storm.

Is Guy still your fave British hunk? Get voting online NOW!

Only when she entered the farm shop, halfway between the pub at the bottom of the lane and the guesthouse at the top, did Jules understand Sally's last comment.

'Sold out,' Stan explained, his hand passing over the remaining newspapers spread in front of him.

So far, the balding shop owner seemed to Jules to be the only person in Cottinghale who had not been injected with an overdose of friendliness.

He narrowed his eyes on her. 'But what did you expect, asking anyone who would listen to keep their eyes peeled for stories about you?'

'I said that?' Jules exclaimed, wondering what or who had invaded her body and done the exact opposite of her wishes. Never in her right mind would she have dragged the entire hamlet into her life. Bloody Guy and his newspaper, and bloody Rich with his ridiculous concoctions.

'Yep.' Stan moved out from the long counter covering the wall to the right of the door. Stepping into the middle of the store, he began unpacking a cardboard crate of large earth-covered potatoes into a sloped display next to an array of other vegetables.

'Anything else you were looking for?' he asked without looking up from his task.

'What about the copy that you were delivering to the house? Can't I look at that one?' she asked, ignoring the shop owner's obvious annoyance at her presence and selecting a Curly Wurly from the colourful display of chocolate bars stacked by the till.

Stan let out a deep sigh. 'So you want that now, do you?'

'Yes please,' she responded in the most pleasant voice she could muster. It was only two days ago that she'd had great difficulty convincing Stan to stop the deliveries in the first place.

'Sold that one too,' he replied, his face twisting into an amused smile.

'Oh.'

'I suppose,' he paused, breathing out another long sigh and wiping his hands on his long green apron. 'If you don't mind looking at a creased copy, I could let you take a quick look through mine.'

'Thank you Stan, that's very kind of you,' she replied, gritting her teeth with frustration as Stan busied himself with the potatoes for a few moments longer before stepping back to the counter.

'Here you go then.' He reached under the till and handed the paper to Jules.

'Thanks.'

'I suppose next you'll be wanting me to put one aside for you each morning?' His tone was gruff as he reached for a leather-bound notebook.

'That would be great, thank you.' She had no desire to hunt through a trashy tabloid every day, but after the shock of Guy's visit and her strange behaviour in the pub, did she really have a choice? If she wanted to avoid any more surprises then a walk to Stan's shop each morning would have to become part of her routine for a few days at least.

'You're not in it, but your boyfriend is mentioned somewhere in the middle.'

'He's not my boyfriend,' she muttered, trying to keep the edge from her voice as she rummaged through the pages and found the mention of Guy.

It took two careful checks from front to back before Jules felt confident Guy had been wrong.

Nobody cared about her and nobody would bother speaking to the paper about her. It had all been part of his pathetic games after all, she realised, too relieved that her life could return to normal to feel any more anger at the mess Guy had already caused.

'Everything alright up the house?' Stan's voice interrupted her thoughts.

She folded the newspaper in her hands and passed it back to Stan. 'Yes of course, why wouldn't it be?' she quizzed, handing him the money for her chocolate bar.

'Just wondered if the old tenants minded all the changes going on.'

'Why would they mind?' she asked, puzzled by the shop owner's bizarre question.

'Not my place to say,' Stan answered, busying himself with his notebook entries.

Jules stared at the top of Stan's shining head as he bent over the counter, waiting for him to explain.

He said nothing.

'Right, well, bye then,' Jules said, brushing aside her confusion and continuing her walk up the road.

A sugar hit and a shower and she'd be ready for work, Jules told herself, tearing open the chocolate bar wrapper and devouring it in three mouthfuls.

It was only when the bleary gaze of her eyes fell onto to the tiny bed did she wonder if she could allow herself a quick nap.

Before she had a chance to change her mind, Jules stripped off her clothes and slipped under the cold covers. Feeling the throbbing of her headache slow down, she closed her eyes and allowed sleep to take her.

Ten

Loughborough University (Five years earlier)
THE DAILY
SATURDAY, JULY 2ND
FROST HAS MELTED

Super model Lola Frost (20) has finally dropped her famous Frost-y glare in favour of a super smile. Posing at the launch of *GiGi* sports new swim and leisurewear, the pouting model couldn't hide her more saucy side as she joked with newcomer and the latest face of *GiGi*, Guy Rawson (22).

According to insiders at the launch, held at the exclusive Farnsworth Hotel in Mayfair, the change in Frost's mood is all down to the charms of her gorgeous co-star.

Rawson and Frost are rumoured to have hit it off instantly and are already planning a romantic get-away once the publicity for their new campaign is over.

Juliet shivered as she dragged her body out of the front door. The warmth from the late afternoon sun was unable to penetrate the layer of sadness chilling her to the bone.

Fourteen days, she reminded herself, covering her puffy eyelids with a pair of pink sun glasses, and forcing her feet to move forward. He had been gone for fourteen days.

She had survived the first week in an anaesthetised blur.

The gown fitting; the photographer; the graduation ceremony; dinner with her parents; it had happened. The memories were still fresh in her head, and yet it was as if someone else had done those things. Just breathing in and out had sapped all of her energy.

The shock had worn off after the first week, leaving in its place the deadening reality of her situation.

Guy had left her.

He was gone, she reminded herself again, welcoming the fresh wave of hurt it caused as she dragged her body towards the local shops.

Somewhere along the way, between the numbing disbelief, the desperate hope, and the crushing confusion of their break-up, she had become an emotional self-harmer. Raking over every aspect of their relationship and the day he'd left until the wound remained open and raw.

The day of their argument had been just as hot and balmy. Perfect for the picnic she'd planned.

One minute she'd been absorbing the last rays of afternoon sun, enjoying the taste of ripe warm strawberries, only a week away from graduating university and the next stage of their lives.

They'd planned to stay in Loughborough and find a one-bedroom flat. Just the two of them at last. She'd had an internship lined up with an interior design agency, whilst Guy had planned to pick up a few shifts behind the bar at their local in between his gigs. It wasn't a long-term plan, but it was something they'd decided together, or so she'd thought.

The next minute Guy had obliterated their future and in its place told her his new idea.

He was leaving Loughborough.

He was leaving his dreams of becoming a singer.

He was leaving her.

Three nuggets of information exploding like nuclear bombs in her head.

The memory of his words felt like the twist of a knife in her chest.

The heat of the day now pounded into her brain, but she had to get out. She had to eat. All she had to do was pick up a carton of milk and some bread, and then she could bury herself once more in his smell, still lingering on their bed covers.

It should be simple. Something she had done a hundred times. Yet, in that moment, walking the short distance to the corner shop to buy a pint of milk felt like an insurmountable task.

Suddenly, out of nowhere, she felt his presence.

He had come back.

Juliet stopped dead, twisting her body in a full circle as her eyes sought out the familiar frame of his body. Her heart jumped into her throat and despite the horror of the past fortnight she felt a rush of happiness gush through her veins.

Then she saw it.

Her eyes fixed onto the poster at the bus stop directly in front of her. Guy's life size body stared back.

Her brain failed to compute the information before her. It had to be a hallucination.

Her hand clenched the warm metal of the nearest lamp post, forcing her body to stay upright as she fought the urge to reach out and touch his face.

She knew him inside out. The man in the poster was definitely him. The mop of his messy hair had gone and so had the cheeky lopsided grin, which never failed to turn her stomach to mush.

She searched his face for some sign of familiarity but nothing but the stony pose of a model stared back.

She had to get out of the sun. Spinning around, Juliet dived into the cool interior of the mini-mart, the cool air from an electric fan prickling against her skin as her eyes adjusted to the change in light.

What had just happened? Guy, the scruffy musician who wore torn up jeans and faded t-shirts; the love of her life who never bothered to brush his hair or look in a mirror; how could that same person be modelling sports clothes?

As her legs regained their strength, Juliet moved back in the direction of the doorway. She had to see it again. But before she could step back outside, something in the corner of her eye made her hesitate.

Turning slowly, she scanned the newspaper display by the door. Her breathing felt hurried and erratic as if a part of her mind already knew the image about to assault her.

Then she saw it. On the front page of one of the brightly coloured tabloids was another photograph of Guy.

'No.' The cry escaped her mouth as she absorbed the picture of him staring at the camera, his arm looped around the shoulder of a skinny brunette.

Grabbing the paper, Juliet read the article, each line causing fresh pain to cut deeper inside her.

Two weeks without a single word; countless unanswered phone calls; and then this. She could not grasp the reality laid out in print before her very eyes.

'Miss, are you alright?' a voice called out to her from somewhere further into the shop.

She lifted her head in a slow nod as she felt something disintegrate inside her.

Now she understood what she needed to do.

Turning quickly around she grabbed a basket and began to fill it.

Guy had destroyed her. She didn't have to think anymore.

Juliet lifted the cheap plastic bottle to her lips, taking another swig of vodka and ignoring the carton of tropical juice unopened on the bedside table.

The first half of the cheap translucent liquid had burnt her throat raw, no doubt doing the same to her insides. Not that it mattered now.

At least the second half seemed to be slipping down a little easier, she thought as she flopped her body onto the bed.

Pulling the rim of the bottle from her lips, she fumbled with the volume remote, forcing the stereo to vibrate against the shelves as their music blared out into the messy bedroom, still filled with his belongings.

The bittersweet tunes caused a mixture of comfort and crushing sadness to wrap itself around her.

Propping the vodka bottle against his pillow, Juliet ripped the lid from the chunky cardboard box, her swollen eyes gazing at the contents spilling onto the bed, as if it had the power to save her.

She pressed her fingers against the protective foil packets, popping the white tablets one by one onto the bedcover until all the packets' contents had been emptied and a tiny mountain had formed before her.

Any minute now, she told herself as a flood of fresh wet tears sprung from her eyes. The salty solution burning like the vodka against the sore rims of her eyes. How could there be more tears?

He had gone, leaving behind an eerie devastation that haunted her day and night. As if he'd ripped out a part of her and taken it with him.

She had nothing left.

She had been living under a thick veil of grief and disbelief, but everything was clear now, she realised, thinking back to the lightning bolt of horror that had struck her only a few hours earlier.

Her watery gaze fixed onto the mound of tablets, the smudged newspaper now a blur in the corner of her eye. Their glossy faces grinning at her, mocking her existence.

Any minute now, she told herself again, her thoughts almost lost behind the blaring noise of the stereo.

She let her head fall against the bed, its cool fabric soothing the heat from her puffy face.

What was she supposed to do now?

She forced another mouthful of vodka down her throat, wishing the drink would numb the pain, but not even the dizzying hit of drunkenness could lessen the reality of what she'd lost.

Juliet reached a shaking hand towards the tablets, brushing the tips of her fingers against the powdery shells. She felt her heart quicken with anticipation and fear.

'Any second now,' she mumbled to herself, holding a single pill in one hand and the almost empty bottle of vodka in the other.

If only she could undo the past. Rewind the last two weeks and return to the park. She wouldn't let him leave again, no matter what. But there could be no going back. Guy had moved on, deleting her completely from his life as if their love had never existed, as if she had never existed.

Soon she wouldn't, she thought, placing a single pill on her tongue and washing it down with another swill of fiery liquid.

Her heart thundered in her ears, muffling the noise of the stereo.

She had started now. There could be no going back. She had nothing to live for.

Juliet reached out to the mountain of tablets, grabbing a handful in her fist.

If only she could undo the past, she thought again. If only they had never met. If only she'd ignored the exotic pull she'd felt from that first day. She could have ignored her feelings, ignored the dishevelled boy offering to help her and carried on walking. Maybe then she would have spent her time at university studying and having fun with friends, instead of wrapped in the bittersweet bubble they had made for themselves.

She had allowed herself to be consumed by their love until she was nothing without him. She was trapped.

Hopelessly trapped, she thought again as she threw the pills into her mouth.

Juliet tipped the vodka bottle almost vertical, causing the liquid to stream down her chin as it filled her mouth.

Just as the pills began to slip down her throat an image of a morgue flashed in front of her face; her naked body lying on a cold metal slab; her parents standing over her.

Suddenly she couldn't swallow. The tablets felt like acorns at the back of her mouth.

Panic hit like a hard blow to the head.

She bent forward, opening her mouth and letting the remaining liquid drip over her. But the tablets refused to budge as they clawed their way into her body.

In a flash she felt an overwhelming will to live. The sense so strong it cut through the alcohol running through her veins and drowned out the pain Guy had caused.

Without another thought to her despair, Juliet threw her body off from the bed, crashing hard onto the floor.

The pills grated against the inside of her neck causing a gag reflex to push up from her stomach.

Seconds past and nothing happened.

Then the retching began. Long heaving wretches as her stomach pumped the vodka and the pills out of her body.

For what felt like hours, she knelt on her hands and knees next to the bed she had shared with Guy, crying and vomiting until nothing remained inside her.

She leant exhausted against the bed. The tears and the music had stopped, causing a silent calm to consume her.

With slow deliberate movements she pushed her body from the floor and began to clear up the mess of her life, starting with the sick and finishing with five bin bags full of clothes and make-up she would never wear again.

Only the cheap white shirt and black skirt she'd worn to graduation hung in the wardrobe. It was all she needed. Tomorrow she would buy new things and move away. Start over and forget Guy had ever existed, just as he had done to her.

Eleven

THE DAILY
SATURDAY, FEBRUARY, 22ND

GUY'S GAL "DESTROYED ME"

In an exclusive Valentine's interview, Gorgeous Guy Rawson revealed his love for ex Juliet Stewart (right). Now we can also reveal that the famous singer is not the only person to be heartbroken by his sexy ex.

Phillip Williams (32), a property manager from Nottingham, dated the star's ex-girlfriend four years ago when the pair met at his father's property business. "We hit it off straight away. We were both really ambitious. Jules had a real spark for business and it wasn't long before the sparks were flying between us too."

But their relationship took a turn for the worse when Phillip, then 28, wanted to get serious. "We'd invested in a property together and things were going really well. But the minute our flat was ready for sale something changed. One day she was warm and loving, the next she was a b***h... She just packed up and left."

"I can appreciate Guy's pain. Juliet broke my heart too. I now realise she was just using me to help her career. She destroyed my trust in women," claims Williams, still single.

Wherefore art thou Juliet? Heart-broken Phillip has no idea where Juliet is now, but maybe you do? Call Sara-Marie Francis on 0800 559 119 NOW!

Right: Juicy Jules, then 23, shows off more than her property assets in a minuscule bikini whilst holidaying in

Spain with "heart-broken" ex-boyfriend Phillip Williams, above.

'Good morning dear,' a voice called from behind her as Jules stepped into the dining room.

'Morning Mrs Beckwith.'

'Lovely and bright out there today. Was it a bit warmer on your run, dear?' Mrs Beckwith's singsong voice asked as she shuffled out from the kitchen.

'A little,' Jules replied, taking a seat at the single place set in the middle of the long dining room table.

'Lovely,' she sighed. 'Spring will be here in no time.'

'Let's hope so.'

'Righty-ho, shall I pop your toast on? One slice, or two?'

'Two would be great. Thanks.'

Jules had no idea if it was any warmer outside. The bitterly cold wind had still felt like a brutal assault against her skin as she'd pushed her body up the valley, but she found it much easier to agree with her landlady's opinion on the weather each morning than embark upon a lengthy discussion. Especially before she'd had a chance to digest a cup of Mrs Beckwith's treacle thick coffee.

As her elderly landlady moved back to the kitchen Jules shook a heap of cornflakes into the bowl, drowning the orange flakes in a large helping of cold milk and shoving a heaped spoonful into her mouth.

Every day that had passed in Cottinghale, Jules found herself adding a little more to her breakfast portions. The long runs, country air, and full days working on her house not only put her to sleep the minute her head touched the pillow each night, but also left her stomach growling like a ferocious dog each morning.

As she stuffed another crunchy mouthful into her mouth, it took Jules a moment to register the kitchen door as it swung open and the man carrying the tray of coffee and toast towards her.

'Hi Rich,' Jules said, swallowing her mouthful so fast that the cornflakes scratched her throat. 'And Max,' she added, bending down to fuss over the young Springer and allowing her a moment to hide the flush she felt spreading across her cheeks.

'Morning Jules. Sorry for barging in on your breakfast.'

'Oh, it's no problem. It's great to see you. Nice weather today. Mrs Beckwith thinks spring might be on the way.'

'It could be.'

'Are you on your way out for a walk? I'd love to join you but I've got to get up to the house this morning. I've forced Terri and the boys to take a day off so I need to crack on.' Jules clamped her mouth shut. She was babbling like an idiot.

'Well, we are, but that's not why I'm here,' he replied, sliding the tray of coffee onto the table and pouring two cups from a steaming cafetiere.

The memories from the last time she'd seen him had yet to fade. Her drunken behaviour, her pathetic attempts to seduce him, and waking up in his bed. The embarrassment never failed to unleash a red heat into her body whenever she thought about it.

She had managed to avoid him in the four days since that horrifying episode. Refusing Terri's offers of a drink after work, and going out for a run at the crack of dawn. In a small place like Cottinghale, she'd known they would bump into each other eventually, she just hadn't thought it would be over breakfast in Mrs Beckwith's dining room on the day she'd agreed to have dinner with him; a tiny fact she'd hidden in the back of her mind until that moment.

Only as he sat down in the chair across from her did she see the all too familiar blue logo of the newspaper sticking out from under Rich's arm.

'Is that what I think it is?' she asked, the embarrassment she'd felt moments earlier now insignificant as her mood plummeted into the pit of her stomach.

'Err, yes. It's why I'm here,' he nodded, passing the newspaper to her. 'Stan grabbed me as we were heading out. I thought you'd prefer to see it sooner rather than later.'

'Thanks,' she replied. How could this be happening again?

'Page seventeen.'

It took a few seconds for Jules's shaking hands to find the right page, and several more seconds to believe what she was reading.

'I... I can't believe this,' she cried out, slumping her body back into the nearest chair. 'This is total bollocks. How can they print this stuff about me? It's all lies.'

'So you don't know this guy?' Rich asked in reply, taking a seat opposite Jules.

'Not exactly. His dad gave me my first job out of uni.'

'But you didn't actually date him then?'

'We never invested in a property together. It was his dad's company who fronted me. And we definitely never went on holiday together. This photo,' Jules stabbed at the page, 'was taken on Brighton beach.'

'Right.' Rich nodded, taking a long sip from his cup.

She lifted her gaze towards him, battling the conflicting urges to explain everything and run away.

She remembered Phillip. How could she forget? She had forced herself to accept his offers of a drink after work; then dinner, and everything else that followed. But it had nothing to do with her career, or with him for that matter. She'd done it to prove she was normal, and being in a relationship with someone, anyone, proved she had moved on from Guy.

Phillip had been right about one thing. Their relationship had ended rather abruptly when she'd found a new job away from Nottingham, but there was no way he'd been heartbroken.

'I just can't believe this,' she said again, her mind unable to comprehend the millions of people that would be reading about her, let alone ogling at the picture. 'Why would he do this? They make it sound like I'm an evil slapper.

'Juicy Jules,' she read aloud, shaking her head as the words sunk in.

She pulled the newspaper up to her face for closer inspection. She was sure she'd destroyed that photo. Phillip had taken the shot before she'd been able to protest. Her body looked scrawny, almost malnourished. Her hands were up in protest, her unsmiling face turned away from the camera.

'You know, I meant what I said the other day,' Rich began. 'You should seek legal advice on this. I'm sure you could get an injunction to stop them printing any more stories. There are laws to protect people from this kind of invasion of privacy.'

'What about freedom of speech? If I tried to stop them it would only make things worse.'

'What about speaking to them directly then? If you gave your side of the story then they'd probably—'

'No,' she cut him off. 'I can't... I won't. It's what he wants. I won't give him the satisfaction.' Jules grabbed her coffee, taking two quick gulps. The buzz of caffeine felt instant as it mixed with the anger pulsing through her.

'So what are you going to do?'

'Nothing,' she replied, lifting her eyes to meet his.

He looked different. His hair, still damp and smelling of limes, had yet to be battered by the wind. And his blonde stubble had been replaced with smooth skin, still shiny with moisturiser.

'This will all go away,' she added.

Rich said nothing as the silence grew between them.

Jules could stand it no longer; she had to say something. 'Look, about tonight. Would you mind if we postponed it? What with the long days at the house and now this, I just don't think I'd be very good company.'

'I figured as much,' he replied with a shrug. 'When I didn't see you this week, I thought you might be avoiding me?'

'What? No, of course not,' she lied, feeling the guilt glow on her cheeks. 'I've just been busy.'

'No problem.'

'Thanks. Another time definitely.'

'Okay,' he nodded. 'But can I ask you something, then?'

'Sure.'

'Isn't it letting them win? I mean, I understand if you want to hide from all this,' he began, nodding his head towards the newspaper. 'But you've been in Cottinghale how long? A week? And you go from here to your house and back again. It's not much of a new start, is it?'

Jules felt the breath leave her lungs as a fiery rage engulfed her. 'And what would you know about it? Has anything like this ever happened to you?' she snapped.

'No, but—'

'Well then, stay out of it, okay? You're right, I've been here a week, so don't pretend you know me.'

She pushed the chair back and sprang to her feet, almost dragging the lace table cloth and the bowl of soggy cornflakes with her.

'Jules, wait; I was only trying to help,' he explained, his tone remaining even.

She stared down at him fighting the anger throbbing in her head. 'I know,' she sighed. 'I'm sorry for having a go at you. I guess that's why they say that you shouldn't shoot the messenger. Thanks for bringing this over.'

'Don't mention it.'

She could tell by his tone that Rich was still annoyed about her outburst, or about cancelling dinner, but she couldn't think of anything else to say.

'I'd better go,' she said, grabbing the paper and striding from the room without waiting for a response.

As soon as she unlocked her car and slipped behind the steering wheel she felt better. Her house sat less that a ten minute walk further up the road, but something about driving soothed her.

What had just happened? She knew Rich was the last person she should be angry at, but for some reason the more he tried to help her, the harder she pushed him away.

The vibration of her mobile saved Jules from thinking any deeper about the reasons for her strange behaviour towards Rich. She dug her fingers into her pocket and snapped her phone open.

'Hello,' she said.

'Hello Juliet, this is your mum here, just calling to see how your new property is coming along, give us a call—'

'Mum, I'm here,' Jules interrupted, balancing the phone in the crook of her right shoulder, freeing her hands to start the car. She couldn't bear the thought of seeing Rich again now.

'Oh, hi darling, I thought it had gone straight to voicemail.'

Even with her mind clouded in anger Jules felt the familiar churn of guilt. She hadn't spoken to her parents in months; preferring instead to exchange voicemails every couple of weeks when she knew they would be out at their book club. Their cheerful answer phone message never asked awkward questions she didn't have the answers to.

'How are you? Did Guy manage to find you? It was only after he left that I realised our road map might be a little out of date.'

Jules slipped the gear stick into reverse and guided the car out of Mrs Beckwith's driveway. It took her a moment to register her mother's comment.

'Mum, why did you tell him where I was?'

'Why? Shouldn't we have done? He told us all about the newspaper story and sounded so apologetic, not that your father and I could figure what exactly was going on, but it was lovely to see him again. I don't know why it never worked out between the two of you.'

Jules heard the deep sound of her father's voice bellow in the background as she moved the gear stick into drive and sped up the road.

'Oh, yes, yes that's right, you were too young.'

Another thrust of frustration reared inside her. Her mother's ability to make everything seem so simple never failed to drive her crazy.

Her parents, Nora and Bernie Stewart, still lived in the same 1950s semi-detached house on the outskirts of Bath where she'd grown up. For over thirty years they had run a tiny museum, bookshop and local tour dedicated to Jane Austen.

It always surprised Jules how two people who lived with their heads in books could manage to organise themselves enough to get out of bed, let alone run a successful tourist spot in the heart of the city.

With no brothers or sisters, the three of them had always been close. When she'd introduced her parents to Guy on one of their regular visits to see her at Loughborough University, they had accepted him like a son, showering him with presents and encouraging him to pursue his music.

Neither of her parents had once questioned their love, and at the time Jules had loved them even more for it.

Things had changed when Guy had left. Like every other aspect of her life, he'd ruined her relationship with her parents too. They'd never said anything, but Jules had seen the sadness and disappointment in their faces when she'd told them he'd gone. She'd let them down.

Since then, with the exception of a flying visit at Christmas and sporadic phone calls, she kept her distance. It just seemed easier that way.

'Hello? Juliet, are you still there? Bernie, I think she's gone. I told you these portable phones weren't as good—'

'Mum... mum, I'm here.'

'Oh, jolly good. Well as I was saying, we weren't sure if the directions we gave him—'

'Look mum, if anyone else asks you for my address, please don't give it to them, or tell them anything, okay?'

'You're not in trouble are you sweetheart? I hope you're not worrying about that good for nothing so-called paper.' Nora paused for a moment, her tone turning serious. 'We brought you up to laugh at nonsense like that Juliet. Guy was so worried about you, bless him, but I told him you wouldn't mind.'

Jules released a long breath, pushing her foot harder against the accelerator and revving the cold engine.

'No, mum,' she sighed, 'I'm not in trouble. I'd just prefer it if you didn't give out any personal details about me, okay?'

'Oh, we wouldn't speak to anyone who didn't know you of course. It's funny actually because just yesterday we had a nice friend of yours pop into the shop for a quick chat.'

'Who?'

'Oh I can't remember her name now, something unusual. The kind you wouldn't find in an Austen.'

'What did she want?' Jules racked her brains. She couldn't remember the last time she'd mentioned her parents to anyone.

'Just to see how you were getting on.'

'Did she say where she knew me from?'

'Reading, I think, but I could be wrong. Or maybe it was school, she was very interested in the photos, you know the ones we have pinned to the corkboard by the counter?'

'I don't have any friends in Reading.'

'Oh well, somewhere else then.'

She didn't have any friends anywhere else either, but she couldn't admit that to her mum.

Jules spun the wheel towards the narrow entrance of her overgrown driveway without reducing her speed, narrowly missing the skip as she slammed her foot against the brake pedal, bringing the car to a jolting stop.

'Mum, I've got to go. The builders are on my doorstep,' she lied.

'Oh...Okay then, well take care won't you Juliet. Are you eating enough? You're not too lonely up there I hope.'

'I'm fine mum. Are you and Dad okay?' Jules added as an afterthought.

'Of course we are. In fact, we are opening a new tour – famous characters of Bath. You must come see the costumes we've got and the local drama kids helping us. It's all so theatrical.'

'Okay mum, I will. I'll call you soon. Bye.' Jules clipped the cover of her mobile shut without waiting for her mother's response.

Twelve

A magnitude of thoughts battled for attention inside Jules's head as she made her way into the house.

Something her mother had said troubled her, but before she could put her finger on it, another wave of guilt had started to works its way into her body, curdling the hot anger marching through her veins.

Why had she flipped out at Rich? She wondered again.

She seemed incapable of being her usual cool self around him. He had nothing to do with *The Daily*'s story and could hardly be blamed for Phillip spewing his pathetic lies to the trashy tabloid. She would have to apologise, Jules thought with a sigh of resignation. But for now she had her house to herself for the first time since arriving in Cottinghale and an unending supply of hot energy to expend.

Despite her dark mood, Jules felt her spirits lift as her eyes scanned the progress they'd made. In the four days since she'd woken up with Max's tongue slobbering in her ear, the old living room ceiling had been torn down, and just as Terri had promised, her brother had plastered the lot, hiding any trace of the hole that had been there only last week.

Even the majority of the dust had gone, thanks to Dan's and Jason's endless sweeping.

Tomorrow she would pack up her belongings from the guesthouse and finally get the peace she'd longed for since the first time she'd set foot in the house. Even with the beautiful landscape stretching around it, Cottinghale had taken on a suffocating feel. She seemed incapable of taking two steps out of Mrs Beckwith's front door without someone stopping for a friendly chat.

With Terri's help also coming to an end, she could finally be alone again.

The feeling of relief did not last long. Jules soon found her mind jumping back to Philip's story about her. She didn't know why Philip would do it, or how Guy had arranged it, but she knew Guy was behind it somehow. There was no level that he wouldn't stoop to in order to boost his career, she thought as the anger and frustration wound its way around her body in a tight grip.

It hardly seemed real. The millions of people that would be reading about her, not to mention staring at her picture as if she was just as famous as Guy; and yet every time she allowed herself to relax, to believe the newspaper had moved on, another story appeared.

For the first time since it had begun Jules allowed herself to wonder if another story would follow. A sliver of fear embedded itself under the surface of her thoughts like a splinter. Jules pushed it away, shifting her focus back to the house.

Scanning the empty rooms, she searched for something that would release the hot energy bouncing through her. If only she had a spare wall to knock down, she thought.

Then her gaze fell onto the dirty grey carpet that covered the hallway and the stairs. She'd never taken up a carpet before, but how hard could it be? Jules wondered, eyeing the disgusting threadbare wool, which she suspected was the cause of the lingering stale smell that flooded her nostrils whenever she entered the house.

Springing into action, Jules jumped up the creaking stairs and dived into the bathroom. In less than a minute, she had swapped her jeans for the loose freedom of her overalls and was back in the living room, a Stanley knife in hand.

Gripping the knife in her clenched fist, she drove the blade into the carpet, dragging it the entire length of the room. She wanted to picture Guy's face, or even *The Daily*'s bright blue logo underneath the sharp gleam of the blade, but she had to stay in control or she risked damaging the floor underneath.

Although knowing her luck in the house so far, the floorboards would be rotten.

Suddenly, as she worked her fingers between the slit she'd made, Jules heard something from upstairs. She held her breath, listening to the sound of floorboards moving above her, her anger momentarily forgotten.

'Hello,' she called out. 'Terri? Is that you?'

A slow breath eased out from her lungs as silence filled the house. Old houses always made strange noises. She berated her foolishness and turned her attention back to the floor.

The carpet seemed unwilling to release its hold on the house. Each tiny piece Jules managed to pry away felt like the tight fingers of a grip clinging to life.

Rolling up the sleeves on her overalls, Jules wormed her fingers under centimetre after centimetre of carpet, ignoring the painful cramps gripping her hands and thinking of nothing but the slow progress she was making.

By the time Jules had worked her way to the stairs, the light had begun to fade from the sky. She had moved non-stop, freeing chunk after chunk of carpet and dragging them outside before heaving them into the skip.

With the carpet gone, she could just make out thick planks of rich dark wood hiding underneath another decade's worth of dust and dirt. With a good scrub and a treatment of varnish, the swirls of the natural wood would match perfectly with the skirting boards, picture frames and doors.

At last something was going right, she thought, allowing herself to smile for the first time that day.

Jules felt suddenly exhausted. As the day had worn on, the anger had melted away with it, leaving behind a tiredness that lay heavy on her mind and body. She should stop. Go back to one of Mrs Beckwith's delicious casseroles and crawl into bed. But as Jules looked towards the final bit of carpet covering the stairs, she forced her throbbing muscles to continue working. Another few hours and she would be finished.

Keeping her head down and her jaw clenched against the exhaustion, Jules plied the carpet away from each stair as her tired limbs moved up the staircase. She could think of nothing but finishing the job.

Suddenly, a noise broke through her concentration. It sounded to Jules like twigs being snapped beneath her. Before she had time to comprehend the strange noise growing up around her, she felt the first movement from under her feet.

That can't be right, Jules reasoned as she tried to steady herself. It had to be her own exhaustion which made it seem like she was suddenly on a swaying rope bridge, instead of a safe and sturdy staircase. But even as the thought raced through her head, Jules knew it was something more. The entire staircase was moving around her.

She flung her arms out on either side, one hand scraping against the bare wall, searching for anything that would support her, the other reaching instinctively for the banister, which had also started to sway.

For what felt like an eternity, Jules remained in limbo, unable to move as she waited desperately for the staircase to steady itself. Something which seemed to be less and less likely with every passing second.

Then it happened; a strange sensation of weightlessness overtook her as the stairs beneath her fell to the floor with a deafening crash. With nothing to support her, Jules was powerless to stop her body falling with it.

The time between the stairs falling away and her body crashing to the floor could have lasted no more than a second, but it was long enough for Jules to wonder if the entire day had been a terrible dream.

Another horrifying story in *The Daily*, her rudeness towards Rich, the beautiful floors too good to be true, and now the collapse of the stairs from underneath her.

Just a dream, Jules repeated to herself, as thick clouds of dust flew up around her and she hurtled down over the wreckage, a yelp escaping her mouth as much from landing hard against the floor as from the banister, still in one piece, which crashed on top of her.

Thirteen

'Well, if it isn't Cottinghale's very own celebrity,' she heard Stan's gruff sarcastic tones call out as she unlatched the heavy pub door.

It took a moment for her eyes to adjust to the flickering light of the fire as she entered.

The spinning had subsided on the slow walk from the house, but she couldn't shake the feeling of detachment pressing down from the back of her head, or the musky smell of sawdust lingering in her nose.

Jules had no idea how much time had passed between the fall and the moment she'd realised it hadn't been a dream, but it was long enough for an ache to overtake her entire body, pulsing all the way to her bones.

One by one, she had wiggled each of her fingers and toes, relieved to find them still responding to her commands. Somehow she had managed to freefall onto a pile of rubble, with a banister crashing on top of her, and not broken a single bone. Although based on the cries of resistance from her body as she'd clambered to her feet, it had been a close call.

'Jules.' Rich strode out from the behind the bar. 'Are you okay?'

'I'm fine. The stairs fell on me,' she replied, stepping slowly into the cosy warmth she remembered from her last visit.

Rich's forehead creased with concern. 'What? Are you okay?'

'I think so. I can't get to my car keys, purse... clothes... in bathroom,' she babbled, unable to string the thoughts together in her mind, let alone form them into sentences. 'I couldn't think of where else to go.'

'Crikey,' an elderly man chirped from a table by the bar.

Jules turned to the sound of the voice, the movement causing a strange weightlessness to float over her, as if the room was swaying around her.

Within a second, Rich had jumped to her side. Catching her arm in his large grip, he half lifted, half dragged her to the nearest seat beside the man who'd just spoken.

'Jules, can you hear me? Are you okay?'

'Yes I'm fine, why?' she replied. Actually, she felt a little sleepy despite the soreness resonating from her limbs.

'Don't move. I'll get you some water.'

'Whiskey, give her some whiskey, boy,' the same elderly man called out from next to her.

'I'm really sorry Rich,' Jules called out to the room.

'What are you sorry for lovey? It weren't your fault,' the elderly man interjected.

'Sorry,' she repeated again as Rich placed a pint of water in her hands.

At that particular moment she couldn't quite put her finger on what she needed to apologise for but she said it again anyway.

'Don't worry about it Jules. Drink the water and then I think you need to go to the hospital or at the very least lay down for a while.'

'All my stuff is upstairs. It fell right from underneath me. Bloody house.'

The elderly man cleared his throat. 'It's Mrs Mayor.'

'Don't start on that now Ben,' Rich cut in, dropping his knees to the patterned red carpet so his head was level with hers.

'It's true; she doesn't like people meddling with her house.'

'What? Who's Mrs Mayor? It's my house anyway.' Jules looked between the faces that seemed to float around her.

She shut her eyes and waited for the spinning to subside again.

'She used to live there,' Ben continued, his voice rising to include the spattering of people sitting at the bar. 'Still does, if you believe that sort of thing. Died about fifteen years ago now, but Jimmy, her husband, swore blind she was still there nagging him day and night. He even left money in his will to send a newspaper up there for her every day. That's right, isn't it Stan?' he called out to the corner.

An indistinguishable grunt resonated from the lone figure on the other side of the room.

'If she's dead, how can she mind what happens to the house? Oh I get it, you're suggesting my house is haunted,' Jules exclaimed, suddenly making sense of the rather strange conversations she'd had with both Rich and Stan the previous week.

'It's true. Mum swears she hears her, it, talking.' A voice Jules recognised joined in the conversation.

She narrowed her eyes towards the young couple perched on the barstools.

'Jason?'

'Dan,' he corrected. 'And this is my girlfriend Molly,' he added, wrapping his arm around the stick thin teenager next to him.

'Oh sorry. But,' Jules's mind struggled to make sense of the situation. 'This is ridiculous, why did no one tell me?'

'We did. The other night, you were the one who agreed to the exorcism,' Dan replied, spinning on his stool to join in the conversation.

'What? No I didn't.' She looked towards Rich, still propped on his knees beside her.

To Jules's surprise he nodded in response.

'Where is Terri?' Jules asked. She would be able to make sense of this.

'At the footie. Should be back any minute.'

'She likes football?'

'Yeah, ever since dad left us she's not missed a Cheltenham home game.'

'Oh. Where did he go?'

'Last we heard he is in Spain. Not that we care. I deferred my place at uni for a year to help mum with the business. Jason's doing the same once his A levels are finished.'

Jules felt the room closing in. She'd never stopped to consider the reasons behind her rather odd building team. There seemed to be more to these gangly teenagers and their mother than she'd first thought.

'So about this exorcism,' Ben began again. 'We were thinking we could combine it with a little gathering. Like our very own bonfire night.'

'You've got to be joking.'

She could have fallen from the roof straight onto her head and she still wouldn't be dazed enough to agree to having a party.

'Look the stairs fell down because… well, because they are old stairs,' she stammered, pushing away the memory of the unexplained creaking floorboards and strange chill which had tickled her skin just before the fall.

Jules ignored the pain that shot from her feet all the way to her head as she stood up, only remembering afterwards that she had nowhere to go.

'My keys,' she exclaimed, patting the pockets of her dusty overalls, as if they might magically appear.

'Jules you really shouldn't be…' Rich called out.

The rest of his words disappeared under the sound of a loud phone ringing from somewhere in the pub. Coloured spots filled Jules's eyes and she felt her body tumble to the floor for the second time that day.

Fourteen

'Jules? Can you hear me?'

'Umm.' She opened her eyes, blinking through the clumps of sawdust and dirt that had stuck like glue to her eyelashes. A soft glow from a bedside lamp illuminated the room.

'Jules, how many fingers am I holding up?' Rich's voice broke into her consciousness. She could smell the soft hints of his aftershave and felt the warmth of his body leaning over her.

Running a finger across her eyelids, she removed the grit and focused her gaze on the hand waving in front of her face.

'Four?'

'Good.'

'Did I pass?' she mumbled.

'Yep, you'll live. Had us scared there for a while though,' he replied.

'I seem to be making a habit of waking up in your bed.' Jules lifted her head from the pillow, relieved to find her vision had stopped spinning.

'What can I say? I'm irresistible,' Rich replied, his eyes crinkling with his smile as he sat down on the edge of the bed. 'Can I get you anything? Water? A three-course dinner? Cup of tea?'

'What time is it?'

Rich pulled up the sleeve of his pale blue jumper. It matched the colour of his eyes perfectly.

'Seven-thirty.'

'Feels more like midnight.'

'You've had quite a day.'

As if to remind her, *The Daily*'s headline from that morning bounced back into her mind, causing a flush of heat to travel across her face.

It made no sense. A national tabloid had published a story about her. Not Guy, the one who was supposed to be famous, but her. She was nobody. And then, it turns out, her house is supposedly haunted by an old woman who caused the stairs to fall down on top of her.

If it wasn't for the ache pouring out from every muscle of her body she might have laughed at how ridiculous it all seemed.

'Hey,' Rich said, his hand resting on her shoulder, 'Are you okay? I could drive you to A&E?'

Jules's eyes looked towards him. The blonde stubble on his face had returned.

'I'm fine really. I was just thinking, it feels like all I ever say to you is thank you and sorry, but I am sorry for what I said to you this morning. I was upset but I shouldn't have taken it out on you.'

'Hey, it's fine.' Rich removed his hand, raking it through his hair. 'I have no idea how it feels to have half the country know about my past, but I'd probably react in the exact same way you did.'

'I doubt that.' Jules thought back to her earlier outburst. 'It doesn't seem like much fazes you. And thank you for helping me and carrying me up here too.'

'Well, thank Stan and Dan too. It took all three of us to get you up the stairs.'

'What?' Jules pushed her body up, resisting the desire to cry out as pain shot through her limbs.

'Sorry, bad joke.'

'Ha ha,' she replied with a smile. 'Just for that you can make me a cup of tea.'

'Coming right up.'

Jules dragged her body up to sitting, resting her back against the pillows as she realised with horror just how much dirt had covered her in the fall, most of which had transferred to Rich's navy bed covers.

With as much movement as her arms would allow, she swept her hands across the bed, pushing the powdery grey dirt to the floor before Rich returned and she'd have to apologise for something else.

'Err, Jules, what are you doing?' Rich appeared in the doorway, a tray in his arms.

'Sorry, I just... I've made a right mess of your sheets,' she replied, scrunching her face in embarrassment.

'I don't know if you've noticed,' he began, stepping towards her, 'but Max is hardly the tidiest of housemates. Anyway, here you go, tea as promised, and I thought you could do with eating something,' he said, placing a black round tray on her lap.

Jules's stomach churned at the sight of two thick slices of white toast, smothered in melted butter. A low grumble escaped from her body. Apart from the half-eaten cornflakes, she hadn't thought about food all day. No wonder she fainted, Jules thought, berating her own stupidity and taking a huge bite of the fresh crispy bread.

'I got Dan to call Mrs Beckwith. She's left a key underneath the front doormat for you,' he said, taking up his perch next to her again.

'Thank you,' Jules replied between mouthfuls.

'But you're welcome to stay here if you don't feel up to walking back,' he added, placing a hand on her leg just as Jules stuffed another oversized piece of toast into her mouth.

'Oh,' she replied, between chews.

A long silence hung between them as Jules's mouth battled with the clump of toast, her appetite disappearing as quickly as it had returned.

'I...' she began after several swallows. Washing the lump of food down with a sip of hot tea. 'I...' Jules said again, grappling for a response.

Why shouldn't she stay? Rich had been so sweet to her over the past couple of days and the warmth of his flat felt so inviting; not to mention his deep blue eyes. She definitely found him attractive. If only she could be sure that the butterflies in her stomach were for desire rather than despair.

She really did want to say yes, but the memory of Phillip's woeful story was still fresh in her mind. Everything with him had been a lie. She hadn't wanted to be in the same room with him, let alone date him. She'd done it anyway though, just so she could tell herself she was over Guy.

In fact, at that moment, lying on Rich's bed, Jules couldn't remember feeling much of anything for the handful of men she'd dated since Phillip.

Jules shook her head, grateful for the dizzying headache washing away her thoughts. Now was not the time to be digging up her past. *The Daily* was doing quite enough of that already.

Eventually, she looked up at Rich, meeting his gaze. 'I'm not really with it tonight, Rich. Rain check?'

'Sure, no problem. I'm here if you need me.' Rich stood from the bed, his frame towering over her.

'Thanks,' she replied with relief.

'How about I walk you back to Mrs Beckwith's then?'

'Thanks, but there's no need, I know the way.'

Rich let out a large sigh. 'Jules, you've had a nasty fall. I'm not trying to be a knight in shining armour here. I just want to make sure you don't faint again, okay?'

'Okay,' she agreed with a small nod.

Jules lifted her face towards the cloudless sky as they walked slowly up the lane. A thousand stars shone back, glimmering like a spray of glitter against black paper.

'How are you finding it here?' Rich asked, breaking the silence between them.

Jules didn't answer for a moment as she thought of the beautiful valley she'd looked across on her first day, the people she'd met – Terri, Dan, Jason, Rich, and all the others hell bent on befriending her. Their desire to interfere infuriated her, yet how far would she have gotten without their help?

'Good, I think.'

'Will you stay?'

'I don't know yet,' she answered honestly. Only as the words left her mouth did she realise she had actually been considering living in the house herself. She pushed the thought away. There was nothing here for her. She would move on eventually, she always did.

They fell silent, neither pushing the subject further. Jules felt suddenly nervous as they approached the glow of Mrs Beckwith's porch.

Something in her relationship with Rich had shifted. The easy banter had been replaced with a stiff tension crackling between them in the crisp night air.

As if reading her thoughts, Rich turned his body towards her, his wide chest covering her view as he stepped closer.

Slipping one arm around her waist, she felt his strength sweep her towards him. Stooping his neck to the side, he scraped his stubble gently across her face as he moved his lips towards her, sending a fizz of *déjà vu* hurtling through her.

A suffocating dizziness took hold as Rich's mouth touched her. It had been a long time since she'd felt the sweeping wave of desire, but something didn't feel right. She couldn't breathe, she realised as panic took hold.

Struggling to unravel herself from his arms, she pulled herself back, gasping the air from the night.

'Sorry, I…' Jules spluttered. She had no idea what happened. She liked Rich, didn't she?

'No, I'm sorry,' Rich cut in, pushing both hands through his hair. 'You've had a big day; I don't know what I was thinking.'

'It's okay. It's not you, it's me, the concussion,' she blurted, cringing at her own weak excuse.

They stared at each other for a moment, neither speaking.

Rich took a breath. 'Well, good night then.'

'Good night, and thanks again Rich, for everything.'

'Anytime.' He nodded. Then with a short wave he turned back to the road and started walking.

What had just happened? Jules wondered as she retrieved Mrs Beckwith's spare key from under the mat and slipped into the silent house.

She brushed the tips of her fingers against the spot where Rich's cheek had grazed against hers. For the smallest of moments she'd thought of Guy and the way his stubble used to rub her skin raw.

The suddenness of the memory filtered through her body in a desperate longing before she could stop it. She fought back a sob threatening to burst out, blocking Guy from her thoughts with a tight grind of her teeth.

It was just the fall, she told herself. Guy was not, and would never be, a part of her life. It was Rich she should be thinking of, Jules told herself as she filled the bath with hot water.

The next time she found herself in Rich's arms she wouldn't pull away.

Fifteen

THE DAILY
SUNDAY, FEBRUARY 23RD
CELEB SLOT

Gorgeous Guy performs live

Record breaking singer Guy Rawson will be performing songs from his debut album 'Regret' tonight for the sell-out crowd at the O2 Brixton Academy. Seeing the star? Text Celeb Spot to 88309 and be one of our *Reader Reviewers*.

'You were amazing,' Sonja screeched into his ringing ears as he stepped backstage.

'Thanks,' Guy replied, running a hand across his damp forehead.

'Loved the pause in the middle of "A Goodbye Fool". You had the crowd gagging for more.'

'Really?' Guy searched Sonja's glistening face for the hidden meaning in her comment. The heat from the stage lights had melted her make-up into a slippery sheen, as if at any moment it would slide from her face and reveal a different person underneath.

Like so many publicists and media types he'd met, her features seemed sharper than most. Guy often wondered if a special human sub-breed had been created for their unusual mix of celebrity pandering and killer media instinct.

'Totally.' Her narrow eyes caught his.

She must have known that the pause had not been intentional. He had choked; plain and simple. The silence of the crowd had felt as deafening as their cheers.

Usually he clicked onto autopilot when he stepped onto the stage, ignoring everything except the movement of his fingers across his guitar strings and the sound of his voice reaching into the crowded room.

The set had been going well. He'd warmed up the audience with 'Regret' and kept them going through the song list stowed in his head. But something had changed. The opening chords of the fifth song had reached deep inside him, digging out the emotions of the lyrics and catching in his throat like a noose tightening around his neck. The seconds had ticked slowly by as he'd found himself unable to breathe, let alone sing.

'Awesome set mate.' A backstage technician clapped a hand on Guy's shoulder, breaking his thoughts. 'Come on, it's this way guys.'

'Cheers,' Guy replied as the man led them through the dark narrow hallway and through to the dressing room.

The space doubled as a storage area, with stacks of chairs lining the back wall. Depending on the line-up, the windowless room could have up to twenty musicians crowded into it. The nerves and the adrenaline made for a lethal mix when it came to sharing the space, and Guy was relieved to find it empty.

'Anything you need?' the technician asked with a friendly smile.

A hot shower, a cold beer and an early night, Guy thought. He had no idea when Sunday night gigs had become so popular, but he missed Debbie's roast dinners and an evening sprawled in front of the telly.

'Guy?' Sonja prompted.

'Sorry, no I'm good thanks, mate.'

'Well hang around as much as you like, we'll be closing up in about an hour, but the band before you are over in the Far Side Bar if you fancy a pint.'

'Maybe next time,' Sonja answered before Guy had a chance to accept. 'We've got somewhere else to be tonight.'

'No worries, see you around,' the man replied, already moving back through the doorway.

Sonja spun on the points of her vast heels, turning her sizable cleavage towards him. 'So shall we head off then?' she asked with an arch of her pencilled eyebrow.

For once, Guy did not need an interpreter to find the meaning behind her words. After all, they'd been building up to this moment for most of the week.

It had started with the flirtatious dinner the night he'd returned from seeing Juliet. However much Guy hated to admit it, he'd enjoyed the attention after his earlier knock back. Sonja had an amazing knack for making people feel good. It seemed to be the way she said things rather than what she said. Touching his hand when she spoke, or staring intently into his eyes when he talked.

Before he knew it, she had proposed a celebratory drink after his set that night, with more than enough suggestion in her voice for Guy to catch her drift.

It had seemed like a good idea at the time. He was supposed to be getting back in the game after all. But something didn't feel right. He was living the dream – the rock and roll lifestyle – a packed-out performance followed by a shag with a gorgeous woman. So why did he wish he would just wake-up from it all?

'Guy? Did you hear me?'

'Absolutely,' he nodded, pushing his face into a smile. 'Let's go.'

Guy gave himself a mental slap. He needed to stop thinking so much. Sex with a good looking woman did not require the same level of contemplation most men put into a marriage proposal. It was no wonder he'd had a problem last time.

'Fabulous,' she purred, her hand touching his arm as they negotiated their way through the corridors and out the back door.

Guy unlocked the front door of his large studio flat, pushing it open for Sonja to enter first.

'Can I get you a drink?'

'Twist my arm, why don't you,' she replied, with a giggle that sounded to Guy like something from a David Attenborough documentary on jungle mating calls. It had taken the mercifully quick car journey home for him to realise just how annoying her laugh was.

Don't think, he reminded himself as he moved into the spacious kitchen area and yanked open the door of his huge silver fridge.

His gaze fell straight to the slim green beer bottles lining the top shelf. Their smooth German taste had become a customary part of his post-performance wind-down. Somehow he couldn't imagine Sonja's bright red lips wrapping themselves around the bottle.

Instead, Guy reached for the bottle of Bollinger that had lingered at the back of his fridge for longer than he could remember.

'Ooh, lovely,' Sonja cooed as Guy handed her the tulip glass and fell onto the opposite end of the sofa.

In a single movement, she threw back her head of dark red hair and emptied the contents of the glass.

'Thirsty?' He forced a smirk.

'You'd better believe it.' Sonja shifted her body along the sofa towards him.

Before he could find a reason to move, her face was looming next to his. He let his lips part and felt the smoothness of her tongue dart across his own as she leaned against him. This was the point he'd expect the first yearn of desire to move beneath his jeans. Instead, Guy felt an emptiness so deep it filled him with a terrifying sadness.

Out of nowhere, Debbie's voice jumped into his conscious: 'You're not happy.'

Whether it was the sentiment behind the voice or the fact that it came from his sister, Guy had no idea, but it unnerved him.

He pulled his head away, fighting the urge to push Sonja back.

'Is everything alright?' she asked, reaching for the glass in his hand and taking a long sip.

'Yeah of course. I'm just going to grab a quick shower. That stage was pretty hot.'

'Want some company?'

'Err,' Guy wrestled for a response other than the rude retort balanced on the tip of his tongue.

'I was kidding Guy, go on, I've got a few phone calls to make anyway,' she replied, pulling her enormous purple bag from the floor.

'Great, I won't be a sec.'

He forced his body to move at normal pace as he escaped from the sofa. He loved the large open space of his studio apartment in the nice end of Camden, only a few roads away from Regents Park. But all of a sudden he wished he had another room to hide in. He suddenly felt very conscious of his bed, lying empty just across the room from where Sonja sat.

His flat would probably be described as minimalist, something that seemed to be considered as a good thing on the rare occasions he invited colleagues and acquaintances in for drink. Only Debbie laughed at his inability to buy furniture or decorate. But to Guy the place had never felt like his.

He had bought it outright after his second contract with *GiGi* had been signed. A trendy flat in a trendy location for a so-called trendy model. It had taken him until recently to realise that the studio had never felt like home. Home was the messy room he'd shared with Juliet at university, or Debbie's house, full of life and love.

Grabbing some fresh clothes from a long mirrored wardrobe, Guy stepped into the black and white tiled bathroom and locked the door.

Within seconds, his naked body stepped underneath the powerful spray of hot water.

Guy closed the lids of his eyes and dropped his head, relishing the pricks of heat bouncing onto the back of his neck.

As he felt the adrenaline from his performance slip away and his muscles unwind, her image floated back into his head. The way her face had softened when she'd seen him, the widening of her already huge green eyes.

Juliet's face had been haunting him for days, keeping him from sleep at night and nudging him awake each morning.

With his eyes still closed, Guy moved his body to face the water, twisting the dial to cold. With a sharp intake of breath he felt every inch of his body break into goose bumps as the icy water flooded over him.

Still her face danced in front of him.

Maybe, just maybe, Guy let himself wonder, as he turned off the water and reached for a towel, a part of her had been pleased to see him.

It felt good to stop hiding from it. Maybe he had been right after all. He had hardly stuck around long enough to find out, he thought, reaching for the door handle.

Suddenly, Guy remembered what awaited him from behind the single lock of the bathroom door and his spirits sank. He couldn't do it. It had nothing to do with his body; his heart just wasn't in it.

He dressed quickly, pulling on a fresh pair of jeans and an old grey t-shirt and stepped bare foot from the steamy bathroom; his lungs filling with a sharp intake of breath as his eyes took in the view in front of him.

Sonja sat exactly as he'd left her, with one small difference. She was naked.

Instinct pulled his eyes to the curves of her enhanced breasts, following the line of her petite body all the way to her feet, still encased in her giant heels.

'I've got a surprise for you,' she purred.

'I can see that,' Guy responded, rooted to the spot as he struggled to regain control of his wandering eyes.

'Well, two surprises then.' A wide smile crossed her face. 'I've just got off the phone with my contact at *The Daily*.' Sonja paused to take another sip from his champagne glass.

If he'd felt the slightest bit aroused by the naked woman perched on his sofa, it evaporated at the mention of the tabloid, which seemed to have dominated his life of late. Although he only had himself to blame for that.

Sonja finished the fizzing liquid and continued, 'They are doing a double page spread in tomorrow's paper.'

'Really? What's the angle?'

'Well it's actually on that girl they're fixated on, but they're only doing it because of you.'

Shit; this could not be good, he thought.

'They've found some more people to go on the record then, I assume?' Guy asked.

'Like you wouldn't believe. Apparently she's been a bit of a slapper since you broke up with her.'

'Damn.'

'I have to say Guy,' Sonja continued as if he hadn't spoken. 'I was a bit sceptical about how the lost love angle would play, but you've handled it perfectly.'

'It wasn't like that,' he mumbled. 'This is very bad.'

'Don't worry babe, you're still mentioned throughout the piece and I gave them a quote to juice it up a bit.'

'I wish you hadn't,' Guy responded, thinking of the anger in Juliet's face last time he'd seen her.

'That's my job. But hey, I think that's enough work for one night, don't you?' She stood from the sofa without the slightest hesitation and crossed the room towards him.

Guy could not stop his gaze from falling back to her huge breasts. They remained perfectly pert as she sauntered towards him.

Panic crept over him. He had to get this woman out of his flat before he lost his resolve.

'Actually Sonja, my sister called just as I was getting out of the shower and she needs someone to babysit for her, it's an emergency,' he lied.

'What's happened?' Sonja demanded, stopping a metre from where he stood and placing her hands on her hips.

Guy dropped his gaze, unable to look at her without staring at the hard points of her nipples.

'Apparently Carl, her husband, is in A&E and she needs someone to watch Sam whilst she goes to get him.'

'Can't someone else do it? We haven't even started to have fun yet.' A slow smile spread across her face.

'I'm really sorry Sonja, I've already agreed.'

'I could wait here for you if you like,' she said, unwrapping her arms and taking another step towards him.

'Well actually, Debbie is dropping Sam over on the way.'

'So I could stay then? Surely he'll be asleep.' She reached out to touch his arm.

Come on, think, Guy implored his mind. He had to find a way to put her off. 'Yeah that would be great,' he began. 'I'd love some help. Sam's got chicken pox at the moment and is throwing up everywhere.'

Guy watched the workings of Sonja's mind as she processed his lie. He had no idea if children were sick when they had chicken pox, but he guessed Sonja didn't know either.

'On second thoughts, I've got an early meeting tomorrow,' Sonja replied, smiling tightly.

If she'd guessed he was making up an excuse to get rid of her then she had the class not to point it out, Guy thought with relief, saying a silent prayer to Debbie, Sam and Carl as he waited for Sonja to get dressed.

Ten minutes later, Guy slid his body beneath the smooth cotton of his bed sheets, his mind racing too much for sleep. He needed a plan this time.

He'd given up far too easily last time he'd seen her; something he couldn't let happen again. Not if he wanted to spend more time with her, let alone win her back. The thought launched a barrage of nerves in his stomach. It was the first time he'd let himself admit his intentions. Despite the nerves, it felt right.

Sixteen

<u>Loughborough University (five years earlier)</u>

The remnants of their picnic lay scattered around them as they lay motionless, enjoying the warm rays from the afternoon sun.

Guy opened one eye and stared at the beautiful girl lying next to him. Even with her eyes closed, half asleep, her lips remained fixed in a grin. He could feel the warmth of her bare legs tangled in his; her tiny white dress barely covering a bright pink bikini and the curves of her otherwise slim frame.

Eyes that swim like an emerald sea

Can't you see, can't you see, you're drowning me?

The lyrics had been haunting him for weeks. From the moment he'd walked out halfway through his final exam and his days as a student had become numbered.

He'd sat for hours desperately trying to construct another verse, but those two lines had stuck like a scratched CD, stuttering on the same bit of music and driving him crazy.

The feverish humidity of a week-long heat wave had finally drawn it out of him. It had been prickling under his skin for months, but it had taken the inescapable heat suffocating him day and night to surface into his thoughts. Now it was there, he couldn't think of anything else.

Guy swallowed hard as he felt his stomach curdle. He had to do it, before it ate him alive.

'I'm going to London Juliet.' The words left his mouth before he could put it off again.

'Don't forget the graduation party is next week,' she mumbled sleepily.

'No, I mean I'm moving there... for good.'

She pulled her body up to sitting and pushed her pink sunglasses onto the top of her head.

By some small miracle they had discovered a quiet space in the otherwise heaving park as every person in a twenty-mile radius scrambled to enjoy the weather.

Perhaps more quiet than he'd have liked, Guy realised as the piercing green of her eyes bore into him.

'What?' she asked, her voice already wavering with emotion.

He took a breath, unsure if the feeling of asphyxiation had more to do with the humidity or Juliet's stare. The latter, he thought.

'I'm moving to London.'

'But you can't be. What are you talking about?'

'Remember that woman who offered me her business card a few months ago?'

'The modelling thing? I thought you threw that away.'

'No I was going to, but...' he paused, trying to find the words to describe the feeling that had been building inside him. 'I thought what the hell. I went for an audition last week and they liked me.'

'Last week? When?'

'Tuesday.'

'Tuesday,' she repeated. 'Whilst I was taking my final exam? And when your phone was off and you told me it had run out of battery?'

Guy didn't respond.

'But you've always thought modelling was stupid,' she exclaimed.

'They've found me a job,' he continued with a shrug, ignoring her comment.

'I don't understand. Why didn't you tell me? When are you going?'

'After graduation.' The lie rolled easily off his tongue. He should have told her the truth, but it seemed too cruel to put into words.

In reality, the modelling agency was expecting him in London in two days. His sister had promised him her sofa to sleep on and he'd booked a seat on a coach leaving in just a few hours' time. He could have gone and come back for graduation, or even waited until afterwards before moving, but he didn't want to. It didn't feel like there was anything left for him here.

'Guy, why didn't you talk to me about this?'

'I don't know.'

Her large eyes fixed on him.

'I really don't. It just sort of happened,' he added.

'What about your music? I thought you wanted to stay up here and pick up some part-time work until—'

'Until what?' he interrupted, sitting up to meet her gaze. 'You should see the old timers playing the same pub circuits as me. All old students, all stuck in some hellish office job, all still waiting for a break. I won't do it. I can't do it.'

'Guy, you're panicking, we all are. But you've got to hold out for what you believe in. It will happen. You're too good for it not to, I promise.'

'For God's sake Juliet. Wake up, will you. This is not a dreamland where everything works out. This is real life.'

He watched her eyes widen at the harshness of his tone. He hadn't meant it to sound so aggressive.

The silence grew between them.

'Baby,' she whispered, 'I'm sorry, I… I didn't mean…'

He jumped to his feet. The anger in him exploding out of nowhere, as hot as the sun burning against the back of his neck. 'You are so fucking optimistic it's pathetic. Fuck reality. Fuck needing to earn money, that's not for us then?'

'I didn't mean that,' she replied, her chest heaving with a sob.

Guy stared down at her as a slow rage unleashed itself within him. He wanted her to argue back. To scream at him for being such as bastard, but he knew she would never do that.

'What did you mean then? Because it sounded to me like you don't want me to be successful.'

'Guy, how can you say that?' Water began to stream from her eyes, mixing with the charcoal of her eyeliner and running in long black streaks down her face. 'You're a fantastic musician, and you're going to make it, I know it. I just don't want you to sell yourself short.'

'It's modelling Juliet, not McDonalds. It's a great opportunity to get somewhere. Anywhere but here.'

'But what's wrong with here?' she sniffed.

'Everything,' he shot back, turning away and shoving a bare foot into one of his discarded trainers. He couldn't look at her face any longer.

'Wait, Guy, I'm sorry okay. I didn't know you felt this way.' Juliet took a shaky breath and wiped a hand across her face, leaving long smears of black across her cheeks.

'You never said anything,' she continued. 'But look, I haven't accepted that design assistant's job yet. We can have a fresh start. Find a flat share in a cheap part of London. You can do modelling if it's what you want and I can get a different job. It will work out.'

'I'm going alone,' he replied in a low voice, forcing his remaining bare foot into the other trainer as the hatred hammered through him. 'I can't do this anymore.'

'What can't you do? I don't understand.'

'This. Pretending every day that it might be the day I get my break. Watching the doubt and the pity in people's eyes when I tell them I'm trying to make it as a musician. I need to do something else. Be someone else. Away from here and away from you.'

'No, you don't mean that, you can't,' she cried, clambering to her knees. 'Why are you doing this? Baby please, whatever it is, we can work it out, I… I can change. We love each other, that's all that matters, please…' her voice trailed off into wrenching sobs.

He wanted to turn around and hold her. To cry with her and beg for forgiveness, but he didn't. He'd only meant to suggest they spent a few months apart, but as the words had left his mouth, he'd realised it had to end. If he was going to start over, then he needed to do it alone.

So instead, he started walking, his body feeding from the anger as he broke into a run. Not stopping to take a breath until he'd taken his seat at the back of the coach.

<u>One week later</u>

Guy stepped into the empty warehouse, two miles walk from High Barnet tube, the last stop north at the end of the Northern line. It looked like the last place on earth anyone would choose to hold a photo shoot.

Two rows of steel pillars ran the length of the warehouse, supporting a windowless concrete ceiling. With the exception of a scattering of damp cardboard boxes, spread around puddles of grey murky water, the space was empty. Only the fluorescent tubes dangling just below the ceiling, and the huge metal door large enough for a lorry to fit through, allowed any light into the gloom.

He looked down at the dog-eared A-Z map he'd borrowed from Debbie as if the tiny black and white street names might have changed in the last thirty seconds.

'Hello?' his voice echoed into the emptiness.

'Hey man.' A short man in tight black leather trousers and a t-shirt came up behind him. 'If you're looking for the crew, they're setting up in the car park round back.'

'Great, thanks.'

'What do you think of my creation?' he grinned, waving his hands out into the warehouse. 'Magnificent, isn't it?'

'Err, yes,' Guy nodded, looking back into the derelict warehouse just in case he'd missed something. It still looked like an abandoned rat infested concrete block.

'One of my best. Oh, that reminds me, if you spot Liam on your travels, tell him to get his arse in here with the other bag of artificial dust before I die of old age.'

'Right, will do,' Guy replied, stepping back into the sunshine. He was starting to feel like he'd fallen down the rabbit hole. Or jumped down it head first.

What was he doing? Guy asked himself for the tenth time in as many minutes as he negotiated his way around the building, only to come face-to-face with a sprawling hive of activity. Dozens of people dashed around him, in and out of five insanely long and very clean white trailers. They stood alone, with no sign of the vehicles that had brought them there, as if they'd grown up from the cracks in the concrete.

He stood still for a moment, wishing he had somewhere to move to at the same rate as the people pushing past him, just so he wouldn't feel as out of place as a pair of flat shoes in Juliet's wardrobe. Guy smirked at the analogy, before he remembered what he'd done.

'Guy,' a female voice called out in front of him.

'Sidney, hi,' he replied with relief as his agent air-kissed him three times; another thing in the long list of new phenomenon he had yet to understand since his move to London.

'How are you feeling?'

'Great.'

'Good,' she smiled. 'Well come on, it's this way. You'll be a hero around here today. You're the first model to arrive, although you'll soon learn the power struggles that go on between the models and the crew.'

He felt like an obedient puppy as he followed the tall body of his agent through the maze of equipment and vehicles.

Sidney was unlike any woman he'd ever met. He could only guess that her age fell somewhere between forty and sixty, but with her slim frame and smooth skin, Guy guessed she might pass for thirty from a only a short distance. And despite the fact that she spent most of her days among young beautiful models, she still managed to ooze a level of confidence he'd never seen before.

Guy had only to sit silently beside her whilst she'd furiously fought over his contract with the people from *GiGi* to know that he had one of the most intimidating and successful agents in London.

'Ah look, perfect timing,' Sidney said, coming to a stop by the door of one of the trailers. 'Here are your hair and make-up girls, Janine and Mandy. Girls, this is Guy.'

'Hi, nice to meet you,' Guy said, smiling through another bout of nervousness.

'Hi Guy,' the two blondes echoed back.

He could feel their eyes appraising his face, doing some secret calculations he couldn't begin to understand.

'So, how much time will you be spending with each model today?' he asked.

To his surprise, the three women laughed.

'Guy, Janine and Mandy are your hair and make-up artists. They'll be working on you alone,' Sidney explained. 'By the end of the day, you'll be running off to the loo, just to get five minutes to yourself. Although, be warned these two have been known to follow models anywhere.'

'Hey,' Mandy exclaimed with a smile. 'That was one time, and to be fair she was three hours late and hung over.'

'Talking of late, what time are we expecting Lola today?' Janine added.

Sidney winked at Guy. 'Don't worry,' she said turning to the girls, 'I warned her *GiGi* wouldn't be standing for any of her usual tricks.'

'Lola? As in Lola Frost?' Guy exclaimed.

'Sorry darling. I was waiting until the contracts were signed to tell you. Lola will be modelling *GiGi*'s new swimwear range. We only had it confirmed this morning.'

'Great,' Guy replied. It seemed to be a word he was using a lot recently. When Sidney had introduced him to the *GiGi* team; when he'd signed the contract and seen the ridiculous amount of money they'd be paying him; when Debbie had asked him how he was finding his new life in London. His only response was 'great'.

Now he was not only meeting, but working with an international supermodel, and there was that word again, summing up a cocktail of emotions and thoughts in a tiny one-syllable word.

Sidney patted his arm. 'I'll leave you in the very capable hands of these two for a little while, but don't be afraid to ask if you have any questions. Remember Guy, *GiGi* picked you because you have a totally fresh look, so no one is expecting you to know what you are doing. If you're not sure about anything, or you need a break, give me a nod. I'll be here all day.'

'Thanks Sidney,' Guy replied, swallowing back the million questions that he could feel lingering on the tip of his tongue. Like, what the hell was he doing as a model? Somehow, he didn't think Sidney would have the answer to that one.

'Right. This way Guy,' Mandy said, as she stepped into the trailer. 'You've got all of this to yourself today,' she added with a grin. 'But don't get used to it. More often than not, everyone is crammed into a backstage area the size of broom cupboard.

'Believe me, until you've experienced twenty hairdryers all going at once, you can't even begin to understand the meaning of the word hot.'

Guy nodded but said nothing as he stepped through a small kitchen and into a seating area. The clean grey leather chairs looked a lot more comfortable than Debbie's sofa bed. It was hard to take in. This was his trailer. Someone had hired this thing just for him.

'If you can take a seat here,' Mandy said, urging him towards a director's style chair, 'we can get started.'

'Yeah, of course,' he replied, moving through to the back of the room, and sitting down.

'Now sweetie,' Janine began, coming up behind him. 'I see you haven't shaved this morning.'

'Err, no,' Guy stammered. 'Sidney mentioned that it would be best—'

'Relax, Guy,' Janine laughed. 'I was just going to say thanks. It makes our life a whole lot easier if you leave it for us to do.'

'Sure,' he replied, feeling like a total idiot. What was he doing here? He wasn't a model.

'Oh, and this one is important,' Janine added with a grin. 'If you wake up with any spots, whatever you do don't squeeze them. Don't even touch them. We've got products here that can work miracles, but only if you leave them alone.'

'Right, will do,' Guy said, trying to work his face into a relaxed smile.

'Now sweetie, you just take a load off. You'll soon get used to us fussing around you, so read a mag or make calls, whatever you like,' Mandy said, giving his shoulder a squeeze.

'Thanks,' he replied, reaching into his jeans for his new mobile. He couldn't wait to tell Juliet. She would love the endless rows of hair and make-up products spread on the counter in front of him. But just as the tip of his thumb stretched automatically over the keypad, he remembered. Shutting his phone with one swift action, he pushed it back into his pocket.

He'd been doing the same thing all week. They'd spoken so often that it felt as natural for him to dial her number as it was to drink a glass of water. Every time he slipped his phone back into his pocket, it felt as if he was cutting off a part of himself.

Instead, he sat still, staring at the bright bulbs bordering the mirror and the dozen or so pieces of equipment sticking out from circular holes on his right. The top one looked like a giant hair dryer, but the rest looked like they belonged in a torture chamber rather than a make-up trailer. Although as Mandy's face loomed into his, her hand wielding a sharp pair of tweezers, Guy started to wonder if the two were all that different.

It seemed to go on forever.

His arse ached from sitting down for so long. His eyes hurt from staring at the bare white bulbs, his ears throbbed from listening to Janine and Mandy's gossiping, but worst of all his mind wandered. No matter which magazine he tried to read or what topic he tried to focus his thoughts on, it always seemed to lead straight back to Juliet and the last time he'd seen her.

A whole week had gone by. One of the craziest weeks of his life and yet no amount of time or distraction could ease the burning sensation which circled around his chest.

He'd made a mistake. Whatever he'd been hoping or trying to achieve, he hadn't meant to break up with her, had he? It had taken the seven tedious hours sitting at the back of the coach, with the overworked engine rattling noisily in his ears, to fully understand what he'd done. Totally fucked up, that's what.

So why hadn't he called her and begged for forgiveness? Why had he ignored her calls and changed his mobile? Why was he throwing away the only thing he believed in? The questions dogged him constantly but there never seemed to be any answers.

He had no idea what he was doing with his life, why he was sitting in a trailer someone had hired just for him, whilst two complete strangers shoved tweezers up his nostrils. He couldn't bear to drag Juliet into his abyss.

To his relief, Sidney's smiling face appeared behind him in the mirror, dragging his mind back to the relative safety of the day.

'Wow,' she grinned. 'What a transformation. I mean, we all knew it was possible but still, Guy, you look totally hot.'

Guy felt his cheeks flush. She was his agent, it was her job to compliment him, he reminded himself, glancing at his reflection for the first time in the hours since Janine and Mandy had been working their magic.

'Holy shit,' he said, moving his hand to his face.

'Wait, Guy,' Mandy cried out grabbing his arm. 'Whatever you do, don't touch your face.'

'Oh right, yeah of course sorry. I... I just can't believe it,' he stammered.

If someone had shown him a photograph of the face in the mirror, he wouldn't in a million years have guessed it was his own. They had cut his hair. The longish unkempt curls had been replaced with short straight spikes. It looked somehow messy and yet every hair was in its place.

His cheekbones seemed suddenly more defined, which would have made him look feminine if it wasn't for the designer stubble. If he didn't know any better, he would have thought he'd been sitting in the trailer for weeks based on the amount of facial hair he now seemed to have.

He looked like a model, he realised with a sudden bout of nausea.

'We're glad you like it,' Janine said, blowing him a kiss in the mirror.

Sidney nodded. 'So Guy, if you're ready let's get you next door to wardrobe for your first outfit.'

'Great.'

'No, hang on, what am I thinking, let me introduce you to Lola first.'

Guy said nothing. His palms felt suddenly sweaty and his heart seemed to have jumped into his throat.

Before he had time to think, he'd said goodbye to Janine and Mandy and had followed Sidney into the trailer next to his. Right before his eyes sat one of the most beautiful women in the world.

A man and a woman bustled around her, oblivious to their arrival.

'Guy, I want you to meet Lola.

'Lola, this is Guy.'

She looked up from her mobile with a curt nod, but her thumbs kept moving. She said nothing.

'As part of the *GiGi* promotions, you two will be spending quite a bit of time together,' Sidney began, with a smile of encouragement at Guy. 'We've agreed with the PR team that you'll be photographed together on three occasions between now and the launch next week. I've arranged for one of those times to be later today. You can grab a quick coffee during one of the set changes. Then a new club opening on Wednesday night which I'm sure you'd both have been planning to go to anyway. And the third time we can arrange for an early morning snap near South Kensington.'

'What's in South Kensington?' he asked.

Lola rolled her eyes. 'Me.'

'Oh, I see,' Guy replied. He didn't have the first clue what they were talking about.

'It's all perfectly normal, Guy,' Sidney explained. 'Many of the advertising campaigns are teamed with some form or PR activity. Rumours of a budding relationship always cause a storm of interest.'

'Relationship? But we don't know each other.'

'Please tell me he's not for real?' Lola cut in, her face showing a mix of disdain and indifference as she stared at Guy through their reflections in the mirror.

'As I said, Guy, this is all perfectly normal and written in the contract you signed as part of the promotional activity. We'll arrange for the paparazzi to see the two of you together; they then supply the photographs to the tabloids, who in turn sell more papers. Everyone loves reading about the love lives of celebrities.'

'But don't the papers know it's not real?'

'Of course they do. Anyone with half a brain knows it's total rubbish. But they sell papers, which in turn raises the profile of you and *GiGi*. Everyone wins. Christ, Guy, half the relationships out there are nothing more than a mutual agreement to boost publicity. It's just the way things are done.'

'Right,' Guy nodded. It was like he'd stepped into a parallel universe where nothing made sense.

'And don't forget to tell him about my rules, Sidney,' Lola said, turning to their agent as if he wasn't there. 'He must never speak to the paps whilst I'm with him, or even smile at them.'

'Darlings, we'll get to all that. Don't worry. Now, let's get started.' Sidney turned to Guy. 'Are you okay with all this, Guy?'

'Yep, I'm great,' he lied.

'Good, because there's no going back now,' she replied with a flash of white teeth.

He nodded, trying to smile as he followed Sidney out of one trailer and into another. She was right, he realised as he stepped into the clothes he'd been told to wear. There was no going back.

His life with Juliet was over. He hadn't just burnt his bridges; he'd dropped a nuclear bomb on them. How could he possibly go back now? So much had changed in a week. The world seemed a different place and he might as well get used to it.

Seventeen

THE DAILY
MONDAY, FEBRUARY 24TH
IS THIS GUY'S NEW BABE?

Has Guy got a new girl? The sexy model turned singer likes to keep people guessing when it comes to his love life, but this snap of the star looking flirty over dinner with his publicist, Sonja Morton, suggests the singer could be mixing business with pleasure.

Jules lifted the newspaper from Stan's display rack and smiled at the image of the big-breasted woman in the photograph with Guy. If *The Daily* had found the life of another unsuspecting woman to pry into then she was off the hook.

It was over.

The Daily had moved on, and by the looks of it so had Guy. With just one sentence, it was as if everything with Guy and *The Daily* had been nothing more than a bad dream.

Jules slipped the newspaper back into place on the rack. She wouldn't be taking it with her today, or ever again for that matter.

'You're in early today,' Stan grumbled, making his way out from the back of the shop, a sack of potatoes in his arms. 'I've not even had a chance to look through the papers.'

'No need thanks Stan,' Jules smiled. 'Looks like they've given up on me at last.' Not even Stan's cantankerous demeanour could dent her sudden good mood.

'If you say so. How's your head?' he asked, busying himself with the vegetable displays.

Jules lifted her hand to the sizable lump on the back of her head and gave it a gentle prod, feeling nothing but the tenderness of a bruise. The throbbing pain which had resonated from it like a homing beacon had disappeared.

'Better. Much better, in fact.' She smiled again.

'Good,' Stan mumbled.

'Right, well I'd best be off. No need to keep a copy of the paper aside for me anymore, Stan. See you later,' she said with a wave as she left the shop.

Stepping into the lane, Jules felt her eyelids scrunch at the bright February sunshine streaming out from a cloudless blue sky. Had it been this nice on her walk to the shop? She couldn't remember.

It took Jules twenty minutes to walk the short distance in the bright spring sunshine to her house. The dizziness clouding her head may have disappeared overnight, but the aching from her limps had not. Deep purple bruises had appeared all over the back of her body like a rash, causing a nauseating pain to attack her any time she moved her body too quickly.

She could barely lift a kettle without feeling a stab of pain, let alone start clearing the rubble that had once been her staircase. So when Terri had dropped by on Sunday and offered to work another week, she'd forgotten about her desire to be alone in the house and agreed, extending her stay with Mrs Beckwith for the same length of time.

A good decision, Jules decided as she made her way slowly up the driveway, an easy smile touching her lips at the sight of her building team already there, huddled over an open copy of *The Daily*.

'Morning guys,' she called out. 'Don't worry, I've already checked it.'

Three pairs of eyes shot towards her.

'What is it?' She felt a laugh build inside her at the stunned faces staring at her.

'Are you okay, lovey?' Terri asked, her gaze turning to the paper in Dan's hands before resting on Jules.

'Of course I am. Guy can do whatever he wants with whoever he wants. As long as he doesn't mention me, why should I care?'

'But you are mentioned. A lot, in fact. It's just so... so unbelievable. I mean if it was me I'd be cowering in my house for weeks.'

'Terri, what are you talking about?' Jules felt a prickling of unease travel across the back of her neck as she took another step towards them.

'The story... here.' Terri nudged her eldest son. 'A whole two pages on... well, on you.'

Jules took a final unsteady step forward as Dan turned the paper around for her to see.

She hadn't checked the whole paper, she realised just as her vision focused on the headline reaching in giant blue letters across the entire middle section on the paper:

GUY'S GAL'S A MANEATER

A shocked laugh escaped her throat, the sound mixing with a sharp exhale of air to create a howl like noise.

How could she have been so stupid? Jules wondered as a tidal wave of nervous adrenaline flooded her system, sucking the air from her lungs. They had not given up on her. It was far from over.

Rooted to the spot, her body frozen, Jules could only stare at the story Dan held in front of her face. She felt her eyes widening further and further as she read the paragraphs laying out her life for the world to see:

MONDAY, FEBRUARY 24TH
GUY'S GAL'S A MANEATER
When heart-throb, Guy Rawson, revealed in an exclusive Valentine's interview that his heart belonged to former girlfriend, Juliet Stewart, *The Daily* couldn't resist playing cupid. But in an unexpected twist to the couples' story, we can report that gorgeous Guy's Juliet is nothing more than a callous man-eater with more ex-boyfriends than we've had lawsuits.
Juicy Jules's path of destruction

1.   Bath born Juliet has always had a way with men, according to estranged parents, Eleanor and Bernard Stewart.

Left: The picture of innocence, Juliet poses for school photo, aged 11.

2.   A-lister Guy Rawson met and dated Juliet during their student days. According to close friends of the couple, Guy and Juliet were inseparable until Juliet broke his heart by running away shortly after graduation.

Facts
Location: Loughborough University
Dated for 3 years
Heartbreakometer: 9/10
Despite Guy's declaration of love, the sexy star has gone on to have worldwide success as the face of *GiGi* Sports and has recently catapulted to the top of the UK singles chart.

Above: The couple celebrating their final exams just weeks before Juliet (22) ran away.

3.   The blonde bombshell moved on to property manager, Phillip Williams, using him to launch her career as a property manager. Williams is still single and claims he will never trust again.

Facts
Location: Nottingham
Dated for 1 year
Heartbreakometer: 8/10
Left: Juicy Jules in skimpy bikini, then 23.

4.   After getting a taste for heartbreak, Juliet set her sights on married father of two, and older man, Steven Alton. Alton's now estranged wife claims the man-eater destroyed her family.

<u>Facts</u>

Location: Slough

Dated for 9 months

Heartbreakometer: 10/10

Juicy Jules broke the hearts of the entire family when she stole Alton.

Right: Juicy Jules, now brunette dresses for seduction in a Karen Millen suit, then 25

5.   From married man to toy boy, Juliet dated student Daniel Barnes, 6 years her junior. "She could have been the one" claims Barnes.

<u>Facts:</u>

Location: Reading

Dated for 4 months

Heartbreakometer: 4/10

Right: A casual Juliet, then 26, plays the role of modern day Mrs Robinson in skinny jeans and Parka

6.   Who's next? *The Daily* can report that Juliet is still breaking hearts wherever she goes. In a recent move to a small community in Gloucestershire, the man-eater is now on the lookout for her next victim.

Below: This recent photo shows Juicy Jules embracing the country life. The longhaired beauty is now looking for her next heartbreak.

Sources close to the Guy camp say the star is "not surprised" by our revelations and is currently very happy with new girlfriend and celeb publicist Sonja Morton. It looks like *The Daily*'s attempts to play cupid have backfired! Good luck Guy.

Time stood still as her gaze flicked back and forth over the double page spread. How could so many lies and photos be printed about her for millions to see?

Then, as Jules's arms finally regained their movement, she snatched the paper from Dan's outstretched hands, her eyes narrowing on the final photograph. When had it been taken?

The loose hair, the pale frown – Wednesday, her walk back from Rich's. At least they hadn't known that, she conceded. But how long until they did? she wondered suddenly.

Jules thought back to that morning less than a week ago, unable to recall a parked car out of place, let alone someone lurking in the bushes with a camera. How did they even know where she was? Her mind answered instantly: the same way Guy had found her. The supposed 'friend' who had spoken to her mum.

A surge of anger seized her. 'How can they do this to me?' she cried out.

'It's crazy alright,' Jason spoke up. 'You're a celebrity.'

Jules swallowed the urge to lurch forward and lash out at Jason. It wasn't his fault. But she was definitely not a celebrity. She was a victim. A victim of what, she couldn't find the words to explain, but most definitely a victim.

She turned her pale face back to the paper gripped between her fingers. 'It's all lies,' she stammered.

'Of course it is, lovey,' Terri replied.

'Seriously,' Jules fought the urge to shout. 'Like this here,' she continued, shaking the paper like a rag doll. 'I'm not estranged from my parents; I spoke to my mum two days ago.

'And... and this, Steve, he was already in the divorce courts when I met him. It was his wife who was having the affair, with the kids' school teacher. I had nothing to do with ending their marriage.'

Jules looked up, shifting her gaze between Terri, Dan and Jason, searching their faces for reassurance. 'You have to believe me... I need you to... I just...'

Terri spoke first. 'Of course we do. Nobody in their right mind would take a word that paper said as anything more than a bit of fun, I promise you that.'

'Fun? How is this fun?' Jules yelped, her eyes continuing to flit between the three people in her driveway.

'Boys,' Terri began, turning her attention to her sons and digging out a five pound note from the pocket of her dungarees. 'Drive over to Marlene's Cafe and get yourselves some breakfa—'

'Cool,' they replied in unison, taking the money and moving towards the van before Terri had finished talking.

'But be back in an hour, we've got a lot of clearing up to do today,' she yelled after them.

As Dan negotiated the van out of the driveway, Terri stepped towards Jules, taking the paper from her hands and steering her gently towards the stone wall surrounding the property. 'Take a seat here for a minute, lovey. I'll be back in a jiffy with a cup of tea, okay?'

Jules nodded, unable to speak as she felt the tears teetering behind her eyes and a painful lump form in her throat.

She had to get control of herself, she thought, taking a shaky breath. And yet her mind refused to budge as she fought to push the image of *The Daily* away.

'Here you are then lovey, drink this,' Terri said as she handed a steaming mug to Jules. 'I know you don't normally take it, but I popped a bit of sugar in there, to help with the shock.'

'Thanks,' she began. Terri's kindness was the final straw of emotion, breaking her fight to remain calm as tears flowed down her face. 'I'm sorry,' she sobbed. 'I don't normally cry, it's just I... I can't believe this is happening.'

'Of course you can't. The whole thing is utter madness.'

'I'm sorry,' she repeated, 'I know it's stupid and I know that no one will remember this in a few weeks, but I feel so... so... naked.'

'You've nothing to apologise for, lovey. Why, if it was me, I'd be on the first plane to the back end of nowhere until not even my boys could remember my name. You're strong though lovey, you'll get over it. It's the shock more than anything. Nobody expects to wake up in the morning and find this kind of thing.'

'Thanks Terri,' Jules sniffed, wiping her hands across her damp cheeks. 'I don't know what I'd have done without you these past few weeks.'

'Hey, now you've nothing to say thank you for either. You wouldn't believe the amount of times I cried when my Kevin upped sticks with that tart from the next village. Not so much as a note. Just this business and a mountain of debt. And even though only a handful of people knew about it, I felt so humiliated – cried for months.'

'That's awful.'

Terri nodded. 'Yes, it was. But if it had been in the papers as well then I don't think I'd have ever stopped crying. Well maybe just long enough to track him down and kill him.' Terri grinned.

Jules couldn't help but feel better at Terri's humour.

'Now obviously I'm not suggesting you should kill this Guy fella. It seems there's still something between the two of you, and—'

'No there isn't,' Jules jumped in. 'Other than last week, we hadn't seen each other for years.'

'Maybe not, but by the way you two were arguing it seems there's still a lot of unfinished business at least.'

'There really isn't. I hate him, Terri. He's the reason the paper is doing this. It's all part of his publicity campaign. He's using me to sell records.'

'Right.'

Jules lifted her gaze to Terri's face, reading her quizzical expression. 'What?'

'Well, it's just if Guy only did what he did for publicity, why did he drive all the way up here to tell you it wasn't?'

'I... I don't know. He probably thought if he could get me to do an interview it would carry more weight with the story. But whatever the reason, there is nothing between us, okay?'

'If you say so lovey. Now look, the best thing you can do now is try and forget about this newspaper article. I know it's embarrassing but without a time machine there is nothing you can do to undo what's happened.'

'You're right Terri,' Jules agreed, wiping the remaining tears from her face. 'Thank you.'

'Oh, I almost forgot,' Terri began, digging out a dusty catalogue from the pocket of her dungarees. 'I found this in the back of the van. It's a staircase catalogue. God knows how old it is, but I thought at least it would give you a few ideas.'

Jules took the catalogue, grateful for something else to focus her thoughts on. 'Thanks, Terri. For everything I mean. Helping me with the house and being so nice to me. I know I'm not the easiest person, I just...' Jules stopped, unsure what she was trying to say.

'Oh you daft thing, what are friends for. Now why don't you hold the ladder, and I'll pop up and get your car keys. They're in the bathroom, you said?'

'Yes, that would be great, thanks,' she replied as they stood up and walked towards the house.

As Jules flicked through the catalogue, she was surprised to see that fitting a new staircase would be simple. Rather than build the entire structure from scratch, she could simply pick out a readymade one and it would be delivered and fitted like any other piece of furniture.

'I still can't believe how much carpet you managed to take up all by yourself,' Terri said. 'And such nice floors, why would anyone want to cover...' her sentence trailed off as Terri stepped through the doorway.

'Sorry? I didn't catch that,' Jules said, entering into the hallway behind Terri.

'Oh, nothing lovey.'

Jules saw the nervous look that crossed Terri's face and guessed the woman's sudden change in mood. 'Terri, you can't seriously believe this place is haunted?' she quizzed.

'I don't know,' she answered, dropping her voice to a whisper, 'but how else do you explain the ceiling and stairs both falling down? It's not right.'

'Honestly,' Jules said, smiling at Terri as she rolled her eyes. 'This place is just old, that's all.'

'I'm sure you're right lovey, but maybe just to be on the safe side you could reconsider the other thing.' Terri scrunched her face into what Jules could only take as some form of wink.

'If you're referring to what I think you're referring to then absolutely not,' she replied, finding her own voice had dropped to a whisper as she tried to ignore the tingle running down her spine.

Ever since Jules had been told her house was haunted it seemed the whole of Cottinghale had been asking about an exorcism. Although she strongly suspected it had more to do with the idea of a party than any concern for her own safety.

'So these stairs,' Jules prompted again, eager to keep her mind focused on her house.

'Yes, right,' Terri nodded causing a wisp of blonde-grey hair to escape from its scrunchy. 'Now, I don't know what you had in mind but I've always thought the old staircase was too narrow for this space. And now that you have the chance to change it, I thought something like this would work well,' she added, pointing to a photograph of a deep rosewood staircase, which started further out at the bottom and swept in a small half circle towards the wall and the second floor.

'I know the last few steps would come out further into the hallway, but you've got a lot of space here and…'

'It's perfect,' Jules interrupted. 'Really perfect.'

'Great. Well, I'll have a word with the company and see if they still make it, and we can get someone in to give you an estimate. But first, I think it's time me and the boys started clearing this mess.'

'Yes,' Jules replied, turning her head to look at the space where her stairs used to be.

Somehow, the destruction of the entire staircase had left little more than a few jagged gaps in the plaster of the wall. A flap of carpet hung from the empty space on the second floor.

She took a step forward, her gaze falling to the flattened area where her body had fallen. Just to the left, three rows of long rusted nails jutted out from a piece of wood. If she'd fallen even a few centimetres in a different direction then she would have suffered a lot more than just bruising.

Something Steven Alton had once said sprung to the forefront of her mind: 'You can't do everything alone, Jules. If you don't let people in one of these days, you are going to land yourself in a mess and nobody will be there to help you out of it.'

As *The Daily*'s story flashed before her, Jules wondered for the first time if he might have had a point.

'Are you okay lovey?' The soft tone of Terri's voice interrupted her disjointed thoughts.

Jules shook her mind clear, turning away from the mess. 'Yes I'm fine, just lost in thought there for a minute.'

'Are you sure? You look terribly pale.'

'Just a bit shocked by it all still, I'm fine though really,' she reassured Terri and herself. 'Now shall we get to work?'

'Well, me and the boys can tackle this by ourselves. You've had quite an upset this morning. Why don't you do something else today, take a drive somewhere maybe?' Terri promoted gently. 'It would be good to get some paint on the walls before the new staircase arrives. You could go to Cheltenham and look at some colours?'

Jules lifted a hand to the bump she'd received the last time she'd thrown herself into work following one of *The Daily*'s stories. 'I think you might be right.'

'Good then. Well, grab the other end of that ladder for me, lovey, and I'll get your things down in no time.'

As Jules climbed into her car she had every intention of heading to Cheltenham, but as she pulled out of the driveway a feeling of dread began to creep through her.

How many of the millions of readers of *The Daily* would she have to meet if she left the hamlet? She wondered.

The irony of the situation did nothing to improve her mood. Just a few days ago she had found the tiny community suffocating, but now the small row of houses tucked between two valleys felt like her only haven.

Until she came to terms with the paper's horrifying attack she needed to stay put.

Applying gentle pressure to the accelerator, Jules eased her car back in the direction of the guesthouse.

Maybe she would visit Rich, she pondered, thinking back to Terri's misinterpretation about Guy and her previous resolve to take things a step further with Rich. That is, if *The Daily*'s destructive reach hadn't stretched to the delicate relationship she seemed to be forming with him.

Then another thought struck her. No matter how fictional the tabloids accounts of her previous relationships, they had been right about one thing: in every place she'd moved to, she'd had one short relationship. She had never been the one to suggest taking things further and the relationship had always died when she'd moved away. Or did she move away to end it?

She thought she liked Rich. He made her laugh and he didn't take life too seriously, but maybe he was just another stop gap she would end up moving away from the moment the house was finished.

All of a sudden, she had no idea how she really felt or what she should do. She needed to think.

Eighteen

What the fuck was he doing? Guy asked himself as the dry edge of his index finger pressed against the doorbell.

Guy listened to the slow movement of footsteps from inside the house, suddenly aware that the plan he had spent hours formulating in the early hours of the morning did not just hinge upon getting Juliet to listen to him, it was the plan. Hardly worthy of an *Ocean's Eleven* plot line.

'Jules, Jules, Jules,' he repeated the name under his breath, recalling the look of venom that had crossed her face on his last visit to Cottinghale.

An elderly woman with a tight grey perm and a floral housecoat opened the front door. 'Hello?'

'Hello, Mrs Beckwith?'

'Yes dear.'

'I'm Guy Rawson, we spoke on the phone.'

'Oh, yes of course, do come in.' Mrs Beckwith shuffled her blue slippered feet back, allowing Guy into the guesthouse.

'Now remind me, Mr Rawson, you've booked for a week, is that right?' the landlady asked as she pushed the door carefully shut.

'Yes please, Mrs Beckwith. Although I may extend it, if that's not a problem?'

'Oh, not at all dear. There's not much call for my rooms until hiking season, and even then I'm empty more often than not. Not that I mind these days though,' she sighed. 'Now, let me give you a quick tour and then I'll leave you to settle in. This is the key for the front door, and one for the room,' she said as her cool wrinkled hand pressed two keys into Guy's palm.

'To your right is the dining room where I serve breakfast, and beyond that is the living room with a television and a few books, that kind of thing.'

Guy followed Mrs Beckwith's short shuffles as she led him through the various rooms; each one appeared more cluttered than the last as his eyes fell upon the dozens of strange brass animals and lace cloths.

'I've got another guest staying at the moment too – Miss Stewart. Although I doubt you'll have a chance to get under each other's feet much as she's out most of the day. I've been making toast and coffee for her around eight each morning, but I can do two servings if you'd prefer a different time?'

Guy felt his mouth dry up. He tried to swallow but couldn't. He hadn't thought about where Jules had been staying until that very moment. He'd seen the derelict house; it was unliveable. And yet it had never crossed his mind that she would be staying in the guesthouse too.

It could be perfect, he reasoned as he processed the information Mrs Beckwith had shared with him. He'd planned to go up to the house the minute he'd dropped off his bag, but this way he could simply wait for her to return. She would be on her own then at least.

But would she listen?

'Mr Rawson?'

'Eight is perfect, Mrs Beckwith, thank you,' he responded with a smile as he followed Mrs Beckwith up the stairs.

'There aren't a lot of places to eat around here, but I fix an evening meal most nights. It's nothing exciting mind you, just casseroles and such. I pop it in the oven in the kitchen to stay warm and that way you can help yourself whenever it suits you. Just leave the dishes in the sink when you're done.'

She stopped on the landing, her hand gripping the top of the banister as she took two long intakes of breath.

'Well, here we are.' Mrs Beckwith opened one of the doors on the landing in front of him to reveal a small bare room, in complete contrast to the clutter covering the rest of the house.

'Err, lovely thanks,' Guy said as he entered the room. He couldn't remember the last time he'd slept in a single bed, he thought, dropping his holdall to the floor.

'Good, good. Now, the bathroom is to your right and if there's anything you need I'll be in my little annex at the back.'

'So,' he began before Mrs Beckwith could leave. 'The other guest, is she is a hiker or something?' he asked, trying to hide the curiosity from his voice.

'Oh no. Miss Stewart is one of us really. She's bought the old house at the top of the lane. You probably past it on your way in. It's been empty for months. Nobody seemed to want it until it caught Miss Stewart's eye. She's just staying here until it's in a fit state to be lived in again.'

Without needing to be prompted further, Mrs Beckwith continued: 'It's so nice to have a fresh face around here, and such a beauty too. Already snapped up by the landlord. They make a lovely couple,' Mrs Beckwith sighed. 'She's had a terrible time of it though.' Her voice dropped to a whisper. 'I'm not one to gossip, you know, but she's been in the newspapers this week. Some nonsense caused by a nasty ex-boyfriend as far as I can figure. The poor thing has been in angst about it all.'

'Oh.'

He turned to the thin framed window, hiding his expression from the elderly landlady as he looked out to the tree lined slope that dwarfed the village, separated from the house by a small garden turned parking space, currently taken by his Jaguar. He was suddenly glad he had tucked it out of sight. If Jules knew he was here, she could just as easily turn around and leave again and he'd be none the wiser.

Although maybe he was too late anyway, he wondered, fighting back a wave of nauseating fear at the thought of Juliet in love with another man.

He'd wasted five pointless years without her. All that time they could have been together if he hadn't fucked it all up.

He had to believe it wasn't too late. She had loved him once with all of her heart. It had taken him until just recently to realise he'd never stopped loving her. Maybe the same could be true for Jules. If only he could make her see it.

'You look very familiar Mr Rawson,' Mrs Beckwith's voice cut into his thoughts.

'Call me Guy.' He spun back towards her.

'Have you stayed here before?' The grey of her eyes, magnified by the thick lenses of her glasses, scanned his face.

'No I haven't, Mrs Beckwith, just one of those faces I guess,' he responded, lifting his shoulders into a shrug.

'Or my eyesight, more likely. It's not what it used to be I'm afraid.' She sighed again. 'Well I'll leave you to it, Mr Rawson.'

'Thank you.'

'You're welcome dear, and remember I'm just downstairs if you need anything.'

Guy stepped back towards the door, closing it behind the guesthouse owner as she left.

Unlike so many of the vain and egocentric models he'd worked with in the past, it had never bothered Guy when people failed to recognise him. In fact, he preferred it that way. He had never once tried to jog someone's memory or list the campaigns he'd worked on. And the last thing he needed right now was a reporter snooping around, dragging Jules further into the mess he'd created and further away from him.

Once he'd heard the slow steps of Mrs Beckwith move below him, Guy crossed back to the window. The crisp February air crept through the single pane of glass, reaching out to him like a cold breath on his skin.

Cottinghale seemed like the perfect place for the old Juliet. A small community with people who cared about each other and always had a friendly word to say to anyone passing by. The old Juliet with her big smile and open nature would have slotted in perfectly. But the new one? He wasn't so sure.

Although maybe this was just another stop on the road, Guy wondered, thinking of *The Daily*'s story. It wasn't the old boyfriends that bothered him, well not much anyway, but the thought of the laughing happy girl he'd once known moving from place to place in a solitary existence that filled him with an unsettling sadness.

At least with the bitter taste *The Daily*'s story had left in the back of this throat, he knew with total clarity that his feelings for Jules were more than just a passing whim.

It had become more than a search for whatever was missing in his life. He had made a terrible mistake a long time ago and now he had to fix it. No matter how long it took or however many rejections she threw at him. No amount of torment could come close to the thought of his future without her.

Nervousness hit like an explosion of sherbet dip fizzing inside him. The thought of what he had to do caused his heart to throb against his rib cage as it doubled in speed. But the thought of what he risked losing again dropped it to his stomach in a sickening flood of fear.

Guy brought back the memory of her face in those first few seconds and clung to the belief that somewhere inside, a part of her still felt the same as she had done years ago.

Unzipping his holdall, he rummaged through the clean clothes he'd packed first thing that morning until his hands touched upon his small black wash-kit. He had no idea how much time he had to kill but he might as well unpack and have a shave, he decided, opening the door to his room and crossing the hallway.

His hand tightened around the cool brass doorknob, twisting it in his hand. Just as he heard the click of the spring he recalled Mrs Beckwith's directions. He had gone straight-ahead instead of right, but it was too late to correct his mistake. The door released under the pressure from his hand and swung open to reveal a room identical to his own, but Guy's gaze could focus on just one thing – Juliet.

She stood in the middle of the room, wearing nothing but a black underwear set. The sight of her body pushed his head into a turbulent spin; the speech he'd practised late into the night disappeared as if someone had pressed the delete button.

Guy watched her, open-mouthed, his eyes unable to move from the large blue bruise that travelled in misshapen blotches out from her underwear and down the curve of her bottom.

'Ahh,' she cried out, her eyes widened at the sight of him as she grappled to cover herself with a flimsy jumper.

'Sorry.' Guy blurted out as he fought to gain control, forcing his gaze away from her legs and up to her face; the green wells of her eyes as distracting as her half-naked body. 'I thought this was the bathroom,' he continued holding up his wash-kit as if it could vouch for his error.

Without waiting for a response, Guy reached his hand back to the door handle, pulling it towards him before she could hear the noise of his heartbeat, amplified to the same volume as the stage speakers he used.

Shit. What had he just done? Walking in on Jules in her underwear was not part of the plan.

He stepped quickly away from the door, relieved to find the bathroom exactly where it should have been at the end of the small landing.

Nineteen

Jules didn't dare move as she listened to the sound of her heart raging through her body.

She wished she could believe the man in the doorway had been a sick mind trick brought on by the shock of seeing parts of her life displayed so callously across two pages of a national tabloid. But the noise of running water coming from the bathroom made the past few seconds impossible to ignore.

Jules pressed a hand against her chest, willing herself to calm down. She had been moments away from being completely naked when the door had opened. It could have been a lot worse, she tried to reassure herself.

In the instant before she had turned towards the doorway she had known it was him. The light had been there again, the feeling of a weight lifting from her body as if she'd taken off a heavy backpack after a long journey. She pushed the thought away before it could settle.

Pulling on her discarded clothes, she stepped barefoot into the hallway, half expecting it to be empty after all. But there he was, standing in the open bathroom. A blue and white toothbrush in his hand. He placed the toothbrush next to hers in the aubergine china holder, like it was the most natural thing to do in the world.

He had remembered to pack it, she realised suddenly as anger and pain swept over her so quickly it brought with it a wave of dizziness. In his rush to pack up his things and run away to London, he'd remembered to pack his toothbrush.

Nausea burned in the back of her throat.

For the first time in all the years since, Jules wondered how long he had planned it. She had always assumed their argument had driven him away, but maybe he had planned to leave her like that all along.

It didn't matter now, she didn't care anymore. She swallowed back the taste of bile rising up from her stomach.

'Sorry about that Jules,' Guy said, his tone impossibly light as he stared at her.

He had called her Jules, not Juliet, but Jules. For a reason she couldn't understand it maddened her more than when he'd called her by her full name.

'What are you doing here?' She forced herself to look at him. His eyes bore into her. She wanted to run away; she wanted to cry; she wanted to hit him as hard as she could, all at the same time.

She clamped her teeth together, willing her body to stop bombarding her with emotions.

'Would you believe me if I told you I fancied a mini-break?' His face lifted into a familiar side grin.

'No, I wouldn't.'

How dare he joke? After the trouble he had caused he still had the gall to joke, she thought. A red heat crept up her neck and onto her face as she struggled to keep calm.

'Alright then, I came here because I wanted to see you.' Guy held his hands up in surrender.

'Perhaps I didn't make myself clear the last time,' Jules began, fighting to keep her voice even. 'I am not going to get involved with you or your publicity stunts, so leave me alone.'

'I'm not asking you to.'

His gaze continued to drive into her, the force feeling like a shove as the back of her heels teetered on the edge of the landing.

'You're not asking me? Since when did you care about asking me? Unless I am mistaken, nobody asked me two weeks ago if I wanted my picture splashed on the front page of that trash like some kind of... of...' Jules struggled to find the right word. Instead she continued, 'AND nobody asked me if I would mind having my life played out in that crap.'

'I know,' he mumbled 'I'm so sorry. I should never have mentioned you, but I really hope you believe me when I say I had nothing to do with the rest of it.'

'Really? And what have you done that would make me think for one second that you are anything more than a selfish pig? And what about me? How many people are going to believe the lies printed about me? It's all well and good for you; I'm the one who's been painted as a monster. Estranged from my parents,' she began lifting her thumb up to count one, but she couldn't remember the rest of the lies. For some reason the comment about her parents seemed to be the only one really bothering her.

Guy opened his mouth, but closed it again quickly.

'What?' she demanded.

'Look, I know it's all complete rubbish, but when I saw Bernie and Nora they mentioned that they hadn't seen you since Christmas. I was surprised, that's all.'

'I love my parents. Just because I don't…' Jules stopped. What was she doing? 'Hang on, I don't need to explain myself to you, so you can stop with the guilt trip, okay?'

Jules closed her eyes, blocking Guy from view, but his image and his words still stuck in her head.

'You're right, I'm sorry. I came here to explain, to make sure you're okay, I know the effect these stories can have and I'm truly, truly sorry.'

She paused for a moment, processing his words, before she said, 'Fine.'

'Fine as in?' Guy questioned, another smile touching his lips.

'Fine, as in thank you for the apology, as you can see I am okay, so if you don't mind I am going for a run, please don't be here when I get back.'

'Great. It's been a long journey and I could do with stretching my legs.'

'No. No way are you coming with me. And since when do you run anyway?'

'Since when do you?' he shot back, his voice remaining infuriatingly smooth. 'Is that a yes then?'

'No it's not.' Jules stormed back to her bedroom, slapping her hand hard against the door. The sting hitting her at the same time as the door crashed shut.

She couldn't get her head around his sudden presence and the reason for his return. He seemed so at ease, like none of the pain he'd caused her mattered.

Bastard.

She could get in her car and go. Drive somewhere far away until Guy got the message and left. The thought of being recognised by *The Daily* readers didn't matter in comparison to spending another minute with him. But why should she? Guy was the one that should be leaving, not her. She had no intention of being run out of her home.

Five minutes later, Jules tightened the laces of her trainers and stepped out of the guesthouse, ignoring the painful bruises on her back and stretching her hands to her toes.

For the first time since Guy had invaded her life, she did not feel the punch of shock from seeing him as he stood by the door waiting for her.

Twenty

'What do you think you are doing? And what on earth are you wearing?' Jules demanded.

'What's wrong with what I'm wearing?' Guy bent his head down, eyeing the mud streaked black shorts and dirty red t-shirt he'd unearthed from an abandoned football kit lurking in the boot of his car.

The t-shirt stretched against his chest, rising up to show an inch of stomach between the painfully tight waistband of his shorts. The last time he'd worn it he had still been modelling, when a beer after work had a penalty worse than death. It seemed the months of Chinese takeaways and bottled beers had taken its toll on his waistline.

'Don't think for a second that I'm going to let you run with me. Go back to London, Guy.'

Her green eyes flashed in the sun light, unlocking a million memories from deep inside the recesses of his mind. It filled him with a longing more desperate than he could have imagined possible.

He had to tell her. Just not now. He'd have to wait until he knew she would listen, and based on her particular outfit, she would most definitely be considered a flight risk.

'So where are we going?' he asked instead.

'I am going up that hill,' she replied, pointing to the woodland sloping up behind the guesthouse. 'You are going back to wherever it is you came from to buy a washing machine and leave me alone.'

Guy ignored the latter half of her statement. 'Great, let's go.'

Jules stretched her athletic frame to the floor and touched her toes. He thought he saw her flinch, but her face remained impassive.

'Seriously, you are not coming with me.'

'Okay then,' Guy conceded.

A look of surprise crossed her face. 'Good then.'

Without saying goodbye, she took a few steps past him, her body springing into action as she strode from the driveway and out of Guy's sights.

'Shit,' he said aloud, sprinting after her.

He made it to the roadside just in time to catch a flash of Jules's body already disappearing up a thin mud footpath to the right of the guesthouse.

Guy could feel the Danish swirl he'd eaten for breakfast lurch to the top of his stomach as he began his chase. How long could she continue at this speed? he wondered as his breath started to shorten under the strain of his sudden burst of exercise.

He had never considered himself unfit before, but Jules appeared to be in a different league, he realised as she accelerated up the steep slope.

Ignoring the sweet smell of fresh earth hitting his nostrils and the tranquil quiet of the woodland, Guy ploughed forward, forcing his legs to keep moving.

'What do you think you're doing?' Her voice startled him from his battle with the hill. The painful cramp snaking across his abdomen like a slashing knife relinquished its fury as he drew to a stop, slumping against the tree next to where Jules stood; her arms crossed and her eyes narrowed on him. She hadn't even broken a sweat.

'Running. Or dying maybe, it's hard to tell at this point,' he gasped between long pants for oxygen.

'I thought you agreed to leave me alone.'

'No,' he replied, drawing in another long gulp of air, 'I agreed that I wouldn't run with you.'

'So what are you doing?'

'What?' he asked in mock innocence. 'I'm running on my own. I just happen to be taking the same route as you.'

'Argh, you are so infuriating.'

'I know,' he said, his reply unheard as Jules sprinted off again.

Surely the valley had to end at some point, he pleaded, pushing off from the tree and feeling a pain grip his thighs as he started striding again.

Guy had no idea how much time had passed. He kept going; head down against the almost vertical hill, his trainers crunching against the burnt orange of the fallen leaves. The chase for Jules was momentarily forgotten as he battled against the cries of resistance from his body.

Suddenly the crowded trees dispersed, allowing sunlight to break in streams around him. He had made it. Guy took a long breath of relief, easing to a stop as he reached a large grassy clearing.

Jules stood a few metres away from him, her body twisted in a bizarre pose as if she was walking a tight rope.

His aching limbs forgotten, he strode towards her.

'GUY, WAIT,' Jules cried out. 'Don't come any closer. The ground is about to give—' she cut off as he reached her and realised too late what she was trying to say.

The long grass of the hilltop had hidden the uneven ground, now crumbling underneath their feet.

Jules went first, her body slipping into the ground. He grabbed her wrist, trying to stop her falling, but there was nothing he could do to stop the ground disintegrating beneath them as they tumbled downwards into the darkness, their bodies tangling as they landed with a heavy thud.

Twenty-one

'Ouch. Now look what you've done,' Jules cried out as she pulled her legs out from under his.

'Hey, I tried to save you.'

'Save me? If you hadn't insisted on following me up here I wouldn't be in this mess. Or better still, if you hadn't used me to sell papers, or come to Cottinghale I—'

'Okay, okay, I get it,' Guy cut in as he scrambled to his feet. 'For the hundredth time, I'm sorry. But blaming me isn't going to help get us out of here. Now, are you hurt?'

She said nothing.

'Jules, please just tell me if you're okay?'

'Well let's see shall we – in the past week I've had lies about me printed in a national newspaper; I arrived at my new property to find my ceiling had collapsed; my back door smashed into smithereens; my stairs fell down whilst I was standing on them, and now I'm stuck in a bloody great big hole with you. So no, I am definitely not okay.'

To Jules's surprise, Guy scrunched his eyes shut and turned away from her, his body shaking.

'Please tell me you are not laughing?' she pushed herself up from the floor, her muscles crying out with pain after the fierce run she'd forced herself to do.

'You do realise that we are stuck in the middle of nowhere with no way out?'

A peal of deep laughter echoed around the darkened space. 'Yes,' he gasped between breaths.

'That's just great.' Jules stepped away, her gaze scouring the darkness for an escape route or something to hit him with. Either would do at that particular moment.

She could see the four square walls of what looked like an old cellar, but no way out. Above them, pockets of sunlight streamed through from across the length of the hole. If she jumped high enough, she might just be able to touch the earthy ceiling, but there was nothing to grip hold of or anything that could be used to climb up.

'Oh come on, it's kind of funny,' Guy said, his laughter abating.

She stared at him, fighting a smile that was threatening to break out. She couldn't give him the satisfaction of laughing with him, however contagious his humour felt.

He stopped laughing and gave an apologetic shrug.

'Come on, give me a bunk,' she said, stepping under the gap of light where they'd fallen.

'What? You can't be serious; you'll never be able to pull yourself up.'

'Yes I will, now come on,' she commanded, with more confidence than she felt.

Guy did not move. He had stopped laughing, but the crooked smile that she remembered so well still touched his lips.

'What?' she asked.

'Was this your plan all along?'

'What plan?'

'Trapping me down here and then escaping. Leaving me to die a slow and painful death?'

'Don't be ridiculous. I'll get help,' Jules replied. Just maybe after a few hours, she added to herself.

'I saw that look. I'm not helping you if you're just going to leave me. Why don't you give me a bunk?'

'Guy,' she sighed. 'I promise I'll get help, now come on.'

Despite the circumstances, Jules felt herself relax in Guy's presence.

'Fine.' He took a step towards her, their bodies close.

If she leant forward just a few inches her lips would graze against the stubble line of his neck. Jules leapt back. Where had that thought sprung from? This was someone she hated with every fibre of her being.

She had to get out.

'Ready?' he asked.

Her eyes met his. With the sunlight shining in from above them she could see the flecks of green in his otherwise dark pupils. They had always been that way. From a distance they appeared almost black, but up close they had speckles of a bright green which seemed to dance when he smiled. She had forgotten how mesmerising those flecks could be.

The heat from his body radiated towards her.

The effect was intoxicating.

For one second, before she could gain control of her thoughts, she wished she was in his arms. But no matter how much her body seemed to react to him, she couldn't do it to herself.

She had to get out.

'Yes, come on then,' she finally croaked.

'Juliet,' Guy said in a deep whisper.

'Don't, Guy. Whatever it is, don't,' she pleaded. She couldn't take any more.

He nodded as if he understood before crouching down and cupping his hands out towards her.

Lifting her left leg up, she rested her trainer on the step he had made, preparing herself to push upwards. She had to get out, she repeated over and over in her head.

'Rest your hands on my shoulders.'

Reluctantly, Jules placed her hands either side of his head, desperately trying to block the sound of the sea rushing in her ears as her heart pounded in response to their touch.

With her right leg she pushed against the ground, leaping up at the same time as Guy lifted with his arms, pushing her towards the opening.

As her head broke into the cool sunshine, Jules threw her arms out over the ledge, pulling with her shoulders to lift herself up and away from Guy's strong hold.

For one moment, as she blinked in the bright daylight, her arms clawing the ground for support, she thought she would make it.

And then she froze.

'You okay?' Guy called out from below.

'Yes,' she lied as she fought to summon more strength from somewhere inside.

Nothing happened.

Her legs tangled heavily back into the darkness.

She scanned the landscape hoping for a bush or anything she could grab hold of, but the only thing in reach was the slippery wet grass surrounding her.

'Sure?'

'I'm stuck,' she admitted through gritted teeth. 'I can't pull myself up,' she said as the weight of her legs began to pull her back into the hole.

'Okay, don't worry, just gently slide back down and I'll grab you.'

'No I ca—' Before Jules could finish her sentence the earth supporting her arms gave way and she found herself in free fall for the third time in as many days.

Jules could do nothing to stop herself colliding with Guy's body as they fell to the ground again.

Twenty-two

The shock of her touch hurtled through him as if he'd connected with a 240-volt current. The dizzying warmth of her body felt like a sickening fairground ride, spinning around and around, blurring his vision and leaving his stomachs in knots.

How had he forgotten that feeling?

It took him a moment to realise he hadn't. He had locked it away somewhere out of reach the day he'd left. It was the only way he'd been able to keep walking.

Only then did he realise that it was that feeling that had been seeping out of its hiding place, making its way into his songs and guiding him back to her.

In that moment, as their bodies collided, it flooded back to him, ingraining itself within his every being. Like an almost forgotten dream, floating on the outskirts of memory until something jogs it into consciousness.

At that exact moment, he knew with sickening clarity that he had made the biggest mistake of his life five years ago. The thought left one question burning into him: was he too late?

'Oh ouch, that hurt,' Jules spluttered.

'Shit. Are you okay?'

Jules did not respond, but Guy could feel her body shuddering from their tangled position on the ground.

'Hey Jules, it's okay, look we're fine,' he tried to reassure her.

'I'm not crying, oh God I can't breathe… fallen three times in three days,' she laughed.

The sound filled him with an intoxicating mixture of desire and hope.

Then her laughter stopped. As quickly as their bodies had fallen to the floor, Jules jumped up, turning her back to him and brushing away the clumps of damp earth clinging to her clothes.

The loss of her touch caused an emptiness to engulf him.

'Why haven't you asked me whether I meant it?' he blurted out, scrambling to his feet.

'Meant what?' She kept her back to him.

'What I said in the interview.'

Jules stopped moving as an unbearable silence grew between them. Finally she replied: 'What difference does it make?'

'Because I...' emotion overwhelmed him. 'I made the biggest mistake of my life leaving you and I have to know if there's a chance we could start again.'

She stood like a statue, as if his words had frozen her. Then she whispered: 'I can't, it's too late.'

'Why?' Guy reached a hand out to her bare arm, twisting her body towards him, her expression still hidden as Jules kept her face tilted downwards.

'I've moved on. I don't feel that way anymore,' she replied, her tone suddenly defiant.

'You don't mean that.' Guy lifted his hand to her cheek, running a finger across the smooth skin and gently moving her face up to his.

As their eyes connected in the dimness, Guy saw for the first time the deep wells of sadness behind her stubborn expression. The emotion jumped between them as he realised the depth of the hurt he'd caused her.

'I do, Guy. I mean it. I can't do it,' she mumbled.

'You can. I know you can. I know we still have something. I feel it every time I'm near you.'

'No,' she protested, her voice barely a whisper.

With shaking arms he pulled her towards him, wrapping them around her slender frame.

Eyes that swim like an emerald sea
What is it you're doing to me?

Guy's body spun into overdrive. His heartbeat raged through his body, his breath quickened as desire strained through him.

He drew her closer still, desperate to hold her tight. She did not resist his movements but her body remained stiff.

Dizziness flooded through him as he moved his lips to hers, unable to breathe through the longing that had overtaken him. But just as he moved to kiss her, she pulled away.

'What was that?' Jules asked, stumbling back to the entrance of the hole and out of his reach.

'What?' He felt his whole being ache with disappointment and confusion. He had been millimetres away from kissing her.

The mix of desperation and desire seemed to fuel him with energy and exhaust him all within the same breath.

'That.'

'I don't hear anything. Jules?'

'MAX,' she yelled, pausing to hear a response. 'MAAAXXX.'

Then he heard it. A dog barking in the distance. Someone had found them; they would be rescued. Fuck. He had been so close.

Seconds later, a brown nose and a dripping pink tongue came into view from the ledge above, followed by a burst of piercing barks.

'Oh Max, thank goodness. Where's Rich? Go get Rich,' she commanded, waving an arm up in the air.

Max continued to stare down towards them, laying his body onto the ground and ignoring her instruction.

'RICH,' Jules's voice yelled out again.

The man's name echoed through the hole and sliced into Guy's chest.

He'd almost got through to her, almost kissed her. But as he looked to where she stood, he could see the wall between them had returned. He'd lost her again.

'Jules?'

She turned her head towards him, her skin glowing in the sunlight.

'I love you. I always have and I always will,' he cried out as desperation engulfed him.

The whites of Jules's eyes widened as her gaze bore into his. He could see her mind processing his words. He did not dare breathe as he waited for a response.

'Hello?' a man's voice called into the hole, cutting through the emotions Guy had laid out.

'Oh Rich, thank goodness you're here.'

'Jules, what the hell are you doing down there?'

'We fell.'

'We?'

'Err, yes, Guy's here,' she faltered. 'He followed me up here.'

For a moment nobody spoke, then Rich called back into the hole: 'Right, hang on.'

Muffled voices travelled down from above, followed by a woman's shriek.

'Right.' The man laid his body on the ground above them, a scruffy blonde head peering over the edge before two muscular arms dropped into the hole. 'Jules. You first. I'm going to try to pull you up, but if the ground starts to shift then we'll have to go and get some rope and a few more bodies up here.'

Guy moved into the light.

'Here, I'll give you a bunk.' He turned to face Jules again, avoiding her gaze as he bent forward into the same position as before.

Once more, Jules placed a foot onto the step of his hands, hesitating for a moment before balancing on his shoulders and jumping up.

This time Jules did not stop. Rich's hands wrapped around her wrists hoisting her out from his reach.

In the few minutes that followed, Guy heard the muffled exchanges of Rich, Jules and another woman. Would they leave him there? He wondered, casting his gaze around the gloom.

'Hello?' he eventually called out.

'Sorry, Guy.' The blonde head popped back over the ledge, the nose of a dog reappearing as Rich knelt down next to the hole. 'Do you think you'll be able to grab my hands?'

'I think so,' Guy replied, trying and failing to rise above the humiliation of being rescued by another man.

Forcing the muscles in his legs back to work Guy jumped up, his hands connecting with Rich's as he felt the strength of his rescuer pull him from the hole.

Twenty-three

Guy fell to the damp ground, his eyes scrunching in the sunlight.

Before he had a chance to breathe in the fresh air, two dogs pounced onto him. One he recognised from the ledge as Max; the other a rotund yellow retriever who had already covered Guy in hair. Their pink wet tongues like a mouldy jay cloth being flapped in his face.

'Hello dogs,' he said, sitting up and patting the excited animals.

'Oh my God, I am so sorry.' A blonde woman with a mass of curly hair leapt forward, shooing the dogs away from him.

'Hey, no problem,' he replied, clambering to his feet and surveying the landscape.

The sun still seemed high in the sky, as if time had stood still during their adventure. He guessed they hadn't been stuck for as long as he'd thought. Most definitely not long enough.

'I'm Sally,' the woman said.

'Guy.' He smiled back.

'Oh I know who you are. I'm a huge fan. I've had pictures of you up in my gardening shed for years. And I love the music too,' she replied, her voice high and squeaky.

'Thanks,' he responded, barely listening as he watched Rich tower over Jules, his head close to hers.

'I know. How sad am I to slobber all over you like Nelson here.' She threw a hand out towards the golden retriever panting on the grass beside them. 'But I am without a doubt your biggest fan.

'If it wasn't for Bill and the kids I'd be stripping naked right now. I seriously think I might be a little bit in love with you,' Sally finished, her pretty face crimson despite the grin.

'Well Sally, Bill's a lucky man,' Guy replied with a smile. 'And lucky for us you were up here when you were, otherwise who knows how long we'd have been down there.'

'We would have found you eventually. This whole area is filled with nooks and crannies for visitors to get lost in, so we generally keep an eye out for people who go missing; especially celebrities. This looks like it used to be the cellar of one of the out houses. This entire place is filled with the remains of the old Cottinghale estate. And lucky for you, you didn't break anything,' she added, eyeing his legs in a way that made him feel naked.

'Anyway, it's Rich you've got to thank really. If I'd have been up here alone I probably would have jumped in with you.' Sally let out a nervous laugh.

'Of course, Rich.' Guy swallowed the pressure building in his chest and turned to face his rescuer. The embarrassment of being rescued was one thing, but it was clear from Rich's posture that he and Jules knew each other well.

'Thanks for the rescue, mate.' He held out his hand as Rich twisted around.

'Don't mention it,' Rich replied with a firm shake.

'If there's anything I can do by way of thanks?'

'No need, I'm glad I could help.'

'Hang on a minute, Rich,' Sally jumped in. 'Why doesn't Guy do a few songs in the pub for us? Draw in a bit of a crowd for you.'

'Err…' Rich looked between Jules, Sally and Guy. 'I'm sure Guy is far too busy to bother with our little local.'

He was the landlord, Guy realised, eyeing the large frame of the man with a renewed wave of jealousy as he recalled Mrs Beckwith's comment.

He swallowed hard before responding: 'I'd be happy to. How about tonight?' he responded, casting a glance towards Jules. He had to show her he wasn't the selfish publicity grabbing celebrity she thought he was.

'Okay then. Thanks, I guess.' Rich nodded. 'And talking of pubs, I'd better get back.'

They made a strange foursome as they walked back through the sloping woodland. The two dogs galloping ahead, then Rich with his long stride, closely followed by Jules, leaving Guy with Sally's lightning speed conversation as she rattled off details of her life on the farm; with the occasional squeal of delight as she declared her love for him over and over.

Despite Guy's best efforts to engage Jules in conversation, she ignored him, refusing to look up from the ground, let alone speak to him.

Whatever had passed between them in the solitude of the darkness had disappeared. He just hoped he would be able to recapture it soon; the feel of her body close to his had left a hollow emptiness inside him.

Forty minutes later, he laid his aching muscles onto the hard mattress of his single bed and let the weight of his eyelids close.

Somewhere along the way, Jules and Rich had sped ahead, and by the time he'd stepped out from the woodland and said goodbye to Sally they were nowhere to be seen. Jules's car had gone from its spot on the road and the guesthouse was empty.

Guy grabbed his mobile. The screen displayed seven missed calls and one text; none from Jules, he noted with disappointment but not surprise.

All of the calls came from Sonja. He didn't have to listen to his voicemail to know they would be of varying degrees of irate as she tried to reach him. He would call her later, but right then he simply didn't care.

He opened the text message instead and read the message from Debbie: Hey little bro, I have been told to rest and sent to bed – BORED! Where R U? I want gossip! Sam says hi XX

He fired a quick response: Hi Debs, hope u r feelin better. I'm in the sticks & just told Juliet I love her. Good enough 4 U? Give the little man hug from me ☺ x

Guy switched his phone off. The last thing he needed right now was to speak to Sonja. He didn't care if he was missing out on playing at a sell-out crowd at Wembley or if he had to work the rest of his life in a chip shop, just as long as he had Jules with him.

He was a massive fool for ever believing he could be happy any other way.

She had stood in his arms and studied his eyes in the same way she'd done all those years ago.

He had to stay. Forever if that's what it took.

Twenty-four

The needle flittered between the eleven and twelve position on the speed dial as the car sped through the twisting single lanes of the countryside.

Jules threw the gear stick into fifth, refusing to release her foot from the accelerator for even a second as she flew into one sharp corner after another. If a vehicle appeared from the other direction she knew she would have no time to stop and no space to swerve. The gamble felt good.

The pounding from behind her temples had yet to subside; the throbbing pain intensified as her mind tried to make sense of the emotional turmoil she'd experienced in just a few short hours. So instead she drove, feeling the tension ease with each mile she covered.

An hour later the ticking of the indicator jolted her from autopilot. She had no recollection of the road she'd covered or the manoeuvres she'd made, but she must have kept her foot firmly on the accelerator because the road sign read only thirty miles to Bath.

Jules noticed the goose bumps on her arms before she realised she'd been cold. She'd left the guesthouse in such a hurry that she hadn't changed out of her running kit, dumping her clothes on the passenger seat and almost knocking down Rich and Max with her car in her haste to escape Guy.

All of a sudden it felt as if her childhood home was beckoning her. As if nowhere else on earth could make her feel safe and warm but the familiar furnishings she'd grown up around.

She had no idea if her parents would be in, but the spare key would be under the third flower pot to the right of the front door, just as it had been her whole life.

The newspaper's accusation about her relationship with her parents had upset Jules more than the tabloid's claims about her past flings. She didn't care about the old relationships, but she did care about her parents. She needed to see them, Jules decided, realising for the first time that she might not be the only person affected by *The Daily*'s attack.

As Jules continued her journey, the early afternoon sunshine illuminated the landscape opening up in front of her. She could see the iconic Georgian town houses, stacked one on top of the other as the city spread itself up the hillside. In its centre, the four turrets of the Abbey's tower loomed above everything else, as if it was watching over its residents.

Despite the familiarity of the city she'd grown up in, Jules couldn't stop her mind returning to Guy. The tension and nausea returned with it. From the quiet interior of the car, the electricity pulling her towards him now seemed even more powerful, as if she'd been caught in an unstoppable force.

Out of nowhere a bright light flashed in front of her eyes.

'Damn,' she cursed to herself. As if she didn't hate Guy enough, she could now blame him for a speeding ticket on top of everything else.

Jules eased her foot from the accelerator and slowed the car to a crawl. No matter how fast she drove, she could not escape the truth: in those out of control moments in the cold abandoned cellar, as her body had found its way into Guy's arms, she had wanted him so badly that it had hurt.

Seeing Guy had unlocked a part of her that she'd buried long ago. The dreamer unable to speak up for herself, the weak girl who had let Guy crush her so easily. It was that part of her that had reacted to Guy, not the real her.

Jules focused her thoughts away from the feelings she'd experienced in the darkness. The past few weeks had dented her confidence but she was still strong. She would not let Guy trick her into being part of his music launch.

He'd lied and deceived her before, and he was doing it again now.

She would wait at the guesthouse for him to finish playing his set at The Nag and then she would make it crystal clear to him that he had to leave. She would find a way to make him listen, she told herself, ignoring the heavy weight tugging on her shoulders and the words he'd spoken still circling in her head.

'Hello, Mum? Dad?' Jules called out as she let herself into her parent's 1950's semi-detached house on the outskirts of the city.

'Juliet?' her father replied, sticking his head out of the kitchen. 'Is that you, love? What the blooming heck are you doing here?'

'Just thought I'd pop in,' she replied as her father pulled her into a tight bear hug.

'What a nice surprise and just in the nick of time. Your mother has been in one of her flaps this morning.' Bernie dropped his voice to a whisper. 'You know what she's like,' he grinned.

Jules smiled as her father continued their embrace. The comfortable familiarity of her childhood home relieved her remaining tension in an instant, just as she'd thought it would.

In that moment she could not remember why she'd stayed away so long. Her parents bordered on eccentric most of the time but she loved them dearly.

Despite outward appearances, her father, with his thinning grey hair, broad shoulders and round stomach, was a scatter brain. He might have been the sensible half of her parents' marriage, but Jules had lost count of the number of times she'd seen him get so engrossed in conversation at their shop that he'd given the wrong change to a customer. It was Nora's meticulous management of the shop accounts that had kept their business in the centre of Bath ticking over for so many years.

'Juliet,' her mother screeched from the kitchen doorway. 'Thank heavens. We've been worried sick about you.'

'Hi mum,' Jules smiled, swapping the large arms of her father for the petite frame of her mother.

'You poor, poor girl. How are you holding up?'

'Me? I'm fine, why?'

'The newspaper of course. I was utterly horrified when I saw it.'

'Oh, that.' With the arrival of Guy and the events of the morning, her earlier humiliation had been pushed aside, returning in a split second as her cheeks flushed a bright red.

'The phone has been ringing off the hook,' Nora began, giving Jules one more squeeze before releasing her and walking back into the kitchen. 'Pop the kettle on Bern.

'We had to nip out and buy a copy first thing and just couldn't believe what we were reading, could we Bern? Your father made me unplug the phone in the end. Everyone we know is calling.

'Would you like a hot cross bun? Or I could heat up some soup? Leek and potato, just like the time you had chicken pox.'

'Thanks mum, but I'm fine really. Just a cup of coffee would be great,' Jules replied, taking a seat at the same table she'd sat at her entire life.

'Nora, leave the girl alone for a minute will you, she's only just walked through the door,' Bernie said from the sink. 'Now, how is everything with your new house?'

Her mother let out a cry. 'How can you even ask such a question when we haven't even told her?'

'Told me what?' Jules looked between the faces of her parents.

'Oh Juliet, it's all my fault,' Nora wailed as she slipped into the seat opposite Jules.

'What is, mum?'

'This story. We feel like complete fools. Do you remember I told you about that girl who stopped by the shop last week?'

Jules nodded. She knew what was coming.

'Well, the minute I saw the name at the end of the article, I knew it was her. Bloody Sara – that was her name. I'm so sorry, Juliet. She was paying me all these compliments about the shop and taking such an interest in you. Before I knew it, she was asking me all these strange questions about how often we saw you. Of course, it was only this morning that I realised that she'd been putting words in my mouth.'

Jules reached out and squeezed her mother's hand. 'Don't worry mum. They would have printed the story either way. I'm just sorry they've got you involved too,' she replied. Seeing her parents' concern for her seemed to have relieved some of the unease she felt towards *The Daily's* allegations.

Bernie placed three mugs and a chunk of fruit cake in front of them. 'Here you are love.'

'So you don't blame us then?' Nora asked, her voice timid as she patted Jules's hand.

'Don't be daft. Of course I don't. The only person to blame in all of this is Guy.'

Nora shook her head and opened her mouth to speak before Jules cut in: 'I'm sorry, mum, I know you both like him and you were upset when we broke up, but he was the one who got *The Daily* interested in me, and it was all to boost the sales of his album.'

'Juliet,' Bernie began. 'Your mother and I were only upset when you and Guy broke up because we hated seeing you so unhappy. Yes we liked Guy, but only because of how happy he made you. You're our daughter; you're the one that matters to us. If you tell us to hate him, we will hate him.'

'But mum just shook her head when I said it was Guy's fault?' Jules quizzed.

'Yes, because maybe you're right and this whole nonsense with the paper has been down to Guy trying to help himself, and if that's the case then he's off our Christmas card list. But these bloody journalists are like vampires. One minute you're having a perfectly friendly chat with them about the weather or what not, and the next minute you find yourself admitting things about yourself you didn't even know were true.

'They suck it out of you is all I'm saying. If Guy said it was an accident, then I can see how it happened. And what with us liking Guy, well, I'm with your father on that one.'

'Oh,' Jules replied. She took a long sip of coffee as her mind made sense of what her parents had told her. 'I thought I'd let you down.'

'When?' Her parents exclaimed together.

'When Guy left. I thought you were disappointed in me for not being able to make it work.'

'I've never heard such rubbish in all my life,' her father exclaimed. 'We could never be disappointed with anything you do. You and Guy were so young. Just because your mother and I met when we were kids, it didn't mean we expected you to do the same. If anything, we were pleased that Guy leaving meant that you could find your own feet a bit more. And look how much you've achieved. We are so proud of you,' her father finished, his voice deep with emotion.

'Thanks Dad.' Jules felt the lump in her throat again. She'd been so wrong for so long about her parents' feelings, and now all she wanted to do was make up for all the times she'd pretended to be too busy to see them.

'Would you come and see my house?' she asked suddenly.

Her parents exchanged smiles. 'We'd love to,' they replied.

'How does Saturday sound? I haven't actually got a staircase or a back door at the moment, but it would still be nice to see what you think.'

Nora rose from the table and stepped to Jules's chair, bending down to give her a hug before replying. 'Saturday it is. Now, how about some soup?'

'Would you mind if I just grabbed a quick shower first? I kind of left in a bit of a hurry.'

'I did wonder about the mud on your face,' Bernie smiled. 'Off you go, then. Gives me a chance to nip out and get some fresh bread.'

'Thanks Dad, and thanks mum. It's nice to be home.'

By the afternoon, Jules felt like a balance had been restored inside of her.

She'd hidden herself away from her parents and from anyone else that had tried to get close to her for so long that she'd forgotten how nice it is to be with people that love her and to love them back. In shutting herself away from her feelings for Guy, she'd somehow cut off her ability to become close to anyone else.

Remaining five miles under the speed limit, Jules drove back to Cottinghale, still determined to get Guy out of her life once and for all, but there was someone else she wanted to see too.

Rich had been so sweet when he'd pulled her from the cellar. He hadn't acted surprised to see Guy, or asked her what they'd been doing. All he'd wanted to do was check she was okay.

With everything that had happened to her over the past few weeks, she felt like a different person. If it was time to move on and start a new relationship, a proper one this time, then Rich was the perfect person to try it with, she decided, putting the sudden bout of nausea down to nerves.

Twenty-five

What was she doing? Jules had no answer to her own question as she crouched low to the ground, leaning against the cold stone wall. The light from the pub above her cast an orangey glow out into the night.

Guy and his bloody note, Jules thought, wishing she hadn't left the guesthouse in the first place, but unable to move from her position under the side window.

It had been written on a small piece of lined paper ripped from a notebook; the same kind he used to keep in his pocket wherever he went.

Jules,
Please come see me play.
Love
Guy

Love Guy. The words seemed stuck on repeat in her thoughts. How dare he? Even when they were apart he still seemed able to inflict an electrical pull on her.

When Jules had returned from Bath a little before seven, she had planned to stay in her room, wait for him to return from playing for Rich and Sally, and tell him once and for all to leave her alone. But she had not anticipated the note, and the effect that the words, written in the all too familiar handwriting, would have on her.

Not this time. Never again, she'd reminded herself, storming towards the pub with every intention of interrupting Guy's performance and telling him to sod off in front of anyone who had bothered to come and watch. It was about time he endured a smidgen of the humiliation she had suffered in the past few weeks.

Yet even before Jules had stepped onto the gravel driveway of The Nag, she could see that the turnout had been better than she'd anticipated. Darting to the side window before she could be seen, Jules had peered into the orangey glow, only to be faced with a mass of bodies, filling every available space, all facing towards her.

She'd dropped to a crouch.

Guy sat less than a metre away, his back towards her as he faced into the pub.

But before she could make her escape, the murmur of the crowd ceased and Guy's voice echoed out into the night. Suddenly Jules found herself rooted to the spot, desperate to run away but unable to make her body move, as every part of her absorbed his words.

'This is one I've been tinkering with for only a few hours, so you'll have to bear with me. It's for someone very special that I think a few of you may know.'

He began to play a gentle melodic tune on his guitar and started to sing.

So many love songs wish true love goodbye,
But I wanted to let you know my love, that's not you and I
I've been away for such a long time, but I still love you so,
In fact, with the dawning of every new day, my love seems to grow
And grow...

'Jules?' a voice whispered from the darkness.

She jumped back, the spell of Guy's voice broken.

'Rich, hi,' she stammered, scooting away from the window. 'You scared me half to death.'

'Did I really?' Rich smirked. 'Sorry about that. Next time I see someone lurking in the shadows of my pub, I'll be sure to make a bit more noise, shall I? Now what on earth are you doing out here?'

'Oh. Nothing really. I was just leaving.'

'Right.' Rich nodded, the expression on his face showing his disbelief.

'Big crowd,' she began, wrapping her coat closer to her body.

'Yeah. I've had to drag Stan and Sally behind the bar to help me.'

'Who are they all?'

'Everyone in Sally's address book, I think.' He smirked. 'Are you sure you don't want to come in?'

'I'm sure, thanks.'

Neither spoke for a moment as an awkward silence fell between them. The husky tones of Guy's voice filled her head causing an overwhelming despair to take hold.

'Actually I'm glad I bumped into you,' Jules began as she tried to muster her earlier resolve.

'Oh?'

'I just wanted to say thanks again for your help today, and to explain really.'

She sucked in a lung full of cold fresh air. 'It's just: I don't think you've seen me at my best. Ever since I moved here it's been one thing after another, but I really think that things will be getting better from here on out and well... what I was hoping was... if your offer of dinner might still be available?'

Despite the outside temperature Jules felt hot and uncomfortable.

Rich ran a hand through his hair and smiled. 'Of course it is. You can come for dinner anytime. I know Max would love to see you. But Jules, listen for a minute, okay? I like you. You are beautiful and funny and strong. But I think we should stay friends, rather than... well you know.'

'What?' she exclaimed. 'But you were the one who tried to kiss me.'

'Yes I know, but that was before I saw you with Guy. It just seems clear to me, and to the entire country for that matter, that you and Guy are meant to be together, and I don't want to be the one to get in the way of that.'

'You're breaking up with me?' Jules asked in disbelief, too shocked by Rich's sudden change of heart to care how stupid she sounded.

To her surprise he laughed.

'How on earth could I break up with you? In what version of reality have we been dating? Not unless you count passing out drunk on my bed, fainting in my pub and me pulling you out of an abandoned cellar, a relationship?'

'I see what you mean,' Jules gave a weak smile. 'But it's not too late. You're wrong about Guy. You couldn't be further from the truth in fact. I'm telling him to leave the minute he finishes playing.'

'Well, you're an idiot then. It's none of my business, and tell me to shut up if you want to, but you're a different person around him. More relaxed or something, I don't know. It's hard to describe. But whatever it is, you'd be crazy to throw it away.

'I can see he must have really hurt you, but everyone makes mistakes, and you can't say he hasn't been trying to make up for it. Every song is about how sorry he is. If you just stopped running from it for five minutes, you might find... I don't know.'

Jules shook her head. She couldn't speak. She had no idea how to respond. Rich was wrong. Guy was wrong. Everyone had it wrong, didn't they?

'And anyway, Max is crazy about you and the last thing I need is him sulking all day because I spend more time with you than he does,' Rich added with another smile.

He touched Jules's arm. 'You okay?'

Jules nodded, still unable to speak. Nothing seemed to be going to plan.

'Come get a drink. I've got another cocktail I've been working on. I'm going to call it The Juliet.'

Jules exhaled in an attempt to laugh and stepped back. 'Thanks Rich, but I think I'm going to pass. I'll see you soon.'

'Are you sure? Do you want me to walk you back?'

She shook her head. Turning away from him, she walked back to the road.

Nothing made sense anymore.

Twenty-six

Jules paced the room as she waited for the sound of his footsteps on the stairs. She tightened her grip on the worn copy of *Hikers Monthly* that she'd borrowed from Mrs Beckwith's living room. She would be ready for him this time.

A sudden explosion of energy travelled through her veins as she heard movements from outside the door. Throwing herself onto the hard mattress of the bed, Jules opened the magazine, her eyes unable to focus on the pages as she waited.

Nothing happened.

She held her breath, straining to hear over the vigorous thumping of her heart. The only noise was the creaking of hinges from Guy's door opening and then closing again.

Damn that man, she cursed to herself, leaping from the bed and deciding instead to confront him. Rich had been wrong about Guy. She wanted him gone. She wanted her life back.

Throwing open her door, Jules flew across the narrow hallway separating their rooms.

'If you're here on some stupid quest to relieve yourself of some old guilt, then you can SOD—,' she half shouted as she stormed into Guy's bedroom, her sentence and her body grinding to a halt at the sight of his bare torso and half-open jeans.

Guy said nothing as he put down the can of deodorant he'd been holding, and then he smirked. 'I was just coming to see you.'

'Guy, we are not living in the past anymore. I've changed, you've changed. You can't possibly expect us still to...' Jules stopped again as her thoughts trailed off.

'What if I do?'

The smirk disappeared as the dark of his eyes stared into her.

'Well I don't, so for the hundredth time please leave me alone.'

She twisted her bare feet against the prickles of the carpet and crossed back into the safety of her bedroom.

She seemed unable to catch her breath as if she'd just completed a hundred metre sprint.

No matter how hard she tried to cling on to it, the anger she'd built towards him always disappeared the minute his eyes met hers.

'I can't,' he replied as he stepped up behind her.

She screwed her eyes shut as she felt the warmth of his body against her back.

'Please go,' she whispered.

'I can't.'

'Why not?'

'I told you. I love you,' he replied.

'But you don't know me anymore. I'm not the weak stupid girl I was.'

She took a step away from him, not trusting herself to turn around.

'I know that. But I'm not either –a stupid boy I mean. And I know that I love your confidence and how stubborn you are. I especially love your temper, the way your face tightens and your eyes glow. And I love the fact that underneath it all, no matter how hard you try to hide it, you are still the kind sweet girl that I fell in love with whilst sitting in a lecture about buttons.'

Like a million shards of glass falling from the sky, his words cut into her.

'It's not real.'

'Yes it is. More real than anything else in the world to me.'

His response startled her. Had she spoken out loud?

All of a sudden she spun towards him. He was closer than she realised and still naked from the waist up.

Her heart pounded so hard she half expected it to explode.

She needed to gain control.

'And what would your publicist think about you saying that?' she demanded.

To her surprise Guy's deep laugh filled the room. 'Right – two things: firstly it's good to see your jealous streak is still alive and well—'

'I'm not—'

'Secondly,' he continued, ignoring her protest, 'You of all people should know not to believe what you read in the papers. I'm not dating Sonja, far from it. I won't lie to you, we kissed yesterday. Well actually, she kissed me. But all it did was reinforce how I feel about you. No one else comes close.'

He took a breath before continuing: 'Jules, you may not have noticed, but I have a single at number one and an album release in a fortnight. I should be spending every second I can doing interviews and performances, but I'm not. I'm here with you and I'm going to stay here for as long as it takes.'

'For as long as what takes?'

'For as long as it takes for you to believe me when I say that I love you more than anything in the world. Until you stop pretending you don't feel it too.'

His fingers touched her neck as he tilted her face towards him, his eyes penetrating hers. 'I know I made the biggest mistake of my life, and I know that I really don't deserve it, but please, Jules, I'm begging you to forgive me. Please stop fighting it for one minute and see what happens.'

'I… I…' She struggled to find an answer. 'I'm not sure.'

Despite her weak protest, Jules continued to stare into his eyes. She didn't know what to think.

'When I'm with you,' Guy continued, his voice shaking, 'Even when we are arguing in a dark hole, I feel complete. When we're not together, all I feel is emptiness, like someone's turned the lights out.'

Jules stopped breathing. He felt it too.

'But you left. You ruined it,' she cried out suddenly.

'I know.' Guy's shoulders slumped. 'It's the biggest mistake of my life. I would give anything to go back and undo it. Anything.'

'But why did you?'

'I can't tell you how many times I've asked myself the same question.'

'And?' For the first time, Jules felt none of the anger which had haunted her for so long. She just needed to know.

Guy moved his arms toward her, taking her hands in his. She didn't stop him.

'It's hard to explain, and even now I'm not sure I fully understand why I did it. But it just seemed like the minute my exams had finished everything changed. Things went from being fun to suddenly needing a life plan. And I didn't have one.

'I couldn't keep playing in total dives for no money just on the hope of being discovered, but I couldn't do anything else either. I barely scraped a pass, remember. When modelling came up it gave me a way out. I could be an instant success without needing to lift a finger.'

'But what about us Guy, it doesn't explain why you did what you did, leaving in the park and—'

'Because you knew the truth,' he cut in. 'You knew me better than anyone else, better than I knew myself probably. You saw through it all instantly, I knew you would. I was selling myself out. I wasn't a success; I was just a skinny kid.

'I was giving up on the thing I loved doing because it seemed so much easier to do that than to try and fail. I thought it was the singing I was giving up, but it was you. I didn't want to fail you, but I couldn't find a way to be all the things you saw in me.

'It doesn't excuse what I did, I know that. And no amount of apologies or explanations can change that. But I was young and stupid, I thought I knew everything, and I'm so, so sorry.'

'It's too late for sorry.'

'Tell me what to say then. Tell me what I can do to, because whatever it is, I'll do it.'

Without thinking, Jules leant forward, pressing her lips to his.

It suddenly didn't matter what he said, nothing could change the past, but she was tired of fighting it. Every single atom of her being had longed for him from the first instant she'd seen him in her kitchen last week.

For just one second, she didn't want to fight anymore.

Twenty-seven

Guy stood frozen, unable to move as a surge of electricity travelled through him, draining the blood from his head and weakening his knees.

Then, like a crashing wave, he regained control and suddenly they were kissing. Their movements increased in speed as familiarity and desire hit him.

He reached his shaking hands towards her, brushing the smooth skin of her neck before his fingers travelled up to the silk tendrils of her hair and down to her waist.

He wanted every inch of her. The desire so much more powerful than he remembered. Then she pressed her body against the erection straining from his jeans and every thought in his head disappeared.

Moments later, Guy felt a space grow between them as Jules pulled her lips away causing a desperate longing to rocket through him as he looked into her emerald eyes.

'Jules,' he whispered. 'We don't have to—'

'Don't say anything,' she cut in, tugging at the waistband of his jeans and pulling him towards the bed.

Time stood still. His mind was unable to imagine a world outside of the cramped bed as their elbows knocked painfully against the wall in the struggle to remove each other's clothes. He didn't care. The last thing he wanted at that particular moment was space.

Her skin felt even smoother than he remembered as his hands roamed the contours of her body. He never thought it could be possible for someone to become so much sexier, but Jules's sleek lines overwhelmed him.

With their naked bodies pushing against each other, Guy dragged his lips from hers, his kisses travelling down to the soft curve of her breasts and brushing the rigid points of her nipples.

Her gasp stretched into the silent room, causing another surge of longing to catapult through him. He wanted her so much and yet he could not let the time between them end.

Guy moved further down her body, his lips grazing the slender shape of her stomach. With a gentle push from his hands he moved her legs apart and continued kissing; his tongue flicked harder against her, his movements guided by her cries. Pulling away only when he'd felt the orgasm shudder through her.

Jules sat up tugging him back towards her, a smile stretched across her face.

'You are so beautiful,' he said, running a hand along the loose waves of her hair.

'You're not so bad yourself.'

Her hand reached for his erection, causing a current of dizziness to sweep across his mind as her cool grip tightened around him.

'Come here,' she commanded in a whisper as her body dropped back to the bed.

He struggled to think as the speed of her hand increased. Pulling away before it was too late, Guy reached for the wallet in his jeans bundled at the bottom of the bed.

Her eyes shone out at him as she watched him open the condom wrapper.

Gently, he laid over her, brushing her neck with kisses as his hands lost themselves over her body.

Only when he could not wait another second did he push into her, the feeling so mesmerising that he felt the instant danger of climax build inside him. Not yet, he begged, as every movement caused another gasp from Jules and an ecstasy he never thought possible.

The room closed in and their breathing quickened. As Jules pushed herself harder against him he stopped fighting it, thrusting again and again until the orgasm overtook him.

The same electricity he'd felt earlier by her touch now magnified by a thousand as the moment consumed him.

With their damp limbs tangled in the bed spread, Guy's fingers stroked the ends of Jules's long brown hair, which had loosened from its grips and spread in waves across the pillow.

'That was...' he began, unable to locate the words to express the emotions still pulsing through him.

'Yes it was,' she smiled.

'Better than running, that's for sure.'

Jules's laugh rang out into the room and she nuzzled further against his chest.

'Why are there none of the weird little brass thingies in these rooms?' he asked.

'People kept stealing them,' Jules replied as her fingers stroked the soft hair on his chest.

'Seriously?' he smirked.

'Yep.'

'I like it here,' Guy said. 'Cottinghale, I mean.'

'Me too.'

'Are you sleepy?'

'No.'

'Me neither,' he added as his hands wandered back across her naked body.

'Guy, you can't be serious?' Jules laughed.

'Can't I?' he replied, turning her head to his and planting light kisses all the way to her mouth.

Only after they lay satisfied in each other's arms again did they really talk. It seemed to Guy as if they'd been separated for five weeks rather than five years, as if the time apart was insignificant.

A feeling of total completeness enveloped him, mingling with exhaustion until finally they slept.

Twenty-eight

The first time Jules felt herself pulled from the depths of sleep, she had been dreaming of paper butterflies flapping in the breeze. The second time it was the slim beams of daylight creeping through the thin curtains that tried to drag her from her slumbers.

Eventually she peeled open her eyes, allowing the feelings of contentment and excitement to drench through her first waking moments.

She could not remember the last time she'd slept so deeply and awoken so refreshed, she thought as she stared at the clock on her mobile, surprised to find it was already a few minutes to ten. Jules snuggled against the creased space on the bed, still dented with the imprint of Guy's body. She took a long breath in, absorbing his smell. It was just as she remembered.

She let her eyelids close again. She could do nothing to stop her mouth stretching into a wide smile as she recognised the sound of plates clattering from the kitchen. Breakfast in bed had always been Guy's speciality, she thought.

Jules drifted into an easy doze and waited for him to return. Her mind dancing through the memories from their night together.

When she looked at the clock on her mobile for the second time the first trickle of fear broke inside her. Another hour had gone by and Guy had not returned.

He must have been held up talking to Mrs Beckwith, or gone for a walk and stopped to talk to one of the residents, she reassured herself as she climbed out from the bed and threw on last night's clothes.

Raking a brush quickly through her hair, Jules bounced down the stairs to find him.

'Good morning, dear. Did you sleep well?' Mrs Beckwith greeted her from the dining room table as Jules entered.

'Yes thank you, Mrs Beckwith. Sorry I missed breakfast this morning,' she replied, unable to stop herself from smiling.

'Don't you worry, dear. I know the effect this country air can have. I can fix you something now if you're hungry?' The old landlady asked, already pushing her china coffee cup aside and moving slowly to her feet.

'No, don't get up, I'm fine thank you.'

Jules felt a ferocious hunger echo in her stomach, but she didn't want to eat. Guy would be back soon. He had probably driven halfway to France to find fresh croissants, she thought.

'I don't suppose you've seen Guy this morning, have you?'

'Well, yes, dear,' Mrs Beckwith nodded. 'Of course, I didn't know who he was yesterday otherwise I would never have let him stay after all that trouble he's caused you. But you've no need to worry – he left this morning, and by the expression on his face, he won't be back in a hurry.'

'He's gone?' Another drop of panic rippled through her.

'Yes, but I thought you'd be pleased.'

'Did he say where he was going?'

'No he didn't and I didn't ask. He just paid up and left. Are you alright dear? You look terribly pale all of a sudden.'

'I'm fine thanks,' Jules mumbled as she struggled to comprehend what could have changed in the few short hours after they'd fallen asleep.

'Well, have a lovely day dear,' Mrs Beckwith called after her.

'You too, Mrs Beckwith,' Jules managed to say as she stumbled into the hallway.

'Oh, I almost forgot – would you like dinner tonight? Lamb hotpot?'

Jules gave a fleeting nod but could say nothing more. A haze of confusion swallowed her mind.

After everything that had happened, Guy would not just leave, would he? Not again, Jules reassured herself, desperate to squash the doubt and fear winding its way through her.

She needed air. She needed to find Guy.

Grabbing her coat and boots, Jules stepped outside, stuffing her hands into the warmth of her pockets as a cold breeze wound its way past her.

After one day of sunshine the contrasting chalk clouds made the sky above seem dull and lifeless. The only evidence of the previous day's mild weather was a scattering of daffodil buds that had shot from the earth along the side of the road, their weak stems swaying in the cold February breeze as Jules past.

With her thoughts elsewhere Jules found herself following the same routine as the previous day, walking along the winding country lane towards Stan's shop.

Guy had been right about her. Over the years she had buried herself under so much hurt that she'd lost sight of who she was. Somehow she had convinced herself that she wanted to be alone. The solitary work redeveloping properties, the quiet nights she'd spent alone, and the occasional failed relationship. No friends, no one to share her life with.

It had hardly been fun. It had hardly been living.

Not anymore, Jules said to herself, picking up her pace and inhaling a deep breath of fresh morning air.

She needed to start trusting again. Starting with the people she'd met in Cottinghale – Terri, Rich, and even Stan. They had accepted her into their community and however much she hated to admit it, she would have been lost without them.

As for Guy, Jules smiled to herself, he would not leave her again. She was sure of that. It must have been an emergency or an important meeting that had made him leave so early. There were a thousand perfectly rational explanations, she just had to wait for him to come back and explain.

A few minutes later Jules stepped into the farm shop, her doubts cast aside and her good mood restored.

'Good morning Stan, how are you today?' she called out.

Stan looked up, turning over the paper in front of him and nodding in response.

'Did you enjoy Guy's performance last night?'

'Um.' He shrugged.

'Fantastic weather we had yesterday. Do you think it will be like that again soon?'

'Not likely.'

'No you're probably right,' she agreed, picking up a small carton of fresh orange and a chocolate bar.

'Just these please Stan.' Jules placed her items on the counter and smiled at the bald shop owner.

'I've got your paper here,' he replied bending down to reach for a stack under the counter.

'I don't need it this morning, thank you.'

As if he had not heard her, Stan folded the paper in two and pushed it towards her.

'No, it's fine actually, thanks. I don't want to look at anything they've got to say anymore,' Jules said again.

'But I've already saved it for you now so you might as well take it. No point wasting it, is there?'

'Err no I guess not.' Jules handed over the money and left. What was with Stan's unusually cryptic behaviour? She wondered.

It did not take long before she understood.

Jules let herself back into her room at the guesthouse, throwing the paper onto the crumpled bed covers and shrugging off her coat. Only then did she see the headline written in big fat letters across the front page and the photograph which accompanied it.

THE DAILY
TUESDAY, FEBRUARY 25TH
GUY RAUNCHSON

Guy Rawson may have thrown his towel in for modelling but the 27-year old hasn't lost his trademark sexy bod or his touch with the ladies based on the smiles of these lucky gals.

Last week's hot tub romp, pictured above, is just one of Guy's celebration nights after hitting the top spot with his debut single, 'Regret'.

The star, also rumoured to be dating celeb publicist Sonja Morton, said: "Of course I'm celebrating, who wouldn't be? This is a great time for me."

She threw herself towards the bathroom, barely making it in time to lift the pink woollen seat cover and watch the Curly Wurly and orange juice make an untimely return to the world.

'Shit,' Jules said aloud as the retching subsided.

A sticky fever had cloaked her skin, mingled with a dizziness that left her feeling detached and floaty.

Only when she knelt by the sink and splashed the cold water against her face did the anger consume her.

He had left his toothbrush. The blue and white neck leant intimately against hers. Snatching it from the holder she threw it in the bin as a white heat raged through her.

He had done it to her again.

It had all been one big game. A pathetic ego-boosting mission. The minute Guy had won his prize, he had left.

Her entire face flamed red as she recalled his lies. How easily she had believed them. Every word he had whispered to her late into the night; every kiss – it had meant nothing to him. The only person Guy was capable of loving was himself.

What a fool she had been, Jules thought, as angry hot tears pricked at her eyelids. She clamped her teeth together until she heard the crunch of enamel.

She would not cry.

Twisting the iron taps of the shower, Jules stripped off her clothes and stepped under the scolding water; grateful for the painful water pricks against her skin as she washed away every trace of him.

The waves of fury refused to fade as Jules tied her damp hair into a tight ponytail. Her hatred towards Guy was a minuscule part of the disgust she felt towards herself. The knowledge that she had made the same mistake she'd made five years ago infuriated her more than she could endure.

'Bastard,' Jules said to the empty room as she threw on her clothes.

She had wasted enough time on him. Now she needed to work.

Twenty-nine

Using an out of date mottled-brown telephone directory she'd discovered in Mrs Beckwith's downstairs hallway, Jules picked up her mobile and started dialling. It took three attempts before she found a window glazing company still in business.

'Robert Winter's Glazing, Bob speaking.'

'Hello. I have a broken window pane in the back door of a property I'm redeveloping,' Jules began in a rushed voice. 'I'd like it replaced with double glazing as soon as possible please.'

'Right love, let me just take some details from you and I'll see what we can do. Can I take your name, address and contact number please?'

Jules reeled off her details and tapped her foot impatiently as Bob talked her through a very detailed price list.

'That sounds fine,' Jules managed to cut in eventually. 'When can you do it?'

'Right, let's see then. I can send someone out to look at it early next week. There's no call out charge for that. And we can get the pane ordered and fitted by... let's say the seventh of March.'

'I was really hoping to have it done this week. Any chance you could send someone out today?'

'Um,' the voice on the other end of the line huffed. 'Well you see Ms Stewart, as I'm sure you can appreciate, one pane of glass is not a high priority for us. I mean, if it was a larger job then of course we would shuffle some things around, and—'

'Right,' Jules cut him off. She knew exactly what he was getting at. 'How about this. You send someone out today and fix my back door by the end of this week, and I will put an order in to double glaze the rest of the house next week.'

'Um,' he said again. 'Well whaddya know, I've just this minute had a cancellation and can come myself this afternoon.'

'Thank you.' She hung up.

Jules ignored the flutter of nerves at the thought of her rapidly shrinking bank balance and dialled the number of the staircase supplier Terri had given her. For a reason Jules had no intention of dwelling on, time was suddenly of the essence.

Running into the same slow schedule and with no additional orders to act as an incentive, Jules had no choice but to offer the staircase manager a cash in hand bonus for delivery and fitting by the end of the week.

Finally, she scrolled through her phonebook until she found Terri's number. Taking a deep breath, she pressed the call button before she could change her mind. On top of everything else she wasn't sure she could handle Terri's friendly concern.

'Helloooo,' Terri chirped on the third ring.

'Hi Terri, it's Jules.'

'Hello lovey. How are you getting on? I didn't see you at the pub last night; mind you it was chock-a-block in there. Did you and Guy manage to sort things out?'

'Not exactly. But I've spoken to a glazer,' Jules carried on. 'Someone will be popping over this afternoon to do some measurements. And I've ordered the staircase we talked about, it should be fitted in the next few days. So if you're okay to stay at the house today and continue with the clear up, I'm going to get some paint and supplies in.'

'Blimey, there's no stopping you is there.' Terri laughed. 'That's fine lovey. You'll be pleased to hear that Dan is just loading up the last of the wood from the stairs. And I've set Jason loose on the garden, I hope that's okay?'

'Yes, that's perfect, thank you.' Despite her mood, Jules felt a wisp of relief for Terri, Dan and Jason. She had no idea where she'd be without them.

'And I thought I might take a crack at cleaning up the kitchen a bit. Those cupboards still seem in pretty good nick, if we could take the paint off them, they might look half decent.'

'You're a lifesaver Terri,' Jules said.

'Oh, I almost forgot to ask,' Terri paused, her voice dropping to a whisper. 'Did you come up to the house last night?'

'No. Why?'

'It's my tools. They've been moved around.'

'What do you mean? Is anything missing?'

'No. Everything is still here as far as I can tell, but well... I'm a very tidy person. I always make sure all the tools are packed up before we leave. But this morning I came in and they've all been unpacked.' Her voice dropped another decibel. 'I found my hammer in the kitchen.'

'Have you asked Dan and Jason? I'm sure there's a perfectly logical explanation.'

'They swear blind it wasn't them.'

'Terri, it's okay. Like you said, nothing's missing. Did you work later than usual last night?'

'Yes, a little.'

'There you go then. You probably left in a bit of a rush so you could make it to the pub on time and forgot to pack them away.'

'I guess,' Terri replied, her tone still doubtful. 'So you don't think it could be the ghost of Mrs Mayor?'

Jules laughed despite herself. 'Don't be daft.'

'You're right,' Terri concluded with an attempt at a chuckle. 'But what am I thinking? Are you sure you're okay? I'm free tonight if you fancied another little chat?'

'Thanks Terri, but I'm fine. Gotta go, I've got a call waiting,' she lied, hanging up the phone and rubbing a hand against her forehead.

It didn't seem possible that only twelve hours ago she was lying in bed with Guy. Pushing the thought aside, Jules threw on her jacket and headed for her car.

She did not allow her mind to drift into autopilot this time. Instead she drove to the biggest DIY store she could find and forced herself to concentrate.

As the day wore on, Jules found herself cramming giant cans of white paint, brushes, rollers, light fittings, wall sockets and every other item she could think of into the boot of her car.

The trip served only to impact her bank balance, but not her mood.

No matter how hard she fought it, she could not stop her thoughts from wandering back to Guy. First to the excitement and happiness she'd felt in his arms, and then like a painful static charge, she felt the shock of truth travel through her, causing anger to flash in colourful blotches before her eyes.

She couldn't wait to climb into bed that night and forget the last forty-eight hours had ever happened, Jules thought as she drove back through the countryside towards Cottinghale.

At a few minutes past six, with the sky already an inky black, she pulled into the empty driveway of her house, her headlights bouncing against the windows.

Suddenly, a shiver raced along her spine. From the corner of her eye, she saw something move inside the house. Her mind alert with adrenaline, Jules switched off the engine and held her breath. It couldn't be Terri, Dan or Jason, or their van would be in the driveway, she reasoned.

Who else had a key?

No one, a voice inside her head answered as another shiver ran through her, taking over her entire upper body.

Minutes ticked by as Jules sat like a statue, her gaze glued to the downstairs windows as her eyes adjusted to the dark.

Only as her heart began to slow to a normal pace again did Jules realise that she'd imagined the whole thing. The headlights from her car had caught the metal on the ladder, or one of Terri's tools, causing a flicker in her peripheral vision, she reasoned.

The quicker she unloaded the car, the quicker she could go back to the guesthouse and go to sleep, she reminded herself.

Retrieving two large tins of white paint from the back seat, Jules made her way towards the front door. But before she could dig her keys out from the depths of her jacket pocket, another movement caught her eye. A shadowy figure had crossed by the living room window. There was no mistaking it this time.

Jules set the paint tins onto the ground, dropping them the last few inches and causing a loud clatter to echo out into the still surroundings. Stepping backwards, Jules stumbled out of the driveway, her eyes never leaving the windows.

She had no rational explanation for her behaviour, but she did not turn around until the curve of the lane had swallowed the view of the house, and even then she found herself looking back over her shoulder every few steps.

It was not until she reached the guesthouse that Jules remembered that she hadn't locked her car. Not to mention the fact that she'd left two paint tins in the middle of the driveway.

On any other day she would have gone back. Correction, on any other day she would have stormed into the house and confronted the intruder, but something she could not explain had stopped her.

Only when she stepped into Mrs Beckwith's warm kitchen and breathed in the rich aromas of lamb hotpot did the creeping sensation tickling the back of her neck disappear.

Grabbing a thick dish cloth, Jules removed the plate from the oven. Without bothering to take off her jacket or even sit down, she tucked in, gulping down the food as fast as her mouth could chew it.

As she swallowed the last hot delicious mouthful, it suddenly occurred to her what an idiot she'd been.

Terri and her nonsense superstitions about the house being haunted had been lurking at the back of her mind. It had mixed with her overwrought emotions and given her the spooks over nothing.

Now that she thought about, she was sure she'd heard a car pass through the lane as she'd stepped towards the house. The beam from the headlights must have flickered through the trees, reflecting on the window like her own had done, Jules reasoned as she washed the plate and made her way up the stairs to bed.

She would have to go back first thing in the morning and move the paint tins before Terri arrived.

Thirty

As Jules's hand twisted the handle on her bedroom door she heard movement from across the hallway.

The bastard was back, she realised. Her heart thundered with renewed anger as the image of Guy's hot tub photograph jumped to the front of her mind.

Without stopping to think, she turned on her heels and threw open the door opposite her own with such force that it bounced against the wall and launched back towards her as she sprang into the room.

'Just who do you think you are?' Jules yelled, her feet grinding to a halt as she realised her mistake.

Standing in the exact spot where Guy had stood just one day earlier was a woman in her early twenties, Jules guessed, with a large cleavage and jet-black hair cropped into a sloping bob. She was wearing shiny black leggings and a short black and white stripy t-shirt dress, which made Jules think she was definitely not from the area.

'Excuse me?' the woman laughed as she turned to face Jules.

'Shit, I am so sorry. I thought someone else was staying here.'

'Hey, don't worry about it. I was beginning to think Mrs Beckwith was the only person around here. I'm Becky, by the way, and you must be Jules?'

'Err, yes, how did you know?' Jules asked, with a sudden suspicion towards the woman standing opposite her.

'The landlady mentioned you when she showed me around, but I guess she didn't have a chance to talk to you. God knows how I came across this place. My sat nav had some kind of severe malfunction and took me a completely bonkers route. I'm supposed to be at a Human Resources conference in Birmingham right now.

'Then my radiator conked out too and it was just by some serious good luck that I happened to be passing this house at the time and the old lady offered me a cup of tea and the number of a mechanic. But of course, they couldn't fix it straight away, so I'm stuck here until tomorrow morning,' Becky finished with a grin.

'Oh right. Well anyway, sorry again for barging in here. Have a nice evening,' Jules replied before turning to leave.

She felt suddenly deflated as the anger that had welled inside her moments earlier slid away.

'Actually,' Becky began. 'I don't suppose you know anywhere around here I can get a drink, do you? It's just after the day I've had, I'd murder a glass of wine.'

'There's a pub about five minutes' walk further down the lane.'

'Super. So it's left out of here, is it? And then do I just carry on walking? Do I need a torch or anything? I never knew it could be so dark outside. Sorry, that's a silly thing to say isn't it?'

'You should be okay. There's a row of houses set a bit back from the lane. They usually have the porch lights on so you can see where you're going.'

'I don't suppose you fancy joining me, do you? I hate drinking alone and knowing me, I'd wander off the road and end up face down in a ditch.'

'Thanks, but I've had a pretty rubbish day myself and I really just want to go to bed.'

'Yeah of course, I understand. If you're sure? A drink might be just what you need.'

'Err.' Jules searched her mind for another excuse.

But before she could say anything, Becky stepped forward. 'Great, that settles it then. I'll just grab my bag.'

She hadn't actually agreed, had she? Jules wondered. Then she thought of Rich's mind-numbing cocktails and shrugged. One drink, or maybe two, could be just what she needed, and by the looks of it, Becky would be doing all the talking anyway.

'Let's go,' Becky grinned, flashing a set of bright white teeth.

'Wow this is lush,' Becky said as they stepped into the empty pub. 'It's so quaint.'

'Hey, Max,' Jules said with relief as the young springer spaniel jumped up to say hello. A headache had begun to wind its way across Jules's forehead, thanks to non-stop jabbering from her companion, she thought.

'Oh, a dog,' Becky stammered, taking a step back.

'It's okay, he's very friendly,' Rich said, stepping out from behind the bar. 'The worst thing he's likely to do is slobber on you, isn't that right Jules?'

'Yep,' she agreed, smiling sheepishly at Rich. With everything that had happened with Guy, she had completely forgotten what a fool she'd made of herself outside the pub the evening before.

'But hey, if you'd rather I stuck him upstairs, it's no problem.'

'Thanks, it's just I've got a real phobia against dogs, and this bag is a Miu Miu,' she replied, holding up a shiny red handbag and flashing Rich a smile.

'Sure. Take a seat, and I'll be back in a minute with your drinks. What are you having?' he asked, staring at Jules.

'Large dry white wine for me,' Becky replied.

'Um, red for me, thanks Rich,' Jules added.

Rich continued to stare at her, his eyebrows raised and his eyes moving strangely, as if he was trying to signal something to her.

Becky slid towards a table in the corner, placing her bag in the centre whilst Rich continued to stare, raising his eyebrows another notch higher. 'You sure you don't want to come up to the bar for a sec, Jules, and pick something else out?'

'No thanks, I think I'll stick to red wine tonight,' she replied, shrugging her shoulders and giving a small shake of her head.

She had no idea what Rich was getting at. No doubt he just wanted to check on her, she decided, following Becky to the table.

Only when they had the second glass of wine in front of them did Becky stop talking. Jules had zoned out after the first five minutes of her relentless chatter. Something to do with someone called Nathan and a failure to commit. She didn't particularly care, but the distraction and the wine was serving its purpose.

Suddenly, as if a switch had been flipped, Becky shut up and turned her attention onto Jules.

'So, how long have you been staying here?'

'Oh,' Jules said, startled by the change in conversation. 'A couple of weeks.'

'It's a pretty remote place to have a holiday, isn't it? You must be bored stiff.'

'No, I'm not on holiday. I've bought a house here actually. I'm a property developer. I'm just staying at Mrs Beckwith's until my house is in a fit state to live in.'

'Really? That's so interesting. Are you planning to stay here for good then?'

'Probably not,' she sighed. 'I'll be moving on once it's finished.'

'Yeah, I can see why. It's a bit of a shit hole isn't it? Aren't the people really nosy in places like this? It must drive you nuts.'

'I thought the same thing,' Jules said, smiling for the first time at Becky. 'But everyone is so friendly. It's a real community kind of place.'

'So people don't stick their noses in then?'

Jules laughed. 'Well they do a bit, but it's only because they care and want to help. I thought my builders were a bunch of interfering hillbillies when I first met them, but they are actually really hard working. I don't know where I'd be without them.'

'What about the bloke behind the bar,' Becky winked at Jules. 'Something going on between you two?'

'Err, no. Rich is lovely, but he's not my type. Besides I think he thinks I'm a piss head with serious relationship issues. Or I would if I was him anyway.'

'Really, why?' Becky asked, leaning forward and nudging her bag closer towards Jules.

'Nothing, don't worry.'

'God, sorry, would you look at me. Now who's the nosy one? You don't have to talk about it.'

No, it's just...' Jules sighed and rubbed a hand against her jaw. It ached to the point of painful. She took a long sip of wine before continuing. 'You are going to think I'm crazy, but for the past few weeks a tabloid newspaper has been writing stories about me.'

'Oh my God, that's so exciting. Which one?'

'*The Daily.*'

Becky giggled. 'Wow. I can't say I've ever read it but still, it's pretty massive. Why are they interested in you?'

'I used to date Guy Rawson,' Jules mumbled.

'No way, that is so cool. Here let me get you another drink and you HAVE to tell me everything. I can't believe I've been wittering on about myself all this time.'

It took Jules thirty minutes and another glass of wine before she finished explaining the events of the past few weeks to Becky.

She would not have thought it possible, but confiding in a complete stranger felt surprisingly good.

'Wow,' Becky said again when she'd finished. 'That's pretty hardcore.'

Jules nodded.

'So you must really hate Guy for the way he's treated you? I'd want to kill him if it was me.'

'Yesh. He is a pathetic manipulative worm. I could strangle him,' she cried out as the effect of the alcohol hit her. 'Ist not just him,' she continued with a slight slur, 'I hate them all. All men are bastards put on this earth to destroy us.'

'Too right,' Becky laughed. 'To the bastards.' She raised her almost empty glass to Jules.

'Bastards,' Jules repeated, dropping her head to her hands as she realised how drunk she was. She'd had way too much wine. What was she thinking? 'I'd better get back. I've got loads of work to do tomorrow,'

'Good idea, let's go,' Becky replied, grabbing her bag.

The cold night air had a sobering effect as they stumbled their way back up the lane. To Jules's surprise and relief, Becky's earlier nattering had been replaced with silence.

By the time they made it to the guesthouse an inebriating exhaustion had wrapped itself around her. With a short wave goodbye and a promise to meet for breakfast, Jules stepped into her room, shrugged off her clothes and climbed into bed.

She could still smell Guy's body on the sheets.

Only then did Jules allow the silent tears to fall as the memories of the previous night circled around her drunken thoughts.

Thirty-one

Guy's bleary eyes stared at the loud ticking clock willing it to shut up. From outside the room he could hear the constant activity of the midwives station and the bewildered screeches of newborn babies crying in the next ward.

He stared at the washed out face of his sister lying asleep next to him. He had never felt so helpless.

He should have been a better brother, Guy thought as he dropped his face into his hands. Debbie had always been there for him. Any time, day or night, he knew if he called her she would answer. The same could not be said about him.

He'd spent years jetting all over the world, attending fashion shoots, premieres, and anything else he'd desired. Months would go by before he'd remember to return her calls or drop by.

It was only recently, when he'd chosen to pack up modelling and pursue his music that he'd spent more time with Debbie, Carl and Sam. Only when the invites had stopped flowing in, and he'd found himself in London with no social life to speak of did he take up residency on Debbie and Carl's sofa. A roast dinner on a Sunday and a mid-week take-away; it did not seem nearly enough now.

He should not have taken no for an answer when he'd offered to look after Sam last week. Debbie had looked so grey and exhausted, but he'd been too wrapped up in his own life to pay attention.

She'd even told him she was ill and all he'd done was type a hasty text and forget all about it.

His own pregnant sister and he hadn't bothered to stick around long enough to help her. She was the only family he had. Fuck, he hated himself.

Without warning, Guy suddenly thought of Jules. Ever since he'd sat down in the hard plastic visitor's chair by Debbie's bedside, his emotions had rocketed from one extreme to the other – the guilt and fear for Debbie and the baby felt like a fist squeezing his heart, followed by a panicked desperation for his relationship with Jules. If he even had a relationship.

Twenty past five. Ten hours since he'd left her. Why hadn't she called?

Every few hours, he would slip out of his sister's room and turn on his phone. As the display fired up, a dozen missed calls and messages appeared. Only a week ago they would all have seemed urgent. But none of them mattered now.

He missed her so much it weighed down on him like a concrete slab.

Why had he not woken her? He should never have left her sleeping, but she'd looked so beautiful by his side that it seemed wrong somehow to disturb her.

'Um,' Debbie murmured next to him, pulling his thoughts back to grey walls of the hospital room.

'Hey sis,' he whispered, giving her hand a gentle squeeze.

'Guy?' she mumbled just before her eyes shot open. 'Is the baby okay?'

He felt a bolt of pain as Debbie's nails dug into the palm of his hand.

'Everything is fine, just relax, okay?'

'Thank God.' She released his hand as fat tears fell down her cheeks. 'Where's Carl?'

'He's gone to check on Sam, but he'll be back soon. Sam's going to stay with Carl's mum and dad for a few days and I'll be dropping by in the morning to say hello and take him to the park for a while.'

Guy squeezed her hand again. 'How are you feeling?'

'Tired and thirsty.'

'Here, drink this.' Guy poured some water into the plastic beaker by the bed and held it to her lips.

'Do you remember what happened?' he asked after she'd laid her head back on the pillow.

'I fell down the stairs,' she sobbed.

Guy nodded. 'The doctor should be back in a minute, he'll be able to explain what happened better than I can. Just rest now.'

'No, tell me now,' she pleaded.

'You fainted as you were coming down the stairs. It was only a few steps, but they think the impact caused you to go into early labour. Carl called an ambulance and they were able to stop it,' Guy explained, his voice cracking with emotion.

'My blood pressure was high. The midwife told me to stay in bed and I didn't listen,' Debbie croaked. 'If anything happens... I'll never forgive myself.'

'The doctors think you'll both be okay, you just need to stay off your feet. And you may be stuck with hospital food for a while, I'm afraid,' he tried to joke.

'Oh Guy, what have I done? If the baby is born this early... I... I don't think...' her voice trailed off as fresh tears flooded her eyes.

'Don't think like that, Debs. You've got to stay positive. Me and Carl will be your servants. Anything you need, just ask. Even a few days could make all the difference. The doctor even said there's a good chance you could continue to full term.'

'Since when did you become an expert?' A thin smile touched her pale face.

'When I realised what a terrible brother I am. I'm so sorry, Debbie. I should have been around to help you out more.'

'Don't be an idiot, Guy. You're the best brother ever.'

Before Guy could respond, the door opened a fraction revealing a fluffy blue rabbit followed by Carl and a giant bouquet of pink roses.

'Carl,' she croaked as the tears fell again. 'I'm so sorry.'

'Hey, hey, hey,' he soothed, striding to the bed and wrapping his arms around Debbie. 'What have you got to be sorry for? I'm the one who needs to say sorry to you, I should have helped out with Sam more.'

'Not you too,' Debbie sighed, her face already brightening by the presence of her husband.

'Sam wanted you to look after Floppy.' Carl bounced the bunny gently on the bed towards her.

'But he never sleeps without Floppy,' she exclaimed with a sad smile.

'He's a very brave boy,' Carl replied.

Without saying a word, Guy slipped from the room. It felt more like five in the morning not the afternoon, he thought, wandering along the shiny grey corridor of the pre-labour ward.

'Oh my God, Guy,' he heard Sonja's shriek before he saw her. 'I came as soon as I heard.'

'Why?' Guy asked, his energy levels too low to appease her.

'To make sure you're alright, silly,' she replied, her heels clattering towards him.

'I'm fine; it's my sister who's in hospital, not me.'

'Yes, yes, I know, but look, there are a few photographers out front. I said you might step out for some fresh air.'

'What? I'm not going anywhere. How did they even know I was here?' Guy asked, his eyes narrowing on Sonja's face, glowing orange under the fluorescent lights of the hospital waiting area.

The idea that the paparazzi had a million contacts across the world and could track down a celebrity any time they wanted was a myth. In reality, publicists, agents and sometimes the celebrities themselves told the photographers where and when to expect a sighting; something both Sonja and Guy knew well.

'Well, I called them. But Guy, something like this is great for your image.'

'Oh right, well I'll tell Debbie that, shall I? I'm sure she'll be pleased to know that whilst she's lying there praying for the life of her baby, my career is thriving.'

'Guy, it's not like—'

'No Sonja, I thought we agreed you would check with me first?' he demanded, the emotion from the day building into anger.

'I know, but I had to, Guy – it's damage control.'

'Damage control for what?' Guy slouched against the wall. Suddenly he didn't care. He wanted to be back with Debbie. As long as she and the baby were okay, and Jules still decided to give him another chance, nothing else mattered.

'Well, if you'd have answered my calls yesterday you'd know,' she responded, throwing her nose into the air.

'Sonja,' he warned.

'Okay, okay, this was in this morning's paper.' She pushed a hand into the depths of her giant black bag and pulled out a crumpled newspaper.

He stared at the photograph, realising instantly why Jules had not called.

'Guy.' She touched his arm.

'But this is from the video I did last month,' he exclaimed, shrugging her hand away. 'How did they get hold of it?' His gaze shot back to his publicist. He had a feeling he knew the answer already.

'I gave it to them, but—'

'For fuck's sake, you are supposed to talk to me about these things,' Guy began, his voice rising as he towered over her. 'First all the coverage with Jules, which I know you pushed even when I asked you not to, then this and now the photographers outside.

'It's got to stop. Do you know how this makes me look?' Guy stared at the plastic smiles of the models in the hot tub, his heart lurching at the pain it must have caused Jules.

'I know, but Guy, I gave it to one of my most trusted sources. They were supposed to make it clear it was from one of your music videos. I wanted to make sure you were still seen as sexy now that all your modelling campaigns have finished.

'But hey,' she continued, her tone lighter. 'They'll put an apology in tomorrow's edition and say some nice things about

206

you, and with a few photos of you looking sad coming out of here, it will all be forgotten.'

'No, Sonja. It won't be.' He rubbed his palm against his two-day old stubble. 'I'm sorry, but I don't want it to be like this. I gave up modelling because I don't like all this shit. All I want to do is write some decent songs and do a few performances. I thought I made that clear—'

'But this is how we get you to the top. Honestly Guy, you've got to trust me.' Sonja smiled at him, her teeth a beaming white against the grey walls.

He could tell from her reaction that she'd had similar conversations with other clients in the past. He paused for a moment, before he said, 'Well, if this is really what it means to sell records, then I don't want it.'

'What?'

'It's over, Sonja. Thank you for all of your hard work, but I will no longer be requiring your services. I don't want to play games anymore. If I can't sell my music on my ability as a singer, then I don't want to sell it at all.'

'Guy, do you have any idea how much time I've spent on you?'

'And I'm grateful, but we're finished.'

'You'll regret this,' she hissed, pointing a manicured red nail at him. 'You will fuck this up without me. I guarantee it. And then you'll come crawling back like they all do.'

'Goodbye Sonja.' Guy turned away from her, moving back towards the ward.

He would check on Debbie and then he would call Mrs Beckwith. He had no idea what kind of message he would— Guy's thoughts broke off as he turned the corner, a crippling fear taking hold of his body as his eyes registered the midwives rushing into his sister's room.

Thirty-two

Jules's fingers rubbed the small folded note in front of her. One side had the jagged edge of once belonging to a notebook. Her name had been scratched in pencil across the front.

Her gaze moved to the glassy grey eyes of Mrs Beckwith as Jules absorbed the last part of her words.

'...the vacuum almost had it but I managed to rescue it. Didn't want to throw it away just in case. Oh that's the toaster, hang on dear I'll have your breakfast in a jiffy.'

If only the note had been lost forever, Jules wished as her hands tightened around the smooth paper. It must have fallen down the back of the bedside table the morning he'd left.

Don't read it, she willed herself.

Nothing in the note would be able to explain why he'd left or justify the photograph, she told herself. Still her fingers kept turning it over and over.

She took a sip of bitter black coffee, the harsh tang removing the dry mouth of her hangover.

How much had she drunk? Three or four glasses?

It felt more like ten based on the queasiness bubbling in her stomach.

'Here you go,' Mrs Beckwith said as she placed a plate with two slices of thick brown toast in front of her.

'Thanks.'

Grateful to have something else to focus her attention on, Jules slipped the unread note into the back pocket of her jeans and pulled the plate towards her.

'You're most welcome. Well, I'd best get on. It's been so busy here the past few days I've been rushed off my feet. Oh, that reminds me – I do hope my other guest didn't disturb you this morning?'

'Disturb me? No, why?' Jules quizzed as she smothered the butter across her toast causing her mouth to water as it melted into yellowy pools on the crunchy warm bread.

'She must have left at the crack of dawn. I know it can't have been later than five because the heating hadn't even clicked on. It was no bother to me as she'd paid in full yesterday, but I was worried she might have been clattering about a bit.

'Now what was her name? Gosh my memory is really failing me if I can't even remember the girl's name,' Mrs Beckwith continued as she packed away the unused place setting on the opposite side of the table.

'I didn't hear anything,' Jules mumbled between crunches. 'Her name's Becky,' she added after swallowing. 'We went for a drink in The Nag together last night.'

'That's nice, dear.'

'How did she get her car back so early?' Jules wondered aloud.

'Back from where?'

'The mechanic,' Jules answered. 'I thought she was having her radiator fixed?'

'Radiator? I don't know anything about that, I'm afraid.'

'Oh. I thought you found the tow service for her,' Jules replied, taking another bite of toast. Had she made a mistake? She was certain Becky had said her car had broken down. Why else would she have been in Cottinghale?

'Oh dear, now I'm getting in an awful muddle. I'm sure I did nothing of the sort, but if she said I did, then maybe I did. My memory is not what it used to be.'

'Don't worry Mrs Beckwith; I'm sure I just misheard her.'

'I guess we'll never know now anyway. Can I make you dinner again tonight dear? I don't want you wasting away whilst you're staying under my roof. Spaghetti Bolognese?'

'Yes please. Last night's hotpot was amazing.'

'Glad to hear it.'

Jules drained the last dregs of coffee from her cup. 'I'd better get going. I'm hoping to move up to the house this week, if I can make it liveable that is.'

'Good for you dear. Although I'll miss having you here, of course.'

'See you tonight then,' Jules said, heading for the door. 'Bye,' she called out as she stepped outside, pulling the collar of her jacket up against the bitter wind.

Jules heaved a sigh of relief as she turned the corner to her driveway a little before eight-thirty that morning. Everything was exactly where she'd left it the previous night – her car, full of the purchases from her spending spree, sat unlocked with the passenger door still wide open, and the two pots of white paint she'd left on the driveway had not moved.

She could unpack and Terri would be none the wiser to her foolish behaviour the previous night. The last thing she wanted to do was fuel her builder's imagination about ghosts in her house.

Picking up the paint, Jules lugged the heavy tins towards the front door, noticing for the first time the difference to the outside of her house. In the grey overcast daylight, she could see the progress Jason had made in the front garden.

The thick green brambles which had acted like barbed wire, stopping anyone from entering the garden, had disappeared. Only their roots remained, poking out from the black earth like giant green worms.

She hadn't realised how much land there was. She could plant rows of white roses bordering her drive, or even build an extension, she suddenly thought. A whole new wing to the house in the same stonework would look stunning. A bigger kitchen, another bathroom, maybe even a study.

Jules stopped herself, cutting the idea dead before it could form any further in her mind. An extension might make it her perfect home, but she would not be the one living in it, Jules reminded herself again.

She would finish the basics on the house over the next few months, maybe less if she worked hard, and then she would sell and move on. Just like she always did.

With an abrupt reminder of the task at hand, Jules threw herself into unpacking her purchases. It took an hour, but by the time she'd finished everything was in its place ready to be used.

Only then, as she flicked the switch on the kettle, did she realise something was wrong – Terri and the boys had still not arrived.

It felt strange without them. Ever since they had helped her move in on her first night, Terri, Dan and Jason had been working alongside her almost every day. The house seemed empty without her three builders bustling around inside.

Jules picked up her mobile from the kitchen counter and scrolled down to Terri's number.

Maybe Terri had another job on today and had forgotten to mention it, Jules wondered as the phone rang.

What to do? Jules wondered, as she found herself connected to Terri's voicemail for the second time.

It would be much easier to paint the hallway before the stairs arrived later in the week. The bare plaster would soak up the paint like a sponge. She'd need to do at least two coats to stop it looking patchy.

It was the kind of job that would take her days to complete, but with Dan and Jason's help, they could get the first coat done in just a few hours. With that in mind, Jules grabbed her car keys and stepped back outside. They needed another batch of tea bags and more biscuits anyway, Jules thought, slipping into the drivers' seat of her car and turning on the engine.

It was still only early morning. Terri would turn up soon enough.

It took less than a minute to reach the store. She'd driven up and down the lane so many times in the past fortnight she didn't even slow down as she moved into each turn.

Drawing to a stop outside, Jules jumped out, not bothering to lock the car as she walked through the open doorway, finding the place empty apart from the bald shop owner standing behind the counter.

'Hi Stan,' she called as she stepped towards the back.

The gruff shop owner lifted his head from his notebook but said nothing as she picked up a box of tea-bags and a double pack of chocolate bourbons.

Jules placed her items on the counter and smiled to Stan as she handed over the change.

'You've got some nerve,' he muttered under his breath.

'Sorry?' Jules questioned. Had she misheard..

Stan shook his head but did not repeat himself as he packed her items into a blue carrier bag and slid it towards her.

It was only when she entered the cold and empty interior of her house and put the kettle onto boil that she noticed *The Daily* poking out from the bag Stan had given her.

'For fuck's sake,' she cried out, ripping open the paper and scanning the pages. There was only one reason Stan would have slipped the newspaper in with her shopping, Jules thought as her eyes searched frantically across the headlines until she found it:

THE DAILY
WEDNESDAY, FEBRUARY 26TH
STAR FACES DEATH THREAT FROM OLD LOVE RAT
JUICY JULES: "I WANT TO KILL GUY"

Former top model, Guy Rawson, is facing death threats from ex-girlfriend, Juliet Stewart, after a night of passion.

This week, *The Daily* has been reporting on the lives of four poor fellas man-hating Juliet destroyed, but now there is a new twist to our story. Just days after Juicy Jules admits to "the most passionate and exciting night of my life..." with the sexy singer she has gone 360^{0} and speaking to our star reporter Sara-Marie Francis, Juliet claims: "Guy is pathetic, if I ever see him again I will kill him."

Police are now investigating the threat further and are thought to be planning to question love rat Juliet in the coming days. Metropolitan Police Commander, Raymond Skelinski, said: "The MET investigates all death threats deemed to be real, and are in the process of speaking to Mr Rawson's security team to establish more details on this matter."

But beware: it is not just Guy this gal is out to get. Juliet also has a thing or two to say about her neighbours in the quaint village of Cottinghale: "All they do is stick their noses in. My builders are hillbillies... the pub owner's an alcoholic... and everyone else in this sh*t hole is deranged. I can't wait to leave."

Sexy star, Guy, could not be available for comment after his sister was rushed to hospital on Monday night with pregnancy complications. The caring singer has cancelled all engagements and set up vigil by his sister's bedside.

Thirty-three

Jules scrunched her eyelids shut as she fought with the overwhelming desire to scream.

A flood of emotions hit her like a punch, pricking her eyes with tears. She slumped against the work surface, allowing her body to slip to the dirty lino as everything clicked into place.

Becky appearing from nowhere and begging her to go for a drink. The incessant talking early on, lulling her into a false sense of friendship, encouraging her to have another glass of wine, and then another.

How could she have been such an idiot?

Jules scanned back over the article and thought back to her hazy recollection of their talk. Becky, or whatever or her name was, must have been recording everything, Jules realised, recalling the designer bag Becky had placed so carefully on the table between them.

Every word she'd spoken had been twisted and manipulated until it made her seem like a monster.

No wonder Terri hadn't turned up, Jules realised as angry tears flooded down her cheeks. They would have picked up *The Daily* on their way to the house, seen the awful things she'd said about them and turned straight back around.

Everyone in Cottinghale must hate her.

As anger and frustration burnt inside her, Jules clasped the newspaper in her hands, pulling it taught as she prepared to shred into tiny pieces. But just as the first tear travelled along the centre of the page a small caption, almost hidden next to an advert for cheap electrical goods, caught her gaze.

APOLOGIES TO GUY RAWSON

***The Daily* would like to apologise to Guy Rawson for photographs of the singer published in yesterday's edition. We reported that the former model had been celebrating his recent singing success by spending time in a hot tub with five glamour models. We have since learnt that the photograph was taken from one of the star's videos "A Goodbye Fool" recorded for his album last month. We apologise unreservedly to Guy and his fans.**

Jules wiped a hand across her eyes, clearing the tears from her vision, and read the paragraph over and over, until horror replaced her disbelief.

In one frantic movement, she twisted her body to the side, digging her fingers into the back pocket of her jeans until she touched the jagged edge of Guy's note.

With shaking fingers, she unfolded the paper.

To my Juliet,

You look so beautiful sleeping bedside me that I can't bring myself to wake you. I need to go back to London. Debbie has been taken to hospital – she's seven months pregnant, did I mention that?

I hate myself for leaving you when we've only just found each other, but I promise you I will be back very soon.

There are no words to describe how much I love you

Call me the minute you wake up – 0763839393

Guy

p.s. Marry me?

Jules sat frozen as the truth behind Guy's disappearance and *The Daily's* apology soaked through her.

Guy had not run away. He had not left her. He had meant everything he'd said.

He loved her.

Jules pulled her jaw tight, swallowing hard as another thought reared in her mind.

What had she done?

What would he think when he read the article? He would have waited for her call all day. Sitting at his sister's bedside, desperate for her support, and instead he would see today's paper.

Guy had no way to know that she hadn't got the note. What would he have thought? That she'd regretted what had happened between them? That she'd gone to the paper to humiliate him and make it clear she never wanted to see him again?

The realisation filled her with a nauseating panic causing her head to pound and her mouth to dry up.

She loved him. She'd always loved him. From the second he'd followed her into the lecture theatre in their first week of university. Even after Guy had broken her heart and destroyed her dreams, she'd not stopped loving him, Jules finally admitted to herself.

The anger that had fuelled her existence for the past five years had vanished. She felt lost without it.

What did she do now?

Jules looked at the note in her hands again, her eyes focusing on the number he'd left as a spark of hope registered inside her.

With shaking hands she punched the number into her mobile, suddenly unable to breathe as she waited for it to connect. But rather than the usual hum of ringing, a mechanical woman's voice echoed into Jules's ear: 'The message box for this mobile is currently full, please try again later.'

'No. No. No,' Jules said to the empty kitchen, slapping her hand against the dusty floor.

She pressed redial and waited, her heart plummeting to her stomach as the same mechanical voice spoke.

After the fourth attempt, Jules pushed herself up from the kitchen floor and put the kettle on to boil for the third time that morning.

In one swoop she had ruined everything. She had alienated herself from the residents of Cottinghale and destroyed any chance she had with Guy.

She might as well get back to work, Jules sighed, changing into her overalls and clenching her teeth together until the urge to drop back to the floor and cry the day away past.

For three hours, Jules worked like a robot, shutting her thoughts away as she focused on painting the wall where her stairs had once been. When a stray memory from the morning escaped from its hiding place and flittered into her mind, Jules clenched her teeth tighter together, forcing her arms to move faster with the roller until the bare brown wall shone a bright white.

Only when she stopped to open a new paint pot and gulp down a glass of water did she find her body slipping once more to the kitchen floor as a desperate isolation surrounded her.

She was alone.

The hermit-like existence which she'd clung to for so long and craved just a few days earlier now felt like a prison sentence.

What was wrong with her? Jules wondered, rubbing her paint spattered hands across her face.

Only when she'd driven Guy away for good did she realise she still loved him.

And only after *The Daily* had printed her so-called interview, and she'd shattered the delicate friendships she'd formed with the residents of Cottinghale, did she find herself suddenly wanting to stay.

The empty house with its creaking floorboards and strange noises suddenly felt like home.

But how could she live here now? No one would talk to her after they'd read the paper; not that she blamed them.

Stretching to her feet, Jules looked around her, feeling the loneliness close in once more.

She looked at the clock on her mobile, surprised to find it already past three in the afternoon.

What was her plan?

Hide in her house until she could sell it. Driving out of Cottinghale anytime she needed something. Praying each time that she didn't bump into anyone?

How long would it take to sell the house? If she used the same estate agent who'd sold it to her, then it could take months, maybe years.

Then what? Jules asked herself. Another house, another town. Where would she find another cosy pub with a roaring fire? And a building team that worked hard and cared about the job they did? A place as beautiful as the view from the top of the hill? Where would she find another friend like Terri?

And if she moved again Guy wouldn't know where to find her, a voice inside her added. She squashed the thought dead. Guy wasn't coming back. She'd made sure of that.

Suddenly, Jules ran from the house and dived into the driver's seat of her car. Leaning over to the passenger side, she tore open the glove compartment, pulling out a stack of receipts and throwing them one by one to the floor until she found the one Terri had given her last week.

Printed at the bottom of the page in small orange letters was Terri's address.

She may have lost Guy but she wasn't about to lose her life in Cottinghale and her home too.

In one fluid motion, Jules turned on the engine and threw the gear stick into first.

'Cherry Blossom Cottage, Hill Lane,' Jules read the address aloud as she drove slowly down the country road, peering up dirt tracks and the occasional road as she searched for Terri's house.

Thirty-four

The black metal gate leading to Cherry Blossom Cottage creaked as Jules lifted the lever and stepped into the garden.

It had taken her less than fifteen minutes to find the row of detached bungalows on one of only four side roads in Cottinghale. As the name suggested, Hill Lane ascended up the same valley on which she had found herself lost a fortnight earlier.

Jules's feet felt like cement blocks as she made her way up the path towards the front door. In her hurry to find her friend she'd not stopped to think about what she would say. But as the gate clanged shut behind her, Jules pushed her fear aside and pressed the doorbell.

For what felt like minutes, she stood like a statue, barely breathing as she listened for movements inside the house.

With half a mind to turn around and forget the whole thing, she forced herself to knock again.

This time she heard the unmistakable sound of footsteps from behind the door.

'Terri,' Jules called out. 'Please open the door. I really need to speak to you.'

Another stretch of time past before the door clicked open and Terri's face appeared.

Even in the growing darkness, Jules could see the puffy red eyes of someone who'd been crying.

'Terri,' Jules began. 'Before you say anything, please let me explain. I am so sorry. I understand why you're so upset, and why you didn't turn up today but I didn't say those things about you. Well I did,' she corrected quickly. 'But I was explaining how my first impressions of you were wrong and how wonderful you and your boys have been—'

'Jules,' Terri interrupted in a croaky voice.

'No wait, I'm not finished,' Jules cried out, the words spilling out of her faster than she could think them. 'From the moment I arrived here you have been a great friend to me. Not just with all that you have done for me up at the house, but other stuff too. Like taking me for a drink even when I didn't want to go because you knew it would be good for me.

'And letting me cry on your shoulder and listen to me rant on about the stories in *The Daily*. I don't know what I'd have done without you.' Jules breathed in a long gulp of air as her eyes scanned Terri's face for a reaction.

'Are you finished now?' Terri asked.

'Err, yes,' Jules stammered, her hand already lifting in protest as she waited for Terri to slam the door in her face.

But to her surprise, Terri stepped back allowing Jules to enter. 'Well, you'd better come in for a cup of tea then,' she said.

Stepping into Terri's house reminded Jules of the show homes she'd visited during her first months as a property developer in Nottingham. The shimmer of gold in the cream lined wall paper, the gleaming mirrors to give the impression of space. The thick red carpet, which ran through the entire house, looked as if it had never been stepped on. Every surface shined the kind of clean Jules thought was only possible in unlived-in houses, and definitely impossible in a home with two teenage boys.

The only thing that seemed out of place was the old grey dressing gown, three sizes too big, wrapped tightly around Terri.

'Wow Terri, this is gorgeous,' Jules found herself saying as Terri led her into an equally stunning living room.

'Do you think so? Thank you.'

'I like the photos,' Jules added, stepping over to a wall of black and white photographs printed onto canvas; each one a different snap of Dan and Jason at different ages, all the way from birth through to the teenagers Jules recognised.

'The boys hate them. They think it's a weird shrine or something. But every time I look at them it makes me smile. Anyway, pop yourself down, I'll be back in a tick with a cuppa.'

Jules sat down on the squishy cream leather sofa and closed her eyes, pushing back the tears threatening to fall.

She had no idea if her welling emotions had more to do with seeing the pain she'd caused Terri, or the realisation of how cowardly her existence had been.

Jules found her gaze stuck on the photos on the other side of the room. Would she ever have that? She suddenly found herself wondering. She'd never thought much about babies. A family had never seemed to fit into her lifestyle, but as she stared at the toothy grins of Dan and Jason as children, she realised again how meaningless her life was.

'So I'm guessing you've started on the decorating,' Terri said, pulling Jules out of her thoughts.

She looked down at her paint spattered blue overalls and nodded. It had never occurred to her to change or even look in the mirror before she dashed from the house. She lifted her hands to her hair, touching a mess of tangles and paint specks.

Terri passed her a steaming china cup and saucer and sat down on the other end of the sofa.

A silence stretched between them.

Jules felt her cheeks flame with embarrassment. 'I am so sorry,' she blurted out, forcing her eyes to meet Terri's.

'Lovey,' Terri sighed. 'What are you apologising for? I couldn't give two hoots about what that trash published. Dan and Jason even thought the hillbilly comment was rather funny. They can't wait to show their friends they've made it into a national tabloid.'

'But you didn't come up to the house today,' Jules exclaimed.

'I know,' Terri sighed, shaking her head. 'I sent the boys out first thing to do a quick estimate before coming over to you and the berks decided to do the job there and then.

'Of course, they only called me an hour ago to tell me it was taking longer than they'd first anticipated. Otherwise I would have called you. I was just about to get dressed and walk up to the house, in fact.'

Jules shook her head. 'You don't need to pretend, Terri. I can see you're upset.'

Terri nodded as she lifted her mug to her lips, blowing on the hot liquid before taking a sip. 'I am,' she agreed in a shaky voice. 'But it has nothing to do with you, lovey, and everything to do with that worthless husband of mine. I'm just sorry you've had to see me like this,' she sniffed, signalling her free hand towards her tatty dressing gown.

'Why, what's happened?'

'It doesn't bear talking about. I can't believe I'm getting upset about it again,' Terri replied with a sniff. 'Now come on, I'll pop my overalls on and we can head back to the house for a few more hours' work.'

As Terri stood up from the sofa Jules shot forward, grabbing her hand and pulling her back down.

'Anything that makes you this upset has to be worth talking about. Now come on, what's he done?'

'It's not what he's done; it's what I've done... I'm getting divorced,' she said with a sob.

'But that's a good thing, isn't it? I mean he's been gone for years, hasn't he?'

Terri nodded. 'I started divorce proceedings years ago but it took my solicitor so long to track Kev down that things just seemed to stall. I guess I wasn't pushing that hard for it either.'

'It seemed like the right thing to do at the time, but as the months went by without a word, I started to think that he didn't want a divorce, and just maybe he was planning to come home. I guess I convinced myself that at any minute he could walk back through the door and we could go on as if nothing had happened.

'Then this morning, one week before the judge would have granted me a divorce by desertion, he sends the papers back, signed and everything. No note... no explanation.' Terri dropped her head to hands and sobbed. 'It's so cruel.'

'Oh Terri, I'm so sorry.'

'I feel like the most pathetic woman in the world for believing he'd come back.'

'But how can you still want him after the way he treated you?'

'Because I love him. Don't get me wrong, I did what you did, I tried to make myself hate him and get on with my life, but somewhere along the way, I just stopped fighting it. If Kev walked back through that door right now, I wouldn't turn him away. I'd make him do some serious begging, but in the end I'd take him back.'

Jules reached out and put her arm around Terri as she cried into her cup. She had no idea how to respond. It seemed grotesque to her that Terri could still love her husband after what he'd done, but at the same time she understood it completely.

'Who else would have me now?' Terri whispered. 'My boobs are half way to my belly button. My bum has so much cellulite on it that it looks like two sagging bags of peas,' she paused for a moment before adding: 'In September I'll be packing my boys off to university and then I'll be all alone.'

'No you won't. I'll be here,' Jules replied, tightening her grip around her friend. 'And so will Rich and Sally, and Stan, and Ben, and everyone else. You will not be alone, I promise you. And as for no one wanting you – don't be daft. There must be a ton of rich widowers or divorcees dying to meet someone as fun and attractive as you. '

'You are sweet, lovey,' Terri sniffed, lifting her head up and wiping her eyes. 'I guess you're right. About having you all here I mean. I'm not so sure about the rich widowers though, definitely not in The Nag anyway.'

'We could go for a night out together somewhere if you like?'

Terri let out a small laugh. 'Only if you wear those overalls. I don't think I'd have much luck with your long legs next to my tree trunks.'

'Deal,' Jules smiled.

'So you're not planning to leave us then?' Terri asked suddenly, lifting her head to look at Jules. 'I thought maybe there might have been some truth in what you said to that journalist.'

'If you'd have asked me yesterday I probably would have said yes, but when I saw those awful comments in *The Daily* this morning it made me realise how much this place means to me. I don't want to leave, but I don't know how I can stay now. You might have thought it was funny, but I can't see anyone else feeling that way,' Jules finished, rubbing a hand over her aching jaw.

'Oh, I've just had the best idea,' Terri said, getting to her feet and turning to face Jules. 'You should have a party.'

'What?' Jules spluttered as hot tea dripped down her chin. 'No one would come.'

'Yes they would. You should have a party on Saturday. I'll get on the blower to Sally and she can ring round the gang. We'll put a sign up in the pub and at the shop. You'll have a great turn out. Sally and Bob can bring sausages and do a bit of barbequing. Rich can bring some dri—'

'Terri,' Jules interrupted, wiping away the liquid she'd spilled. 'No one will come. Not after what I said. Or what *The Daily* reported I said anyway.'

'Don't you worry about that, lovey. Sally and I will explain what happened, and besides there's nothing like a good party to make people forget a scandal.'

'But the house, it's hardly ready for people to see it.'

'Are you kidding? Do you know how many people are dying to get a look inside the Mayor house? And anyway, the stairs are arriving tomorrow. We can get some paint on the walls and make sure the downstairs looks half decent at least.'

'Promise me this is not some crazy exorcism séance thingy?'

'It wouldn't hurt to invite the vicar from the next village.'

'No, Terri. Absolutely not.'

'Fine, but we're agreed – a party on Saturday? If nothing else, it will give me something to take my mind off the divorce,' Terri added with a weak smile.

Before Jules could voice the other protests stacking up in her mind, the sound of a doorbell chimed into the room.

'Who could that be?' Terri wondered aloud as she left the room. 'No one knocks on my door for months at a time and then the minute I'm wearing this tatty old dressing gown it's like Piccadilly Circus in here.'

As the front door opened, Jules heard Terri's surprised voice: 'Well I be damned, you are just the person we wanted to speak to.'

'Really?' a man's voice answered.

If it's Terri's soon to be ex-husband, Jules thought, then I'm going to ram this saucer down his throat.

To her relief, Rich ducked his head under the door frame and strode into the living room.

'So I'm an alcoholic, am I?' he demanded, turning to face Jules.

'Oh Rich, I'm so sorry,' Jules cried out all over again, hiding her face in her free hand.

In her haste to repair the damage she'd done to her friendship with Terri, she'd forgotten all about the comments the paper had made about Rich. 'I didn't say anything like that, I promise—'

'Rich,' Terri cut in. 'Stop teasing the girl. You know full well she'd never say such nonsense.'

'I guess not,' he agreed, 'I thought something was up when that girl just appeared out of nowhere. I should have done more to interrupt the two of you.'

'What? You knew and you didn't help me?'

'Not exactly. It just seemed a bit suspect to me. But then I thought there's no way you'd be stupid enough to say anything to a journalist after everything that's happened to you.'

'Gee, thanks,' Jules muttered, taking a mouthful of tea to hide her embarrassment.

'Enough of that now, you two,' Terri broke in. 'Rich, we need your help. Do you think you could nip to the cash and carry before Saturday? We need some supplies for a party up at Jules's house.'

'So you're going to try and buy our forgiveness, are you?' Rich looked at Jules.

'Exactly,' Terri answered for her.

Rich smiled, 'Count me in then.'

'Brilliant. Now what brings you here?'

'I was thinking of asking the two of you for a favour and when I saw Jules's car outside it seemed like a sign.'

Jules moved her gaze to Terri, exchanging a confused look.

'The Nag needs a serious overhaul. I've been thinking about it for a while now but I just don't know where to begin. It looks okay in the winter months when it's dark outside and you can't see all the cigarette burns in the carpet or the places where the wallpaper has peeled away from the wall, but in the sunlight it looks a bit...well...dilapidated.

'So I thought with your eye for interiors,' Rich nodded towards Jules, 'and your decorating background, Terri, that the two of you might consider working together to give the pub a facelift. I'd pay you, of course,' he added.

A silence fell in the room as Jules and Terri turned to each other and waited for the other to speak.

'Well,' Jules began, 'if I'm staying in Cottinghale I will need a job of some kind, and if Dan and Jason are heading off to uni this year, you might need another pair of hands,' she said to Terri, feeling a sudden bout of nerves float inside her stomach as if she was asking for a first date.

'I don't know,' Terri shook her head. 'You are awfully bossy lovey, and what with the ceiling and the stairs it might be bad luck for me to work with you.'

'Oh.'

A smile lit up her face. 'Lovey, I'm kidding. Of course I want to work with you. I can't think of anything more fun in fact.'

'And speak to Bob and Sally too, I hear they're thinking of converting one of their barns into a lodge for hikers,' Rich added.

'This calls for a celebration. More tea all round,' Terri said, dashing towards the kitchen.

Rich crossed the room, taking Terri's place on the sofa. 'About the other night,' he began in a low voice.

'Shit, I'd forgotten about that too,' Jules exclaimed, her face glowing a bright red. 'Rich, I'm so sorry. I've made a total of fool of myself in front of you so many times now, I don't know what to say.'

'Don't worry. I just wanted to make sure you were okay, that's all.'

'Me? I'm fine,' Jules replied, swallowing back a lump in her throat.

'Sure?'

Jules turned her face away, sucking in her bottom lip as she fought the sudden emotions clouding her vision.

'Want to talk about it?'

She shook her head as the tears began to fall. 'I've ruined everything.'

'Come on, what harm can it do?'

'That's what the journalist said last night,' Jules replied with a weak smile.

For a moment Jules said nothing and then with a deep breath and a pang of regret that she'd not confided in her friends to begin with, Jules starting speaking.

She began with the day Guy had walked her to the lecture hall and finished with the note Mrs Beckwith had handed her that morning and the apology printed below her interview.

At one point Terri had brought a tray of drinks into the room and sat between them on the sofa, taking Jules's hand and squeezing it every so often.

'So, like I said,' Jules added with a shaky breath. 'I've ruined it.'

'Call him,' Rich declared.

'Go down and see him,' Terri added.

'I tried to call but his mobile is off and his voicemail is full. I have no idea which hospital his sister is in, not that I could just turn up there whilst she's ill. It's too late for that anyway. He'll see the paper and think I'm the worst kind of bitch. He has no idea that I didn't get his note.'

'It's not too late, Jules,' Rich replied. 'You may not have heard Guy play the other night, but we did, and he is so in love with you that not even a million stories like this could change his mind. All his songs were about how sorry he is for what he did to you and how much he loves you.'

'But what do I do?'

'There is one thing,' Rich replied.

'What?'

'You're not going to like it.'

'What?'

By the time Rich had finished explaining his plan the three mugs of untouched tea had gone cold and nothing but darkness could be seen outside the window.

'You're right, I don't like it,' Jules said, unsure whether to laugh or cry. 'I thought Terri's idea of a party was crazy, but this is just nuts.'

'I hate to say it, lovey,' Terri began, 'but Rich is right.'

'What other choices have you got?' he added.

Jules thought for a moment before replying: 'None, I guess.'

'There you go then.'

'Just like that?'

'Just like that,' he agreed. 'Here. Use my phone.' Rich pulled out a mobile from his pocket and handed it to Jules.

'Now?'

'Why not?'

Jules paused for a moment, staring at the blank screen as her heart thundered in her chest.

Rich stretched across the sofa and gave her a shove. 'Go on.'

What other choices did she have? Jules repeated to herself as she dialled the number and held the phone to her ear.

A familiar voice greeted her.

Thirty-five

Jules opened her eyes as the first rays of light crept into her bedroom.

Her bedroom, she repeated to herself. She liked the sound of it.

Even though her bedroom had faded pink floral wallpaper, moulding a gloopy brown around the window, and a dirty grey carpet still rolled up halfway into the room where the damage to the ceiling below had been repaired, she loved it.

From the moment Terri and Rich had encouraged her to stay, Jules had found herself falling in love with every rotting, broken part of her home. So much so that as soon as the stairs had been fitted on Wednesday morning, she'd packed her bags at the guesthouse, given Mrs Beckwith a long hug and moved in.

So what if she had to boil the kettle six times to get enough warm water to wash. Or put on a jumper and two pairs of socks on before climbing under the duvet. Waking up in her house, correction, her home, was worth it.

Her knees screamed in protest as she dragged herself out of the bed and shuffled towards the bathroom. The pain was a reminder of the long day she'd spent on all fours waxing the floorboards in the living room and hall.

As she past the landing, her gaze fell automatically to her new staircase.

Jules would never have imagined that something as functional as a staircase could alter the entire feel of the house. She loved to put her hands on either side of the matching dark wood banisters as she descended down each step.

For every steep and narrow step of the old staircase, there were two wide ones to lead her gently up or down.

She even had a favourite step – the fourth one from the bottom. As she made her way down the stairs, it was the first one to twist away from the wall and angle her into the bright white hallway.

It somehow made her feel more graceful. Jules even found herself standing up straighter and lifting her head whenever she made her way up or down the stairs.

She especially liked her descent. Whereas the upstairs of her home still remained untouched, the downstairs had been transformed, thanks to their hard work. Bright white walls greeted her in every room, contrasting to the rich wood of the floorboards, now shining dark brown.

She had no furniture yet, and the lino in the kitchen seemed stuck to the floor, but her house had fast become liveable. If she could pick up a second hand sofa, and find a plumber to fix her boiler, then she would be happy to stay forever.

The forest of weeds in the back garden, the kitchen floor and cupboards, adding an en-suite, removing the carpets and wallpaper upstairs, and all of the other jobs on her growing list would have to wait. As of next week, Jules would be working on her house in what little spare time she had.

News of the design and decorating business she'd formed with Terri had spread faster than Jules could have imagined. They had enough work in Cottinghale and the surrounding villages to keep them busy for the next six months.

Even Stan had grumbled about changing the layout of his shop to include a space for a coffee counter and a few chairs.

When she put down her paintbrush each evening, rubbed moisturiser into the blisters on her hands and climbed into bed, she would close her eyes expecting sleep to come easily. But instead, ideas would bounce around her head until she had to turn on the light and write them down. She'd already filled one notebook alone on designs for Sally and Bob's barn conversion.

Somewhere along the way, Jules's focus had moved from creating a beautiful home to making a profit as fast as possible. She'd forgotten how exciting it was to start with a blank piece of paper and finish with a brand new room. It made her feel alive.

Jules stared at her reflection in the old bathroom mirror as bright sunlight shone through the window. She didn't recognise the person staring back.

Terri had spent an hour the previous day rummaging through Jules's clothes until she found an outfit that she liked. It was a deep purple knitted dress that Jules couldn't even remember buying.

Fulfilling her promise to Terri, she'd let her hair dry in loose curls down her shoulders and for the first time in years put more than just a wisp of mascara on her face.

She'd followed their plans to the letter, and up until that moment had even believed it might work. But now it was happening, she wasn't so sure.

He should have been here by now, she thought.

Her house was ready. Five boxes of wine and extra glasses from The Nag sat ready to be used in her kitchen and Sally and Bob's barbeque had been placed on the bare earth by the driveway, ready for the sausages.

She could hear Terri and the boys moving around below her, opening dips and bags of crisps and adding last minute touches to the house. Any minute now her parents would be arriving, and an hour after that the first of the guests would start knocking on the door.

He wasn't coming. Rich's plan had failed, she thought again with a gripping sadness.

Just then Jules heard the unmistakable sputter of her father's twenty-year old exhaust pull into the driveway and she pushed the thought aside.

She had her home, she had her friends and she had Cottinghale. It was so much more than she'd had for so long and it would have to be enough. Guy wasn't coming.

As Jules stepped into the afternoon sun to greet her parents, she could smell the sweet freshness of spring rolling down from the valley. The air still held a chill, but the promise of warmth carried in the light breeze.

'Juliet,' her mother screeched, jumping from their faded blue Volvo estate. 'You look so beautiful. Doesn't she look beautiful, Bernie? And this house, it's amazing.'

'Thanks mum,' Jules replied, steadying herself as her mother pulled her into the folds of her bright orange pashmina and held her tight.

'Your father and I are so proud of you.'

'Thanks,' Jules murmured through the thick mist of her mother's treacle sweet perfume. The smell flooded her with warm memories of her childhood, the reassurance blanketing the jumble of nerves and disappointment dancing in her stomach.

'Did you find it okay?' Jules asked as she untangled herself from Nora's embrace.

'Just about,' her father smiled, pecking her on the cheek. 'I wrote out the directions last night, but you know your mum, she always knows best.'

'Shut up Bernie,' Nora laughed. 'We found it, didn't we?'

'Yes dear,' he replied, winking at Jules. 'We are so glad to be here,' her father added, squeezing her shoulder.

'Come on in. I want you to meet my friend Terri, and her two sons – Dan and Jason. They've been helping me with the house,' Jules said, leading her parents into the kitchen.

'This is amazing,' her mother repeated as they stepped into the kitchen. 'Oh my, what strapping young men,' she added, catching sight of Dan and Jason hovering by an open packet of cheese puffs.

'Dan, Jason, Terri, these are my parents – Nora and Bernie. Anyone for tea?' she added as they greeted each other.

'Oh, I think we can do better than that,' her mother replied, retrieving a bottle of champagne from the fabric shopping bag she carried with her everywhere.

'Perfect,' Terri agreed. 'Why don't I pour whilst you show your mum and dad around? Dan, Jason, you'd better go too before you eat all the food.'

'Thanks Terri, here—'

'Shhh. Did you hear that?' Bernie asked suddenly.

'Don't you start, Dad,' Jules smiled. 'Terri's already convinced this place is haunted.'

'No I'm serious, I definitely heard something upstairs.'

'It's just the old plumbing. I've got someone coming out next week to look at it. Come on, I'll show you around.'

Before her father could disagree, Jules beckoned them out of the kitchen, leading her parents from room to room, pointing out the work they'd done and talking through the list of tasks still ahead of her.

'Such a lovely staircase,' her mother cooed.

'Thanks mum. Terri picked it out. The old one fell down.'

'NO,' Nora replied in disbelief, running her hand over the twisted spindles.

'There... I heard it again,' Bernie cut in.

'What?' Jules, Dan and Jason asked in unison.

'Shhh.'

No one dared breathe as they listened to the unmistakeable sound of shuffling from above them.

'It's the plumbing,' Jules repeated with a little less conviction.

'It's a sort of flapping noise,' Bernie disagreed. 'Since when did pipes flap?

'And a spooky woman's cry,' Jason added with a grin, nudging his brother.

Bernie turned to his daughter. 'Juliet, have you looked inside your loft yet?'

'Honestly dad, this place is not haunted.'

'I'll get the ladder,' Dan smirked, already moving towards one of the bedrooms where they'd hidden all of the tools.

Two minutes later, they all stood holding the bottom of the ladder whilst Dan balanced on top, sliding the loft hatch out of the way before his head disappeared into the darkness.

'Holy shit,' a voice called down from above.

'What is it?' Jules demanded.

'You'd better take a look for yourself,' Dan called as he hoisted himself off the ladder, his body disappearing into the loft.

'Oh my God, it's a ghost isn't it?' Terri cried in a shrill voice.

Jules hopped up the ladder and poked her head into the darkness. She had no idea what she expected to see, but nothing prepared her for the hollow black eyes that greeted her.

Perched less than a metre away on a long roof beam sat two huge barn owls. Their cream feathers shimmering in the sunlight streaming in from a hole to the side of her house.

'Wow.'

'They are beautiful,' Dan whispered.

'What is it?' Terri called out from below.

'Shhh,' Dan and Jules said together.

At that moment, one of the owls lifted its wings slightly to reveal two small baby owls, one cream and one brown, hiding beneath them.

'They are amazing,' Dan whispered, creeping slowly back to the loft hatch.

'Come on, let's leave them to it,' Jules said, stepping back down.

'Well?' Nora asked.

'Owls,' Jules said.

'A whole family of them,' Dan added, placing the hatch back in place. 'Two adults and two babies.'

'But what about the ghosts?' Terri asked in a timid voice.

'I think they are the ghosts,' Jules replied, placing her arm around Terri.

'Oh.' Her friend frowned, her cheeks turning crimson.

'What are you going to do about them?' Jason asked.

'Nothing for now. They're not going to do any more damage than they already have done. I'll wait a few weeks until the babies are older and then I suppose I'll call the local vets.'

'Right then,' Bernie began. 'Now that we've sorted that one out, how about that champagne?'

'That's why I married you, Bernard,' Nora patted his arm. 'Always the first to suggest a drink.'

Only after Jules had taken a sip of champagne and the bubbles had mingled with the fizzing nerves building in her stomach, did her mother pull out a copy of *The Daily*.

'I assume you've seen this?' she asked.

Jules nodded, the disappointment returning.

'And?' her mother asked in an excited voice.

'Nothing,' Jules shrugged.

'Nothing yet,' Terri added.

'Don't worry love,' Nora began, reading the sadness in her daughter's face. 'The best love stories have to go through turmoil before the happy ending. Just think of Romeo and Juliet. Where do you think your father and I picked your name from?'

'But they died at the end, Mum.'

'No love, they were together for eternity.'

'Oh. I'm not sure that was the ending I was hoping for,' Jules replied with a sad smile.

Thirty-six

Guy eased his foot onto the brake pedal, coaxing the car to a stop as the light turned from amber to red. He glanced back at the solemn face of his nephew, staring out of the window from his car seat.

He had no idea how Sam had survived the week. Or Debbie or Carl for that matter; he'd barely made it himself.

Saturday. Four days since he'd listened to Carl's message and slipped out of Jules's room. Four days since he'd seen or heard from her. Four days since he'd sacked Sonja.

It felt like a lifetime.

Ever since he'd seen the midwives rushing into Debbie's room and felt a crippling fear pierce through his chest, he'd focused on nothing else but Debbie and the baby.

He had the rest of his life to dwell on the bitter mistakes he'd made.

Despite their optimism, Debbie's body had started labour for the second time; the contractions hurtling through her only minutes apart. How they did it, he didn't know, but the quick work of the hospital team stopped them once more.

In the days that followed, he'd sat helpless by Debbie's bedside as she'd received a cocktail of steroids in the desperate hope of maturing the baby fighting for life inside her.

Thirty weeks pregnant. It sounded like a lot to Guy, but as the midwife explained to him, a baby born so early would miss out on ten weeks of development in the womb; when the baby would gain over half its body weight and allow the organs to mature, ready for life outside the womb.

He'd lost count of the times he'd scrunched his eyelids shut and prayed as Debbie and Carl stared helplessly at the clock, continuing to tick loudly into the room.

In his twenty-seven years he couldn't remember ever wondering if he believed. He'd just accepted that something might be out there and got on with it. But when he looked at the terrified expression on his sister's face, Guy found himself promising everything if Debbie and baby would be okay.

Then on Thursday afternoon, just after the lunch trays had been cleared away, Debbie's waters broke. This time there was nothing the team of doctors and midwives could do but assist the delivery.

Guy had been ushered out of the room so quickly he hadn't even had a chance to tell Debbie how much he loved her. For two excruciating hours he waited. Pacing up and down the waiting room and blanking out the excited faces of the other visitors waiting to meet new arrivals. He could only imagine how much worse those few hours had been for Debbie.

It seemed impossible to him, the task Debbie and the other women in the delivery ward had to do, but she did it. Carl's face had poked into the visitors' room to tell him; a mixture of excitement and anxiety etched in lines around his eyes.

But before the new parents could so much as say hello to the three pound seven ounce little girl, she'd been whisked away to the Special Care Baby Unit and attached to a dozen machines as the paediatricians made their assessments.

Debbie and Carl named her Faith, and then the waiting continued.

The paediatrician called it Respiratory Distress Syndrome. Despite the steroids Debbie had received, Faith's lungs were too immature to breathe without the help of a respirator. Her only chance was to gain weight fast; the doctor had explained to them, giving Faith a calorie and vitamin enriched formula through a tube in her nose.

A car horn jolted Guy from his thoughts. He focused his eyes back on the road just in time to see the traffic light turn from green back to amber. He'd been doing that a lot lately – losing track of time as he gazed at nothing.

Not long now, he thought. Two more sets of traffic lights, a mini-roundabout and then they'd be there.

He'd done the journey so many times in the past week that in the rare moments when exhaustion gave way to sleep he found himself dreaming it.

But never with Sam, he reminded himself with a nauseating wave of dread.

Every afternoon, after taking croissants and fresh fruit to Debbie and Carl, he would kiss his sister goodbye and collect Sam from Carl's parents. It took all the energy he had left inside of him to glue a smile on his face and pretend that everything was okay.

But today there was no trip to the park to chase the ducks. Today, as he'd strapped Sam into the car seat, he'd received a text from Carl:

Come to hospital. Bring Sammy.

He had no idea what to expect as he pulled into the parking bay, but nothing could stop the fear rising to his throat. Was this the goodbye they'd all silently feared?

'Okay Sammy,' Guy called, forcing his voice to sound cheery as he unclipped Sam's child seat and lifted him into his arms. 'Let's go see Mummy and Daddy.'

Sam's large blue eyes fixed on Guy's with a mixture of hope and fear. Maybe his 18-month old nephew understood what might await them on the other side of the revolving doors, Guy wondered, gluing a smile onto his face.

As the midwife buzzed Guy and Sam into the Special Care Unit another wave of panic drenched through him. Just a few metres away on the red plastic visitors' chairs sat Carl. His hands covering his face as he rocked back and forth.

'Daddeee,' Sam cried out, stretching his stubby arms out towards his father.

Guy felt the sting of water prick his eyes as Carl lifted his tear streaked face up to greet them.

'Sammy,' Carl said, standing up to take his son and wrapping him into a tight embrace.

Guy swayed back, his body leaning against the wall as the fear in his stomach mingled with the emotions of the week until he didn't think he had the energy to stand a moment longer.

But as he took a step towards the row of chairs, his eyes caught sight of his sister's red and white spotty dressing gown. On the other side of the Perspex glass looking into a room of tiny cots, with wires and machines all around them, sat his sister.

A sob leapt through him as his gaze fixed on the tiny bundle of blankets in her arms and the look of joy on her face.

'Come in,' Debbie mouthed, beckoning to them with her free hand.

'Mummee,' Sam yelled as Carl carried him into the warm room.

'Oh Sammy. Mummy has missed you so much,' Debbie said, kissing her son on the cheek until he wriggled with glee in Carl's arms. 'Sam, I want you to meet Faith. She's your baby sister.'

'Granny,' Sam replied, pointing at the tiny face poking out from a pink blanket in Debbie's arms.

'She is a bit wrinkly isn't she,' Carl laughed, ruffling his blonde hair and gazing down at his daughter.

'They took away the respirator this morning,' Debbie explained, her eyes meeting Guy's. 'She's going to be here for a good few weeks and it's too early to say if she'll have any problems later on, but she's here and she's breathing on her own.'

'Debbie...' Guy croaked, bending down to kiss his big sister.

'Hello Mum and Dad,' a midwife with a thick Dublin accent interrupted as she weaved her way through the rows of incubators. 'And you must be the gorgeous Sammy I've heard so much about,' she said, smiling at the little boy, hiding his face in his father's shoulder, as she strode towards them.

'Now mummy, I've put up with you under my feet for several days now, even mums need their rest just as much as babies. So do you think you can go back to bed for a few hours now that little Faith is doing so well?'

'Will you—'

'Any changes and we'll let you know straight away, but as we said this morning – plenty of food and this little fighter will be home in no time.

Debbie bent her head, planting a gentle kiss on the forehead of her daughter and placing her carefully into the tiny incubator.

'Thank you so much, Georgina. For everything,' Debbie said to the midwife.

'You're most welcome, Mrs James. Now, off you go,' she said, guiding Debbie towards the door and turning back to Guy. 'And Mr Rawson, you might want to read this whilst your sister gets some rest,' she grinned, holding out a tatty copy of *The Daily*.

'Err... thanks,' he replied, taking the newspaper.

'Page five.'

'I'm sorry?'

'The story you'll be wanting to read. It's on page five,' she grinned.

'Right,' he nodded, already peeling back the pages as he followed Debbie, Carl and Sam out of the room.

THE DAILY

SATURDAY, MARCH 1ST

THE NEVER ENDING STORY

Juicy Jules: "I Love you, Guy"

Even we are getting a bit bored with this pair of star-crossed lovers, but we couldn't resist this ending of sweet sorrow.

The former girlfriend of Guy Rawson has retracted her earlier comments to reveal that she is "madly, deeply in love" with the sexy singer.

The property developed from Cambridgeshire said in an exclusive interview with *The Daily:* "I've been running away for five years, and I've made a lot of mistakes, but I won't make the mistake of ruining this chance." The previously hailed man-eater went on to say: "Have you ever touched something and got that spark of electricity from the static? That's what it's like with Guy every time we meet."

"Guy, if you read this, please come back to me. I love you, I always have."

After reuniting briefly, the lovers are said to be separated again, although based on the soppy comments from both Guy and Juliet, we at *The Daily* can't see why. So on behalf of everyone at *The Daily* and all of our readers, please GET IT TOGETHER!

'Wow,' Debbie said, reading the story next to Guy.

'What on earth?' Guy mumbled, scanning the story again.

Why had she done it? he wondered as thoughts of Jules flooded back.

He couldn't understand it. After the night they'd had together, she could have called, but she didn't. So why do this?

'Guy?'

'Yeah.' He turned to his sister, still standing in the hallway despite the nurse's instructions.

'What are you still doing here?'

'What?' he asked, staring at his sister's exhausted face.

'Go get her, for God's sake,' she said, giving Guy a shove. 'And whatever you do, don't muck it up again.'

'I... I can't leave you,' he stammered.

'Yes you can. Look, we're fine,' she replied, wrapping her arm around Carl and Sam. 'Faith is beautiful. She is feeding and she is breathing on her own. Thank you for everything you've done. You are a wonderful brother, but we're fine.'

'Are you sure?'

'Mate,' Carl added, 'Listen to your big sister for once and get out of here.'

'Okay.' Guy grinned, placing a kiss on his sister's cheek. 'I love you, sis.'

'Love you too. Now get out of here.'

Thirty-seven

Jules breathed a heavy sigh as she sat down on the fourth step of her stairs. Everywhere she looked huddles of smiling faces greeted her. Terri had been right; it seemed the whole of Cottinghale had turned out to say hello and look around her house.

No one had mentioned her earlier interview in *The Daily*. Whatever Terri and Sally had said to the residents had worked. Or perhaps it was Rich's plan to call the paper and offer another interview that had trumped their interest, Jules wondered.

It seemed that everyone had the same question on their lips: what had happened?

Nothing. Nothing. Nothing, she thought. Nothing had happened.

Maybe he hadn't seen it. Maybe he'd seen it but it was too late.

Eight million people had woken up that morning and read her declaration. Was Guy one of them?

She swallowed hard, unable to stop the questions from plaguing her thoughts.

She had found a place that felt like home, with a house that she loved, currently full of people. She belonged here. Guy's return into her life had reawakened a part of her. It felt as if she was seeing things clearly for the very first time.

Maybe one day that would be enough, Jules hoped. Her love for Guy had dominated her life in one way or another for seven years. She had tried to forget him, she had tried to hate him and she had tried to reach out to him. At some point she would need to move on. Just not quite yet, she realised as she found herself scanning the crowd for the black eyes with speckles of green that lit her up inside.

'Jules,' Terri called, pushing her way through a group of teenagers standing in the living room. 'Guess who's just arrived?'

Her eyes shot towards the open front door as a mixture of hope and nerves zapped through her veins.

Terri stepped towards her. 'It's that journalist. Becky, or is it Sara? Whatever her name is, she's outside by the barbeque, chatting to Jason.'

'Oh.' Jules sank back against the wall feeling her bubble of hope deflate.

'Oh lovey, I am so sorry, I didn't mean to get your hopes up like that.'

'It's okay.'

'He might turn up tomorrow, you know. He might have a gig to do or is helping his sister still.'

Jules shook her head, fighting the tears building inside her. 'I don't think so Terri.'

'Do you want a drink, lovey? I think Rich is mixing cocktails in the kitchen.'

Jules could not answer. She had heard the question. A response had been resting on the tip of her tongue, but something had stopped her from speaking.

She held her breath as her gaze shot to the doorway, gasping as she heard it again. The notes of a guitar drifted to her ears.

Suddenly she felt it; the fizz of electricity shooting through her.

Guy.

She shot up, jumping towards the doorway just as he stepped through it.

'Guy.' A smile stretched across her face at the sight of his crooked grin. 'I—'

Before she could continue, his hands moved across the guitar in his arms and he started to sing:

In my idle moments when I'm not thinking of much

I hear your distant laughter and feel your distant touch
The memory of my gamble, a youthful losing bet
I lost the love you gave me, you're my one regret
My Juliet
I haven't had a bad life, laughter, fun and friends
I've sped along life's highway leaning over on the bends
But I'm running to your love, the one I can't forget
I can't see your face in rapture, that's my one regret
My Juliet
A drink or two at Christmas with hearts that reminisce
Auld lang syne at New Year but now no midnight kiss
The loving years behind me, these cheeks are running wet
Old photographs remind me, picture my regret
My Juliet
I've told a million stories, sung a million songs
Sold a million good turns and done a million wrongs
But one sum is out of balance, forever in your debt
I'll never pay the price I owe you, you're my one regret
Juliet.

As the final chords hung in the air a silence fell. Jules took a step closer, oblivious to the people around her as she felt his gaze run through her.

'Jules,' he whispered, putting his guitar to the floor.

She felt the heat of his body as she moved closer, the world around her evaporating.

'Guy.'

'I'm sorry,' they said together.

'Hang on,' Guy said, 'I know why I'm sorry, but why are you sorry?'

'Because of the story in the paper,' she replied as his gaze sunk into her.

'No, that's why I'm sorry, the photograph, it was from a video. I didn't—'

'I know, but the one after it, the death threat.'

'Death threat?' Guy smirked. 'I didn't even see it.'

'Really?'

'I sacked my publicist. She was the one behind all the stories, Jules. I'm sorry.'

'What about the one today? Did you see it?'

'Yep, got that one right here,' he grinned, patting his jacket pocket. 'I'm getting it framed tomorrow.'

Relief flooded through her, sucking the air from her lungs.

'I'm sorry I left you.'

'Is Debbie okay?'

'Debbie, Carl, Sam, and my beautiful niece Faith are all doing well. It was touch and go for a while, but everything looks like it's going to be okay. When you didn't call me. I thought—'

'I didn't see the note until a couple of days ago and I couldn't get through on the number you gave me.'

Guy reached out, taking Jules's hands in his; the touch causing a colony of butterflies to flutter in her stomach.

'So,' he began. 'Will you?' he asked.

'Will I what?'

'Marry me, Juliet Jane Stewart,' he said, dropping to one knee.

'Guy, you idiot,' she laughed, suddenly aware of the faces staring at her.

'I'm not getting off from this floor until you answer me, I don't want to lose you again,' he added.

'You won't,' she said, her voice flooding with emotion.

'So marry me then.'

'Fine, I will.' Jules grinned, dropping her knees to the floor and wrapping her arms around him.

She could just make out the noise of clapping over the sound of the sea rushing in her ears.

'Right, does anyone know a vicar?' Guy jumped up, pulling Jules up with him as he looked around the faces.

Jules recognised Terri's voice chirp into the crowd: 'I told you we should have invited him.'

'We don't have to do it now, Guy,' she laughed.

'But soon?' His dark eyes searched hers.

'Yes,' she laughed again. 'Soon.'

Guy pulled her towards him, the familiar touch of his fingers brushing her cheeks as their lips touched.

Thirty-eight

THE DAILY
SUNDAY, MARCH 2ND
GUY'S GETTING HITCHED

Thousands of women will be mourning today, with the news that Britain's sexiest man is getting hitched. Yes, you heard it here first. In an emotional reunion, the successful solo artist dropped to one knee and popped the question to his first love Juliet Stewart at her home on Saturday. The couple are rumoured to be planning an informal summer wedding in Cambridgeshire.

THE DAILY
FRIDAY, MAY 4TH
TV PICKS

Never before has setting your alarm for Saturday morning been met with such excitement. Richard Green, friend and neighbour to chart topping singer Guy Rawson, will be presenting a new cooking programme starting this Saturday at 09.00. The show "Gourmet with Green" will feature easy to do gourmet recipes along with guest appearances from a mix of stars and non-celebrities, starting with, yes you guessed it, Guy and fiancé Juliet Stewart. Tune in to see juicy dishes and some even more juicy details about Guy and Juliet's up and coming nuptials.